I0736273

STARS, STORMS AND THE RIVER OF LIFE

A BRAD WALKER SUSPENSE NOVEL

DALE LOVIN

UPDATED EDITION

STARS, STORMS, AND THE RIVER OF LIFE

A Novel of Suspense

DALE LOVIN

Published by
Illumify Media Global
www.IllumifyMedia.com
"Let's bring your book to life!"

Paperback ISBN: 978-1-959099-37-6

Typeset by Jennifer Clark
Cover design by Debbie Lewis

STARS, STORMS AND THE RIVER OF LIFE

DEDICATION

Stars, Storms and the River of Life *is dedicated to the countless ordinary people who change our world through heroic sacrifices or extraordinary contributions. All too often, they are either not recognized or are too quickly forgotten. In particular, I dedicate this story to two people who were heroic and extraordinary during and after the historic flood of 1908 in Folsom, New Mexico. They deserve continuing tribute.*

Sarah Rooke, a telephone operator in Folsom, New Mexico, refused to leave her switchboard, choosing instead to remain at her post so that she could warn community members of approaching flood waters. She died in the raging flood, her body recovered weeks later and miles away. Because of her commitment to duty and dedication to her neighbors and friends, Sarah is credited with saving dozens of lives. An engraved stone marks her grave in the Folsom cemetery.

\-

George McJunkin, a black cowboy and son of slaves, possessed remarkable curiosity and intellect. After the waters of the Folsom flood receded, McJunkin discovered newly exposed remains of prehistoric bison and human weapons that stunningly altered scientific theories on the progression of man in North America. His revolutionary discovery was ultimately recognized and labeled 'Folsom Man.' However, McJunkin's attempts to alert scientists to what he had discovered were ignored until after his death. George McJunkin died in obscurity and is buried in the Folsom cemetery beneath a simple headstone.

PROLOGUE

And God saw that the wickedness of man was great in the earth, and that every imagination of the thoughts of his heart was only evil continually and it repented the Lord that he had made man on the earth.

And the Lord said, I will destroy man whom I have created from the face of the earth.

And the rain was upon the earth forty days and forty nights.

And the waters prevailed exceedingly upon the earth, and all the high hills ... were covered and all flesh died that moved upon the earth ... all in whose nostrils was the breath of life ... died.

Book of Genesis
(King James Version)

ONE

THE ROAD WAS DARK. Even though the headlights were distant when first appearing in her rearview mirror, they offered a welcome sense of companionship. As slow drizzle transformed into steady rain, the beams maintained a steady and comfortable separation. Wiper blades, in hypnotic throb, delivered a sense of calm. The party atmosphere she had earlier enjoyed faded into rain and darkness.

Sharon Moore knew the twisting mountain road well. She took solace in that only a few more curves remained before it would straighten into a final stretch to her mountain paradise. An unconscious smile appeared on Sharon's face as she thought of her waiting fiancé and the cabin they had rented for the weekend. It was a mountain jewel that they had discovered months earlier. An occasional escape from the hectic city life of Denver was a treasure. As her thoughts wandered, she smiled more openly. Uninhibited sex with windows opened wide to mountain breezes and a dazzling sky was a huge part of why they so loved their retreat.

Sharon peered into rain that had become heavy and was beginning to blow in slanted sheets across the highway. Instead of feeling alarm over the deteriorating weather, she thought of how their lovemaking would be extra special with a storm raging outside their cabin. Only a few more minutes and she would be with him. Ecstasy with the love of her life would conclude what had been a marvelous outing with girl-friends she had known for years.

It was only because of her fiancé's encouragement that Sharon had left the cabin at all. She had wanted to take a pass on the girls' night out and never leave their private Shangri-La. But her fiancé had insisted, and she ultimately gave in. The purpose of the party was to say goodbye to a friend she had known since childhood. The ladies-only farewell gathering was important, and her fiancé had dismissively waved away her objections. As so often was the case, his instincts were spot-on. Non-stop laughter filled the evening as they remembered past escapades and talked of how they would always remain friends. The evening's experience would now be a treasure. Sharon was so glad that she had not allowed the opportunity to slip by.

Only after Sharon had made her way through the mountain canyon and the road straightened did the trailing headlights cease to be a source of comfort and begin to alarm. Having initially maintained a safe and hospitable distance as they had together traversed the winding road, the headlights now accelerated, bearing down upon her with stunning speed. Making matters worse, rain now pounded with increasing fury. She felt winds buffeting her car. Casting frequent glances at the approaching headlights, Sharon frantically fumbled with the control to make her wiper blades keep up with the deluge but discovered they were already operating at maximum capacity. The headlights were approaching at a rate she could not grasp. Try as she might to focus on a road that had become almost completely obscured in rain, Sharon could not force her eyes from the rearview mirror. The glaring beams of light grew in size and intensity by the second.

Her heart altered its rhythm. Wiper blades pounded, whump-whump-whump. The road deteriorated into a wet blur. Should she speed up or make it easy for the encroaching maniac to pass? Having no idea of the right thing to do, she steered as close to the narrow shoulder as she dared. Her tires dropped from the edge of the highway. Gravel pounding on the vehicle's undercarriage reverberated like gunfire. With an instinctive jerk, she over-corrected back onto the pavement and felt the auto on the brink of an uncontrolled swerve. The road before her had become a hazy shroud. The lights from behind, now only feet from her car, went from low to high beam.

What was happening? Something terrible gnawed within her stomach. Again, she inched her tires toward the edge of the road and once more they sank into soft soil of the highway's edge, followed by the sickening teeter of a vehicle on the verge of overturn. Clutching the steering wheel in a death grip, Sharon managed to hold the car steady as she eased it back on to pavement. Without conscious thought, she instinctively lifted her foot from the accelerator as she swallowed a prayer of thanks that she was still on the road and right side up.

Whump-whump-whump. The sound of wiper blades pounded within her skull. Flashing red beacons of a police car now became a part of the blinding headlights. What in the name of God? Instinctively, Sharon braked, slowly bringing her car to a halt.

Pain registered in her wrists. She tried to make her fingers relax but her palms remained pressed hard against the wheel. Rain battering the vehicle had become thunderous and the pounding of wiper blades now hammered their own chorus of panic. Searing light and pulsating red became disorienting strobes. Her eyes dilated as her senses spun with vertigo.

Tasting fear, Sharon desperately sought answers to the last few seconds. Had she been speeding? No way. Her mind flashed back to the party with her friends. Could she pass a sobriety test? Only two glasses of wine all evening, of course she could. This was insanity. Whump-whump-whump. Lightning flashed. Sharon was vaguely aware of thunder. With her fingers tightening even more about the wheel, Sharon dropped her head in an attempt to gather her wits and force her brain to think. As she did so, her eyes froze in dread. Scarcely covered by the short skirt that had ridden above mid-thigh, white flesh of her legs was obscenely exposed. She swallowed. A jacket was in the back seat. Should she draw attention to her discomfort by twisting her body to retrieve a covering? She felt naked. For a fraction of a second, Sharon thought of her fiancé, no more than a single mile away. Whump-whump-whump.

A human torso, bearing a holstered gun, filled the space of her vision.

Time froze. The silhouette of a man stood outside her window. All she could process was that the man must be tall and that he wore a dark shirt. Sharon saw his hands. One held a flashlight, its beam directed to the ground. The other hand was empty but rested on the butt of his gun.

It flashed through her consciousness that the man was not wearing protection from the downpour and that he would be getting drenched as he simply stood outside her vehicle. Whump-whump-whump.

Lights whirling like a strobe disoriented her senses. Sharon saw the man's empty hand leave his weapon and slowly move toward her window. The hand held in midair for a moment before making a cranking gesture. She sucked hard. This couldn't be happening. It had to be a dream. The cranking gesture again, this time more forceful, commanding that she open her window. Did she dare disobey the command of a police officer? What was wrong with the hand? She blinked. Terror rose like vomit from chest to throat and her ears throbbed with the hammering of her heart. A clear rubber glove covered the hand. Was this something new in police procedure, an added protective measure for the officer?

Her mind spinning in uncertainty, Sharon clumsily tapped about the array of controls on her armrest. Her fingers feeling like fat pickles, she searched for the single tiny button that would lower her window. Somewhere in her brain she heard the door lock snap open as she fumbled. Finally, the proper control was pressed. The window lowered. She stopped it after only inches as wind-driven rain splattered over her face. The flashlight rose, stopping for only a moment to focus on her face before being redirected to shine directly onto her exposed thighs. Once settling on her slightly parted legs, the flashlight's illumination held, it did not move.

Sharon felt her heart on the verge of explosion. The gloved hand made another motion to lower her window, impatience now clearly visible in the silent gesture. Whump-whump-whump. Blinding lights. Her throat closed. Could she speak? She had to speak. Her own voice sounded as an echo within her head as words left her mouth, "Officer, please, I don't understand. What is this about? Why are you stopping me?"

Holding himself erect outside her window, the man's face remained invisible. Never moving or shifting his body, Sharon could see that his clothing was drenched. The clinging fabric of his shirt revealed unfastened buttons just above his trousers. Whump-whump-whump. Rain pounded. White light blazed. Red light spun. Sharon felt her thighs naked for the viewing. Something was wrong, terribly wrong. In less than a terrified heartbeat, reality registered within her brain: Run! Run!

Realization arrived too late. Faster than her mind could process the terrible mistake she had made, her door was flung open. A drenched shirtsleeve pressed against her throat, constricting her breath and pinning her against the headrest. A face, mere inches away, blew hot breath over her nostrils. The scent of sweet cologne, sickening and thick, engulfed her senses.

Pressure from the man's forearm threatened to crush the bones of her throat. Furious squalls of water poured into her vehicle, saturating the tiny gasps of air she managed to suck. Sharon felt that she was drowning inside her car.

"Hey, little lady, you need to learn to do what a policeman tells you to do."

Whump-whump-whump. White lights, red lights, vertigo, lungs screaming for oxygen.

"I'm glad to see that you are all buckled up for safety. I was afraid I was going to have to give you a ticket for not being properly strapped in. You look very uncomfortable, let me help you out of this awful thing." Pressure into her throat increased. "I must say, though, a nicely fastened seatbelt does wonders for this marvelous chest of yours. Maybe you should make a tight-fitting seatbelt a part of your wardrobe every day. It goes with the little skirt you were kind enough to wear just for me." A hand on her thigh, creeping upward, fingers brushed between her legs. "Just relax, I'll have you out of here in a blink. I know you don't understand what's happening right now, but you have been chosen."

Hot breath on her face, repugnant.

"As the angels appeared before the Virgin Mary and spoke to her, I come to you and bring you the same message. Blessed are you among women." His face even closer, breath even hotter. "Now, let's get rid of this terrible seatbelt. I will be your protection from this moment forward."

Sharon felt a hand slide across her right breast, lingering, before shifting to her left breast, groping. With her seatbelt unfastened and pressure easing from her throat, Sharon sucked hard, desperate to quench the fire in her lungs. Breathe, breathe. Hands in her hair, a merciless tug wrenched her from the seat of her car. She stumbled, knees scraping over gravel and mud. "Come along now. God has given you to me. He created this storm just for the two of us. We must now follow His will." On her feet again, another fall, being dragged, lights searing. Jumbled images of her fiancé's face whirled through her mind.

She felt his lips. Moistness of his tongue moved about her ear as whispered words seemed to echo from miles away. "Our day has come. It is time for the two of us to begin the journey that God has ordained."

TWO

Darkness would soon succumb to daylight. An owl blinked sad moon-shaped eyes. With a swivel of his head and a fluff of breast feathers, the night's final hoot found its way. The mournful sound drifted through slumbering cottonwoods that seemed to sigh as their leaves rustled in protest of first light. Wisps of smoke ascended from chimneys and the aroma of brewing coffee hovered over awakening streets. The veil of dawn swept over rooftops, transforming shadows of night into rose-tinted glow. Crispness tinged the air, forewarning that autumn's chill and days of slanted light were soon to come.

Dawn, August 27, 1908, arrived over Northern New Mexico and the village of Folsom. The new day was clear and clean, brimming with promise.

A mere twenty-four hours later, dawn of August 28th, the air was stagnant and oppressive, as if a wet blanket smothered the land. If any hint of promise or crispness was to be found, it lay suffocating beneath an oozing glacier of mud. Steam-like vapors rose from the flattened remains of demolished buildings and naked foundations of what the day before had been homes and businesses of this remote settlement. A pall of horror and death hovered over receding waters of the flood that had raged through the tiny town in the black of night. It would take some time to know with certainty but, in the end, the stunned community of Folsom faced the grim reality that, between the sunrises of August 27 and 28, seventeen souls departed this small village for their journey through eternity. Bodies littered the landscape for miles. Some were not to be recovered for months.

———

Folsom practically straddles the line of rocky mesas, scrub oak and piñon pine trees that separates the state of Colorado from New Mexico. On the banks of the Dry Cimarron River, which much of the time more resembles a sandy ditch than a river, Folsom became a community of cattle growers in the 1800s. As ranchers developed their herds and men hammered spikes to create a railroad line through Folsom, these "original" settlers had no idea of the secrets that lay buried beneath their labors. Approximately eleven thousand years earlier, in a canyon now known both as Dead Horse Arroyo and Wild Horse Arroyo, early humans had surrounded a herd of bison, trapping them within narrow confines of the canyon. In the thick of billowing dust and shrieking animals, this band of hunters, armed only with flint-tipped weapons, killed over twenty of the doomed beasts. The animals were butchered and skinned where they had fallen. The precise movements and destiny of the humans in the aftermath of the massacre are a matter of speculation. What is clear is that, for over one hundred centuries, the carcasses of the slain bison and the stone tips that delivered death, lay undisturbed in Dead Horse Arroyo. Ages upon ages, century after century, layers of silt, soil and vegetation accumulated over this desolate area of New Mexico, sealing the remains of the slaughtered bison in a sunless, unmarked and unknown crypt.

———

On the evening of August 27, 1908, the residents of Folsom, New Mexico did not enjoy the colorful sunset to which they were accustomed. Instead, clouds gathered and rain showers fell. Folsom's citizens savored the rain, cleansing and fragrant. In a land where only a few inches of water fall during a year, moisture was always welcomed, especially when it came gently.

However, on this fateful night, as the people of Folsom enjoyed the lullaby of rain on rooftops and windowpanes, they were woefully unaware of the devastation that nature held in store. Miles to the north, where their familiar landmark of Johnson Mesa towered two-thousand feet above the landscape of the Dry Cimarron River, a thickening sky was brewing into an angry cauldron. Clouds grew at an astonishing pace, spiraling upward in massive, anvil-shaped behemoths. Occasional lightning illuminated the growling monsters and, as darkness deepened, a sense of prescient expectancy charged the atmosphere.

Winds began to blow. Masses of green, grey and black roiled across the sky and a perception of danger became heavy in the air. Beginning as periodic flashes, but with increasing frequency and intensity, lightning fractured the heavens. Non-stop blasts of electricity detonated horizon to horizon. With dazzling speed and power, competing elements of nature collided in combat over this tiny segment of New Mexico. Howling winds, fingers of fire and cascades of thunder caused the sky to bellow and the earth to tremble.

Those who witnessed the cosmic battle later spoke of how cattle lowed in panic and terrified dogs wailed as they ran in aimless circles. Willow branches along the Dry Cimarron River, holding birds that had settled for the night, came alive with panicked fluttering and screeches of terror.

Water-laden clouds began to crack. Droplets of rain splattered the ground in sporadic bursts, gathering strength until, finally, the swollen bellies of the clouds ruptured. With sounds of unmitigated fury, torrents of rain were unleashed from the sky. An onslaught of water assailed Johnson Mesa, gushing down its ancient skeleton of volcanic rock into the meadows, hayfields and pastureland above Folsom. Following gravity, torrents of water cascaded over the landscape in a cacophony of terrifying sounds: shrieking winds, bellowing thunder, sizzling electricity and finally, as if coming from the earth's very core, the sickening rumble of deep, violent and unrestrained water.

The assaulting flood swept over fields of freshly cut hay. Low-hanging tree limbs snapped. Entire trees became uprooted. Animals entangled within the deadly grasp of branches and tree trunks quickly drowned, their carcasses swirling within the water became nothing more than debris, spinning like dandelion seeds.

Unaware of the random cruelty of the elements that loomed in higher ground, the village of Folsom prepared for an ordinary night of peaceful sleep. Parents tucked their children into beds and quiet conversations concluded another day.

Upstream, a ranching family recognized the developing catastrophe. A warning call was made to the telephone office based in Folsom. Operator Sarah Rooke, the single person on duty, took the call. Sarah was well-known and liked in Folsom. People of the area fondly called her Sally. Grasping the gravity of what was happening, Sally frantically began calling her unsuspecting community to warn of impending Armageddon.

A railroad trestle spanning the Dry Cimarron stood between the ravage that swirled within the flood waters and the village of Folsom. Supporting structures of the bridge acted as a monstrous net, capturing tree trunks and branches, causing them to entangle and create a makeshift dam and temporary reservoir. As water deepened and expanded from the newly created blockade, Sally desperately continued to make telephone calls, warning her neighbors and friends to run for higher ground. Sally steadfastly refused to heed her own admonitions and remained at her post.

Miles away, the sky continued to empty rain onto the earth with terrifying ferocity. The Dry Cimarron relentlessly funneled the onslaught of water down the valley where it was captured within the confines of the clogged railroad trestle. Wood and metal groaned in the agony of ever-increasing pressure. Steel tracks bowed and swayed over the imprisoned torrent. The makeshift reservoir grew, becoming larger and deeper with passing seconds. Straining and pushing, the seething waters sought release. At first, the sound of a single explosive crack rose above the roar of the storm. Then came another and another. Timbers of the railroad bridge began snapping like twigs and a succession of thunderous booms echoed within the storm. For torturous moments, the railroad trestle fought back, a few surviving supports refused to surrender and stood in heroic defense against the inevitable.

Finally, in a shattering moment, the structure literally disintegrated. With the sound of a runaway freight train, released water and muck now catapulted downstream toward Folsom in blackness and with unfathomable savagery. Trees, that minutes before had been solidly rooted in higher ground, were now transformed into deadly torpedoes. Upon impact with Folsom, the flood's devastation was instant and stunning. Houses floated like children's bathtub toys. Screaming livestock swept from their stalls became dismembered, their severed limbs indistinguishable from tree trunks or branches.

In the telephone office, Sally Rooke spent her final living moments pleading with her neighbors to flee. She refused to save her own life and remained at the switchboard. Her building was swept from the ground as if it were a dried leaf. Weeks later and miles downstream, Sally's body was discovered within in a pile of rotting debris.

Following contours of the land, water plummeted. Through the serendipity of hills, valleys and ancient drainages, deluged channels joined forces as if some divine power was deliberately directing every drop of water into Dead Horse Arroyo. With each second, the rampaging waters gathered speed and muscle until, with deafening concussion, they jettisoned into Dead Horse Arroyo. Boulders were stripped from their moorings to tumble as weeds and layers of the earth were peeled away like rotted parchment paper. Water sliced the canyon as if it was intent on rifting the earth's very mantle. In mere seconds, one hundred years of geology were washed away. Within more enraged seconds, a thousand years were gone, swept into oblivion. Unrelenting, the water seethed, slicing into the arroyo to the time that Jesus walked on Earth. Walls of the canyon quivered and succumbed, crumbling into the torrent and exposing remnants of vanished times and forgotten climates: the age of the pyramids, the era of Stonehenge construction and the days of prehistoric creatures.

The hurling cataclysm of water had no mercy. Five thousand years vanished into froth. Then ten thousand years of geological evolution were sucked into a swirling morass of water, mud and stone, all to be spewed like bits of confetti across the plains of Northeast New Mexico.

Finally, when the clouds had emptied, the waters quieted, and the sun cast its illumination into the canyon, previously buried history now lay exposed in Dead Horse Arroyo, seeing the sun's light for the first time in eleven thousand years.

———

Days later, after the ground had begun to dry, a black cowboy named George McJunkin rode his horse over the ravaged land. He moved slowly, inspecting tangled remnants of fences and assessing the flood's damage. Born of slaves, McJunkin, known as "Nigger George McJunkin," was a man of remarkable curiosity and intellect. Completely self-taught, McJunkin played a violin, was an amateur geologist and archeologist and always carried a telescope while riding his horse as foreman of a nearby ranch. On this day, McJunkin peered into Dead Horse Arroyo and what he saw instantly registered as something far beyond the ordinary. McJunkin saw bones. Not cattle, elk or deer bones. It took moments for full realization to finally settle. McJunkin was a self-educated naturalist and knew that he saw the bones of bison shimmering beneath the mid-day sun. But these were not skeletons of the ordinary bison that had at one time swarmed over this ranch land. What McJunkin viewed were bones of gigantic size, bones that dwarfed those of modern-day creatures. He looked closer. Beautifully carved spear and arrow tips were embedded in the mud and the bones of the ancient bison.

Grasping the significance of his find, McJunkin attempted to alert the scientific world of his discovery by contacting academicians in Denver, Colorado. The leading thinkers of the day, however, were convinced that it was impossible for humans to have hunted this particular species of bison as the animals had been extinct for eleven thousand years. And since these men of science had concluded that homo-sapiens had only walked in North America for about three thousand years, they believed that the encounter of humankind and this species of beast could never have happened. Blindly succumbing to this erroneous mindset, George McJunkin was ignored. A sophisticated dig of the site was not orchestrated until after his death. Once the examination and analysis finally did take place, long-established scientific assumptions of man's progression in the world, specifically in North America, were turned upside down and scattered to the wind.

———

It is reported that as George McJunkin lay dying, he told those gathered about his deathbed that "He was ready to go where all good Niggers go."

———

The bones and flint tips that George McJunkin discovered are now preserved and viewed by thousands each year at the Denver Museum of Nature and Science. The names of the scientists, who for years dismissed McJunkin and his remarkable discovery, are today enshrined in dignified scientific publications and memorialized as pioneers in the study of early man.

———

The man who discovered evidence that established man's presence in North America to be eight thousand years earlier than scientists contended is buried in the Folsom, New Mexico, cemetery with the simple headstone:

George McJunkin
1856-1922

THREE

Ascending embers appeared as orange stars when Kurt Riddle stirred the campfire. "If you two ladies weren't so darned lazy and had gathered us a little firewood, we wouldn't be sitting here on our miserable arses shivering like little wet kittens."

Sam Trathen tilted his cup, swirled bourbon over his tongue and exhaled a sigh of contentment. "Whenever I find myself in the unfortunate position of having no choice but to be around you, I definitely think of something from the feline world but kitten is not exactly the word that comes to mind." Sam paused to let his words take effect. "Just so you know, I ain't shivering and the only way I could be happier is if you wuz a Victoria Secret model." Sam drew another sip and repeated his swirl and exhale ritual as he lifted his head to observe spiraling sparks and the star-filled sky. No one spoke for a few moments as Kurt continued to jab at the fire with a stick and occasionally kick an errant coal with the toe of his boot.

"For heaven's sake, there's half a dead tree right over here." Brad Walker grunted as he placed a cup of bourbon on the ground, stood from his chair and walked away. Leaving the glow of their fire, Brad stepped into blackness and spoke back over his shoulder. "It's a little bit dark over here so I sure as hell wouldn't expect enough bravery or initiative from either of you to tackle such a demanding task." Within seconds, Brad was back beside the fire, dragging a large tree branch that he tossed upon the fading coals. The campfire sizzled with an eruption of sparks. "Heaven have mercy, how is it I keep getting stuck with the two of you?"

Kurt ceased his rekindling efforts and seated himself beside the fire. "You are just one lucky cowboy is the way I see it." The men sat in silence as they watched the fire gather strength. Erratic shadows flickered across the unshaved faces of the three friends who had been sharing campfires for more years than they cared to remember. This was their last night. For the past two days they had waded streams, launched float tubes upon alpine lakes, and marveled at the magnificence of Colorado's Rocky Mountains. Each time they had managed to deceive a trout with a tiny fly, they had hooted like children as the luminescent creature propelled its body from the water in a flash of brilliance, bending their fly rods like willows in a storm.

The men lived for these trips. Tomorrow, their wrangler friends, Bruce and Greg, would come riding into camp armed with jokes and insults. The mountain-savvy guides would lead a string of mules and horses to carry Sam, Kurt, Brad and their gear back to the real world. As in so many times past when the clomp of hooves took them away from their camp, someone would drawl a wistful comment about how an extra horse was needed just to pack out the memories.

Sam, an Aspen police officer, and Kurt, a homicide and robbery investigator for a sheriff's department southwest of Denver, along with Brad, a twenty-year FBI agent, were known in law enforcement circles as 'The Three Horsemen.' Even though they secretly admitted to themselves that they were actually terrible horsemen and the epitome of drugstore cowboys, they relished their glorified reputation. They never passed up an opportunity to enhance their exploits to anyone willing to listen or foolish enough to believe the yarns they spun.

Sam and Kurt were still on the job. Brad had taken early retirement to be with Elizabeth, his terminally ill wife. Nothing could change the bond of friendship between the men. After Elizabeth's death and his departure from the Bureau, a series of incredible incidents had thrust Brad into the midst of human traffickers, white extremist hate groups and thieves of ancient artifacts. With each instance, it was Sam and Kurt who had been right beside him with every step. In some ways, it was almost as though he had never left his career.

A day did not pass without Brad remembering his wife and the three children that they had raised. His love for Elizabeth was as strong as ever. But she was gone, taken from the world way too soon. Somehow, and in an utterly inexplicable manner, Brad's involvement in his post-retirement escapades had led him to Juanita, the woman with whom he was now deeply in love. Coming as a gift from heaven, Juanita filled Brad's life in wondrous ways that he had never imagined to again be possible.

The timing of this fishing and camping trip with Sam and Kurt had been choreographed to accommodate the schedules of Sam and Kurt's wives, as well as Juanita, who was off to Dallas for a regional conference of legal beagles. Juanita was a Federal Prosecutor in Albuquerque. When all-consuming trials or conferences came around, Brad enjoyed heading back to his home in Colorado for time with friends and trout streams. Juanita and he had established a wonderful life together, dividing their time between Juanita's Albuquerque home and Brad's in Colorado. However, when circumstances offered no choice but for them to be separated, the time spent apart was agony, especially nights. They often laughed that they were more hopeless than lovesick teenagers.

Sam topped off his drink and broke their silence with a yawn before speaking. "At least I won't have to endure any more crappy coffee or political soliloquies from you two. Gonna be nice to get back to some sophisticated company and intelligent conversation."

"You wouldn't know sophistication if it slapped you in the face." Kurt's reply was little more than a grunt.

Brad looked across the fire's glow toward Sam and contemplated his reply. "Sam, I think you secretly understand that your only hope for intellectual redemption is to simply listen to Kurt and me converse." Interrupting his observation for a sip of bourbon, Brad continued in a drawl. "Too bad you waited till you were a hundred and twelve to realize that."

"Okay, Socrates and Einstein, listen up." Kurt's voice was now serious as he rose from his chair and crossed his arms over his chest. Maintaining a hold on his cup of bourbon, Kurt began a gentle rocking back and forth on his heels. "When we get down from this mountain and off our horses tomorrow, I've got to hustle back home and jump on a case that's bothering me. In fact, I damned near cancelled out on you boys for this trip, but my partner talked me into going ahead with our plans. He's a great guy and top-notch investigator so I left him to cover things. But I sure as heck want to get back and start carrying my share of the load." Kurt stared into the fire, flames reflecting in his eyes. "Unless something dramatic has turned up while we've been up here in paradise, I'm convinced something bad is in the bushes and it's chewing at my insides."

Realizing that Kurt needed to talk, Brad and Sam both looked attentively to their friend. Seeking to avoid persistent smoke from their fire, Sam picked up his chair and shifted to another position. "Damn, that smoke sure likes me tonight." Sam settled as he looked across to Kurt. "Let 'er roll, my friend, we're all set and listening."

Taking a sip from his cup and holding the fiery liquid in his mouth, Kurt gathered his thoughts. "There was some press coverage, but mostly it was buried on page five, so no big headline stuff. I can't imagine the story made it to Aspen and, Brad, there's no way you would have heard about it down in Albuquerque." Kurt took a deep breath and shook his head, obviously troubled by what he was about to say. "Just a couple of nights before we headed up here for our trip, we had a heck of rainstorm. Denver took quite a dumping. But south and west, in the foothills, some really serious water came down. You know what I mean, one of those tough-ass nights when creeks flood and rocks come crashing down onto roads and highways."

Brad and Sam nodded silently. Both had lived in Colorado for years and understood that when Mother Nature threw a temper fit, there was usually hell to pay.

"Along with horrendous rain, the storm brought some god-awful wind and lightning. After the worst had passed, a slow steady rain just kept on falling and drenched the hell out of everything. In the middle of all this mess, a guy comes along on a desolate-as-hell road off of Highway 285. He's driving slow and safe and paying attention cause the weather is so wicked. He comes out of a canyon onto a straight piece of road and sees a car off on the side of the pavement. He notices right away that the car's lights are on, and the driver's door is standing wide open." Kurt paused to tilt his cup of bourbon. "Now, this guy is squared away and a good dude. He's a volunteer fire fighter and EMT so, of course, he doesn't hesitate. He pulls up behind the car to see if someone needs help." Kurt shook his head. "This well-intentioned young man was absolutely doing the right thing but I'm pretty sure he also did us some damage. He was driving one of those huge-ass pick-up trucks and he pulls his rig right up behind the parked car. The shoulder of the road was nothing but spongy mud after the storm and the weight of his truck tore the dickens out of any chance we may have had to spot tracks from another vehicle."

Kurt took a breath. "But, of course, that realization was to come later. This Good Samaritan pulls up to the car and by now can see that the vehicle is either empty or someone is passed out and lying in the seat. He goes running up to find a perfectly empty car. The engine is still running, lights are blazing, and the interior is totally drenched from rain that's been pouring in. He shouts out, thinking maybe someone is in the woods, sick or needing help, but he gets no response. He makes tracks back to his truck and, with a cell phone and his fire department radio, he's got help on the way real fast."

The campfire was fading again. Brad made a few stirs with a stick but his efforts were halfhearted. This story was sounding too familiar. He didn't like where he was pretty sure it was headed.

Swallowing more bourbon before continuing, frustration filled Kurt's voice as he spoke. "You guys already know where I'm going with this."

Sam and Brad each gave a subtle nod.

"While waiting for help to arrive, the guy takes his truck and cruises up and down the road looking for whatever he can see. Of course, he doesn't see a damned thing but, in the process of looking around, he churns up the side of the road even more. In pretty short order, our department and the state police show up. They make a quick assessment and decide to get some forensic folks and a dog out to help. It all lasts at least a couple of hours. The bottom line is nothing turns up to explain what the heck had happened." Kurt gave a slow shake of his head. "The only thing we found was a big-ass flashlight lying on the floor of the car, up under the steering column. We searched the woods while waiting for a tow truck and the techs did their best to process the scene. But everything was a soggy mess and they got nothing. Even later, after getting the car into a dry place, it was no good."

"Anything on the flashlight?" Sam questioned as he stared into the campfire.

"Nada. The only thing about the flashlight is that it was a pretty unusual design: solid black made from some sort of high-grade titanium. It was heavy duty, Space Age - type metal with a molded grip handle along the length of the battery case. We figured out it's a product sold by a company that caters to police and military folks. All kinds of holsters, ammo belts, that kind of stuff. We're working with the company to find sales records but, so far, it's been up hill. The light actually had a serial number at production, but it had been obliterated. If we come up with a specific name, they can easily run a check for past purchases. Otherwise, all they can tell us is how many of the lights they have sold during a given time period in any given zip code. They can give us a list of the lights shipped to Colorado, or any other state, and who purchased the darned thing." Kurt gave a kick toward the fire. "But that's a pretty desperate lead when a zillion of the things have been shipped all over the country."

"Sounds to me like it was probably a stolen light if the serial number was intentionally removed." Brad looked across the fire at the faces of his friends.

"Yep, that's a good bet," Sam replied with a nod.

"Absolutely." Kurt stepped on an errant ember. "But, trying to track something as small as a stolen flashlight, which in all probability was taken during a burglary or theft with all kinds of other stuff, is a tall order. Where do we start, Colorado or Connecticut? Denver or Dallas?" Kurt took a long drink. "Before we rode off on our horses to come up here, I sent messages to surrounding states asking for help but I'm not overly optimistic on that one. Burglary detectives get buried with this crap every day." Kurt gave a shrug. "You never know, some conscientious investigator may pop up with a lead but it ain't real likely." He kicked at the campfire in a gesture of discouragement. "Big city departments aren't exactly twiddling their thumbs waiting for a chance to spend hours reviewing old reports for something this vague."

No one spoke, each man contemplating embers and wafting smoke of the campfire. After moments of silence, Kurt continued. "We've done the basics. The owner of the car was a young woman, drop-dead beautiful and engaged to be married." Kurt paused, "An architect, smart as hell, and working with a Denver firm."

As if on cue, all three men lifted their cups for a long slug of bourbon.

"Her purse with driver's license, cell phone, credit cards, and all her personal stuff was in the back seat. It appears to have not been disturbed and it looks like nothing at all was taken. She had been to a party in Denver with a few girlfriends. The poor girl was headed to a cabin about an hour out of the city for a weekend with her fiancé. Her car only about a mile away from the cabin where her fiancé waited for her return." Kurt gave another kick to knock a glowing ember away from his boots. "Family, friends, fiancé, all of 'em, we've talked with everybody. We're confident this is not some sort of inside deal. The fiancé is as clean as a whistle and her family is solid. Nothing along those lines smells bad at all." Kurt was quiet before speaking half to himself and half to Sam and Brad. "Another one of these deals where a beautiful woman just vanishes, gone like the wind."

Sam stood up and flexed his legs one at a time. "Sorry, Kurt, I know what you're going through. I hate these damned things. Practically every investigator in the world knows what usually happens in these deals is that the trail goes cold as ice until a body shows up somewhere. Then the investigation starts all over again but from a different place and a whole new angle."

With a shake of his head, Kurt spoke softly. "Yep, I'm afraid you're right. Like I said, maybe something has turned up while we've been up here fishing but, if not, this story may be going on for a long while."

"Yeah, but there's something in the weeds here and it's critical." As Brad spoke, he followed Sam's lead to stand up and stretch. "What made her pull over and stop on a dark road in the middle of a rainstorm?"

"You are spot on with your question and that's why it turned out so devastating that the well-intending guy who initially found her car actually destroyed any chance we had of finding tire tracks from other vehicles." Kurt gave a soft snort, "And hell, he wasn't alone. Responding officers and volunteer fire fighter guys were all over the place in all kinds of vehicles before things settled down to a structured crime scene operation." Taking another hit of bourbon, Kurt continued. "Some sort of staged accident could have caused her to stop but I don't buy it. That's a random technique that offers no control over who comes along or how someone may react. Since none of her personal effects were taken, I'm pretty sure this was not a robbery. I think she was targeted and followed for a very specific reason." Kurt paused and lowered his voice before his next words. "A young and beautiful woman." Shaking his head, Kurt continued. "Nope, she was not a random target of opportunity, no way." Kurt looked across the campfire at his friends. "Now, you boys tell me, what would make a woman traveling alone on a dark stormy night pull over onto a muddy shoulder and stop?"

Sam gave a sarcastic snort and Brad muttered a "Holy Jesus" before they both spoke together, "Cop, traffic stop."

Lifting his face upward and raising his arms above his head, Kurt spoke directly to the night sky, "Well hallelujah and kiss my hairy bee-hind. You guys just might be a tad smarter than I've given you credit for." Dropping his arms and leveling his gaze directly to Sam and Brad, Kurt fired his next words in a near shout, "Hell fucking yes! You can bet the farm. It was a traffic stop. Some son-of-a-bitch with a police light on his car pulled that poor girl over and grabbed her right out of her car. I'm as sure of it as I'm sure that you two bozos are a pain in my ass!"

Silence was loud after Kurt's outburst. Finally, Sam muttered, "I need a refill." He tilted a generous portion of bourbon from a bottle into his cup and then did the same for Sam and Brad. Taking advantage of the moment, Brad stepped away from the fire, returning in seconds carrying another log. "Anything similar to this in recent weeks or months?" Brad asked the obvious question as he tossed the branch over the fire and freshly fueled flames once again danced.

"We're checking but nothing's jumped out at us yet. But, hell's bells, if the shithead – or shitheads - which ever it turns out to be, has done this before, it could have happened in Maine or California, last month or last year. Who the hell knows?"

Nodding in agreement, Sam asked, "Any cameras in the bar or parking lot where she met with her friends?"

"Yeah, we've reviewed all of 'em. Nothing did us any good. We spotted her in the parking lot getting into her car alone and nothing we could see indicated she was being followed. But the bar is in a busy shopping and commercial area. There were lots of blind spots from the camera and people were everywhere. There's no way to be sure."

The men were again quiet. Embers crackled and flames spiraling from the recently added log tinged the branches of surrounding trees with an orange hue. Brad thought of his daughter, Meghan. Before asking his next question, he took a slow draw from his cup. "What's the girl's name, Kurt?" Brad was reluctant to make this inquiry. He knew that these cases became so much more difficult once the victim had a name, a face, a family. A life that could be visualized.

A long silence followed. "Sharon." Kurt lifted his cup to his mouth but, before drinking, he softly spoke the name again. "Her name was Sharon." He took a long swallow. "Sharon Moore. She could be the daughter of any one of us." The burning log popped and sparks drifted upward. Kurt took another long drink. "When we get off the mountain tomorrow, I want you guys to see her. While the girls were partying, they had someone in the bar take their picture. They were five beautiful young women, laughing and absolutely sparkling, every one of them. I've kept the photo with me since this whole thing started. It's in my truck. Hell, I even went ahead and made a copy for you guys. It makes me feel better to share this with you two old goats." Kurt kicked at the fire. "I am so fucking sick of this kind of crap I want to puke." He tilted his cup and drained it.

Sam shook his head in sad understanding and then did just as Kurt had done; he drained his bourbon in a single long gulp before tossing the plastic cup into the coals. Sam eased a few steps around the fire to stand beside Kurt. Briefly placing his hand on his friend's shoulder, he spoke quietly, "Come on, partner. Let's turn in."

With a short nod, Kurt replied, "Yep, I reckon it's time." A second of silence passed. "Thanks for listening, boys. I just can't get that girl's face out of my thoughts. I've had her on my mind constantly, even while we were catching trout. I guess maybe this old cop just needed to vent." Kurt let out a deep breath as he turned to Brad. "You in the tent tonight or out under the stars again?"

Casting a glance to the sky, Brad replied, "Clear night. Think I'm outside. My cot and bag are already set up." Brad pointed into the darkness where he had been sleeping since they had set up camp.

With a head gesture toward Sam, Kurt gave a grin. "The way this guy snores and farts all night, if I wasn't half drunk, I'd stay outside with you." He began to walk away. "But I'm afraid I'd get up to pee and plum forget where I was. I'd probably wander off over a cliff or drown myself in the lake. I love my wife but I ain't letting that woman get my insurance money yet." By the time Kurt had finished speaking, both he and Sam were out of sight, walking toward their tent, disappearing into darkness.

Brad took a seat by the fire that was again faltering, comfortable in being alone for a few moments. Mesmerized by the pulsating embers, he ran Kurt's story through his mind again. It was a tale of wrenching heartbreak that was clearly slicing Kurt to the core. The depths to which human behavior could descend, no matter how many times encountered, always shocked even the most experienced law enforcement officers. But, looking into the campfire, Brad made a silent confession to himself: he missed it. There was something about the challenge, the hunt, and working with good men like Kurt and Sam that was irreplaceable. Even so, Brad knew it was deeper, more complicated than that. It was something much more esoteric. What he missed the most, what gnawed at his soul, was that he still yearned to feel that he was making a difference. He yearned for the gratification that came when handcuffs crimped into the flesh of one who would prey upon a girl such as Sharon Moore. That's what he missed. He missed it down deep inside. He missed it more than he would ever admit to the outside world.

With a final gaze into the campfire and releasing a wistful breath, Brad rose. Grabbing their water bucket, he poured water over the coals, listening to the fire's violent hiss of protest as a plume of smoke and steam erupted skyward.

Turning away from the extinguished campfire, Brad made a slow, contemplative walk through the darkness to his cot. All he had to do was slip off his filthy old running shoes and crawl into his bag. At eleven thousand feet, the night would become cold. There was no need to undress.

Settling into the warmth of his bag, Brad looked to the sky. He loved it. Stars, millions of stars, light years, galaxies, all so unfathomable. From north to south, a satellite crossed the sky in a silent, untethered glide across the cosmos. Traversing space at speed difficult to grasp, the marvel of science sliced the night sky, looking down upon Earth. Watching the craft navigate the heavens, Brad wondered, what did it see – weather disturbances, military maneuverings? The satellite soared from sight.

Brad brought a deep, contemplative breath into his lungs. Had its unblinking eye witnessed the fate of Sharon Moore?

Images of his children seeped into Brad's mind. He saw each one individually. He saw them as babies and as adults. He heard the voice of Meghan as she sang for him, her eyes rolling, but always smiling, as he requested song after song. He saw his sons standing in a river, master casters and lovers of the outdoors. Brad looked to the stars. His eyes saw their beauty, but he looked even deeper into the invisible that was beyond the black void. She was there. How many times each day did he think of Elizabeth, the love they had shared and the children she had given him? Something as trivial as eternity could not alter that.

Brad closed his eyes, wishing to see the face of Juanita. He felt the softness of her touch, inhaled the fragrance of her copper-hued skin. Her eyes were deeper and more enchanting than the night sky. At his beckoning, Juanita came to him, her breath warm and sensuous. Juanita carried Brad into sleep.

———

Three hours in the saddle had been two hours too long. Sam, Kurt and Brad, begging heaven for a shred of mercy, somehow managed to manipulate stiffened legs in a manner that resulted in a most unflattering dismount. While flexing knees and twisting torsos from side to side, profanity-laced groans of agony were the best they could manage for conversation.

The wranglers, Bruce and Greg, maneuvered horses for unpacking. Greg, who had talked nonstop during the entire ride, found the misery of his city-slicker friends absolutely hilarious. Unable to contain himself, he voiced his glee. "Just by looking at the way you candy-assed city boys are waddling around, all stooped over, I'd say you must've ate some barbed wire with your beans last night." Giving a wink to Bruce, he fired his next shot. "Either that or you've got some mighty serious constipation going on." Greg threw his head back and laughed in delight.

Bruce, who shuffled about on legs that were so bowed they suggested he had been on a horse before being weaned, grinned and chastised his partner. "Give 'em a break, Greg. With a little time, I predict they'll be stepping up to the bar, thirsty as hell and hankering for a big ole latte."

"Well, heck yes. Give 'em enough time and they might grow fuzz and turn into peaches." Savoring the moment, Greg pulled a saddle from one of the horses and tossed it over a fence railing. "But there ain't enough time left in the universe for these marshmallows to ever be cowboys." Greg howled at his own humor.

Sam glowered at the two men. "Now I understand why you miserable jackasses demand to be paid in full before the trip even begins." He grabbed a corral post for support as he gingerly bent his knees, lowering his body into a painful squat. "I wouldn't pay you rotten bastards a nickel right now if you were starving and homeless."

Thirty minutes later, dusty gear was packed into respective vehicles and horses were loaded in trailers. With handshakes that silently conveyed the unique bond that is shared only by those who understand the allure of mountains, fly rods, trout streams and nights under the stars, Brad, Sam and Kurt bid farewell to their outfitter friends.

"I'm planning on getting you weenies some satin pillow saddles for your next trip." Greg shook his head in mock sympathy. Thinking for a moment, he again let loose with a laugh. "By golly, I think I've just come up with a great title for a country song, '*Satin Pillow Saddles.*' Bruce here can play the guitar and hum a bit while I croon and drive women right out of their pretty little minds."

Sam, Kurt and Brad were still laughing as pick-up trucks, horse trailers and a cloud of dust carried Bruce and Greg out of sight. Sam was heading back to Aspen while Brad planned some time to fish and explore in Northern New Mexico before returning to Albuquerque and Juanita. Kurt shuffled his feet. "I had wanted to shoot over to Steamboat Springs for a visit with an old buddy." He shook his head in a sad manner. "But that missing woman is all I can think about. I'm making a straight line to the office to see what's happening and get my ass back to work."

"Hell yes. That's exactly what I would do too if I were in your shoes." Brad slapped Kurt's back in a gesture of commiseration as Sam nodded and growled his approval. "You bet. Go nail whoever the hell did it."

"Hang on boys, let me show you that photo I told you about. For some reason, I'm feeling a need to share this." Kurt shrugged. "Maybe it's some sort of subliminal or subconscious mumbo jumbo, I don't know. But it makes me feel better to have you two in this deal with me in some way." He leaned into his truck and came out with photos for Sam and

Brad. "Now, try to tell me you don't see one of your own children in that group of girls. That's Sharon right here," Kurt said pointing.

Sam and Brad each lifted the photograph close to their faces. Brad felt something jolt his heart. Kurt had been spot-on with his analysis. All Brad could see or think of was his own daughter. The photograph was of five lovely girls, late-twenties Brad calculated, each lifting a glass of wine to the camera, their faces smiling and eyes laughing. Sharon Moore was third from the left. The entire group sat with arms draped about the shoulder of the girl seated next to them. Bunched in tightly for the camera, their cheeks practically touched. Brad tried to look at all of the girls but found his eyes riveted upon Sharon Moore. What had happened on the evening of this photo? Such laughter and happiness, life brimming with promise, vanished in a storm of darkness and terror.

Sam and Brad lowered the photo at the same time. For a moment, no one spoke. "I don't know, I don't fucking know. Why does this never seem to end?" Sam's words were spoken to no one as he gazed vacantly back up the mountain they had just descended.

Kurt shrugged his shoulders and shook his head in despair. "I sure as hell don't have an answer."

Bringing the photo to chest level and extending it out for emphasis, Brad looked straight at Kurt. "This stays with me till I get the word that you've nailed the bastard or bastards. Until that phone call, I'll look at Sharon Moore's face every day." Brad placed the photograph in his shirt pocket.

There was nothing left to say. A final handshake and each man climbed into his rig, dreading the long drive ahead.

FOUR

Though barely perceptible, Sharon Moore knew it was real. A hairline fracture of light appeared where plywood had been barricaded over windows. She would not have even noticed the diminutive thread had it not been for the rooster, a creature she had never seen but for whose companionship she desperately yearned. Sharon held her breath, waiting, praying to hear the sound again. The rooster's daily greeting wrapped about her like the arms of an old friend. This was a sound that took her back to the days of growing up on her parents' farm in Southern Colorado. Within her mind, she visualized the bird's cocky strut and the preening thrusts of his head as he announced his importance to the rising sun and all living creatures within range of his ritual.

Over the past days, she had come to love the rooster's raucous morning serenade. But she so dreaded what she had learned was soon to follow. Sharon pulled her blanket more tightly around her body and remained still, allowing her mind a few moments of peace. She had learned the routine. About an hour after the rooster's crowing, he would appear.

Since being dragged from her automobile, Sharon had lost any sense of time or a calendar. If not for the rooster's voice and the teasing sliver of light, she would have no concept of when a day began or ended. She lay still, praying to hear the rooster again, praying that the unseen bird would not leave her.

As black and silent seconds slipped by without additional conversation from her friend, Sharon sighed. It was time. Turning her body, she swung her legs from the cot upon which she had been lying. Bristly grime that was embedded in fibers that passed for carpet scratched at the soles of her naked feet. Maneuvering in darkness from well-rehearsed memory, Sharon counted her steps to the table where her fingers fumbled for the matches she knew to be there. After lighting her candle, she hoisted its flickering illumination to chest level and moved across the room, once again surveying the surroundings that had become her home.

It was a bedroom, almost perfectly square, with those hideous boarded-over windows on three walls. A tiny bathroom, clearly an add-on afterthought, offered a toilet and sink. What was intended to be a hand-held mirror dangled over the sink, held by a rusted nail and twisted wire. Sitting in the sink was a plastic cup that held toothpaste and a toothbrush, gifts from her captor.

Sharon lifted the candle higher and closer to the mirror to enable a self-examination of her face. Considering all that she had been through, she offered a silent congratulation to herself on holding up pretty well. Strands of blonde hair dangled past her shoulders in knotted tangles. Splotches of shadow darkened the skin beneath her eyes. But otherwise, she saw nothing to be alarmed about.

Returning to her cot, Sharon placed the candle on the floor and, as a matter of disciplined habit, folded the blanket she had slept beneath and placed it neatly over her single pillow. Then, with a resigned sigh, she returned to the table and placed her candle in its center. A simple three-legged stool was situated at the table, finalizing the extent of her furniture. Sharing space on the table with her candle was a towel and wash-cloth. Each day the man brought them fresh, whether they had been used or not.

She did not need to explore any further. She had walked the room a hundred times. There was nothing else to be seen or discovered: a bare floor of filthy carpet and naked, colorless walls. After sitting in silence for several minutes, Sharon again carried the candle to her bathroom where she had to position it on the floor while relieving herself. She rinsed her hands before cupping them to splash icy water over her face. From rote habit, she counted the steps back to her stool and table. Sharon waited in silence. The rooster did not crow.

Peering into the inky void beyond her candle, she strained her eyes toward the only wall that did not hold a boarded window. Sharon knew that was where a doorway existed. That's where he would make his grand entrance. He came each morning and evening, delivering food, water, towel, washcloth and a fresh gown. He would return an hour or so later to carry away food and dishes. These simple gestures of servitude were easy enough to handle. It was what he brought just by entering the room, his mere presence and smell, that caused her stomach to curdle.

Sharon listened, her ears and mind on high alert for the sound of footsteps that would signal his approach. He would boldly step into the room, bringing his sickening cologne and lustful gazes. A shudder rippled as she anticipated the repugnance he would bring.

Brief glimpses of what was beyond the door were all she had managed. She had seen enough to know that the room where she was held captive was situated at the end of a hallway that connected to a dimly lit and cavernous structure. He had opened the door only enough to allow for his cautious entries or exits, giving her little opportunity to view what existed outside her room. Gut instinct, probably stemming from being raised on a farm, told her that the hallway she had glimpsed connected to a barn. Perhaps this perception was influenced by the crowing rooster. Sharon couldn't be sure. Gathering resolve, she stood and positioned herself so that when the door opened, she would have the best view possible of what was beyond the door.

The sounds that signaled his approach finally came just as she had expected. Chills prickled her skin. Determined to see past the door but knowing what she was about to face, Sharon inhaled a sharp breath and prayed that her knees would not fail.

The footsteps halted just outside the door. Lock bolts shifted before the door swung open. He stepped into her room.

"Hello, my love. How was your night?" The door closed behind him.

Sharon stood motionless and offered no reply. What had she seen? It surely looked like a barn at the end of the hallway. Her heart drummed within her ears as she fought to control her fear.

"I see you are awake and have lighted your candle."

She watched the man place a large paper bag onto her table.

"Did you know that God sees all lives as candles in the darkness. It is up to each person to make their candle burn brightly and bring light to the world." He reached into the bag and continued speaking as if he were making a grand proclamation of something profound or holy. "I want you to look at what I have brought. This is my gift for you." He retrieved five candlesticks, each in a holder, and proceeded to arrange them in an arc across the table. Lifting Sharon's candle, he used its flame to ignite each new wick and, while in the process, muttered what sounded to Sharon as some sort of low-volume prayer or chant. The array of new candles sputtered to life, casting an eerie glow over the table and about the man's body. Stepping away from the table to view his handiwork, he clapped his hands together as he spoke with satisfaction. "There, that's much better. With what I have brought, you now have six candles. God created this world in six days." He looked across the candle-filled table to find Sharon's face. "You do know the story of creation, don't you?"

Her mind racing for what to do or say, Sharon froze, holding her breath.

The man waited only for a second before a scowl and a head shake of disappointment came across the flickering light. "I was afraid that would be your answer." He sighed. "This must change." Stepping back to the table, he again reached into the bag. Placing a Bible before the candles, he spoke softly. "You shall read this. More candles are in the bag. You have all the light you need for your eyes to be opened so that you may see all that lies inside your soul." His tone gentle but firm, he continued. "Read the words of my Father. Read His words and learn."

Placing his hands on the table, the man leaned forward, bringing himself closer to where Sharon stood. "My soon-to-be wife must understand my Father's commandments. She must study and learn the ways that she is instructed to serve her husband. It is all here." He pointed to the Bible. "In these holy words."

Then it appeared, what she had known would come: the smile she so loathed. She had seen it in her sleep every night since he had taken her. His lips spread so high over his gums it appeared that he had no lips at all. To Sharon, his smile looked like pink plastic from which sprouted teeth that had been bleached to an effervescent white. The light of so many candles dancing over his mouth created an effect even more hideous than what she remembered. A shiver rippled through her spine. She knew what was coming. He would come closer and bring his repugnance to within inches. She could taste her vomit.

Sharon said nothing, unsure of what to do with her eyes. With the added light from so many candles, would he be able see her fear? Perhaps worse, what if she should fail to disguise the sheer revulsion she felt when in his presence? Would that alter her fate?

Her captor stood without moving, his eyes scrutinizing. Sensing that she had no choice, Sharon dared to return his gaze, gulped her fear and resolved to memorize every detail of the man who held her. She knew from when he had pulled her from her vehicle that his body was muscled and held great strength. But up until now, she had seen him only in the obscured light of a single candle. The benefit of newly added light provided her first opportunity for a prolonged and clear view of the man. Feeling her heart hammer, she forced her body to remain rigid as she returned his scrutiny.

Hair, probably dyed, was chestnut brown and lovingly brushed. It hung straight to his shoulders and shimmered in the glow of candles. An immaculately trimmed beard sculpted his jawline and perfectly matched the color of his flowing hair. A tan colored robe draped his shoulders and hung to the floor, swaddling his body and making his feet impossible to see. Sharon felt her breath catch. She knew exactly what he wore on his feet. In an instant of dazzling clarity, she saw and understood perfectly. Sharon recalled days of her youth and Sunday mornings in her family's community church. Images and sounds of Sunday School, sermons, and revival meetings flashed through her mind. She saw the posters and works of art that adorned the walls of the sanctuary and her church classrooms. Sharon knew what the man wore on his feet. He wore sandals. She was looking at the very image of Jesus Christ, the face that she and millions of others had learned while growing up in church or through artistic depictions.

Swallowing hard, she saw the dreaded smile develop again as he spoke softly. "I see that you recognize me." He nodded his head slightly in acknowledgement and lifted his arms as if offering a blessing. "You surely now realize that you have no reason to be fearful." He raised his arms high over his head and lifted his face upward. "My Father has given you to me. Your heart should be filled with joy. You are the chosen one."

Sharon felt disbelief radiate from her face and fear tremor through her bones, but yet she dared not shift her gaze. With his arms elevated, sleeves of his robe slid to his elbows, exposing forearms that rippled with honed muscle.

"The wickedness of humankind grows and grows." The man shifted his head, lowered his arms and cast his eyes downward for a moment before speaking so softly that Sharon had to strain to hear. "This brings great sorrow to my Father." Silence hung for a moment before he spoke again, raising his voice. "His sorrow is so great that He has once again sent me to walk among men."

Placing his hands palm to palm beneath his chin, his eyes never blinked as they again focused on Sharon's face. His gaze intensified before delivering his next words. Raising his voice and speaking with authority, he issued what rang as an edict. "If mankind is to survive, if good shall prevail over Satan and his armies of evil, a new generation of believers must come to the world." The man became silent, holding his breath as he contemplated both his next words and how Sharon was reacting. Pointing his finger to Sharon, he continued. "And that, my child, is why you have been given to me. From our loins, the last hope for all mankind shall emerge. By the joining of our bodies and from the seed I will plant within your womb, you shall deliver this new generation. It shall be the perfect example of what man can be. The example of what man was intended to be." He took a breath as he lifted both arms above his head and clinched his fists before continuing in a near shout. "And then, humanity itself must choose whether to become what you, the blessed mother, have delivered as a representative, God-like specimen, or it will choose to follow wickedness and descend into the depths of hell." His eyes appeared dazed as he became silent and glowered at Sharon.

Candlelight flickered over the man's face. Neither of them breathed. From somewhere outside, the rooster's crow broke the silence.

The man straightened his body into perfectly erect posture, the relentless stare continuing. His face projected a mixture of condescension and pity as he exhaled and stepped around the table. Seeming to glide within his robe, he moved toward her. "Here, my child bride, it is time. I must allow you to feel my touch."

Sharon felt her stomach revolt. His fingers brushed the skin of her cheek, soft as a shadow, tracing a way around her lips before sliding beneath her chin. Then, urging her head upward with gentle pressure from the palm of his hand, he smiled as he spoke. "Father has given me a wife of great beauty." His hand drifted lower, caressing her throat.

Sharon felt on the verge of collapse. Her knees quivered.

His hand moved downward until fingers lingered on her breast in gentle manipulation over the material of her gown.

She squeezed her eyes closed as the pressure on her breast increased.

"Look at me. Look into your husband's face." The command was soft but carried authority. Somehow Sharon managed to open her eyes and peer at the man standing over her. "Father will give the sign of when we are to be joined. I know the sign and I shall wait until it is given." His hand now fully massaged her breast. "I will wait as commanded, but when the time comes you must also be ready." He removed his hand and stepped away. Sternness filled his voice. "You must do two things until Father gives His sign and the time arrives for us to become one." He paused. "Are you listening?"

Sharon forced a nod, her fear smoldering.

"You must read the Bible I have brought to you. You have no choice but to learn the words of my Father. Do you understand?" Another nod of her head seemed to satisfy as he smiled and spoke, "Very good."

The man took another step backwards, away from Sharon. "The next thing I command you to do is to keep yourself clean. I have brought you towels and clean clothes every morning. You are not keeping your body clean." Turning his face toward the Bible, he paused for a moment before speaking again. "My Father's words are clear. In the holy Psalm, he tells the world that before one can ascend unto the hill of the Lord or stand in His holy place, clean hands and a pure heart are required." Shaking his head, he spoke softly. "My Father has given you a beautiful body." Lustful eyes scrutinized Sharon for several seconds before he continued. "My Father has given your beautiful body to me. You are now mine to enjoy at any time I desire. When the sign is given, I shall take your body and fill it with my seed. Then you shall bear my child." His eyes focused on her breasts and lingered. "Your body now belongs to me. I want you clean. That is my wish so therefore it is your command. The moment of our union may come at any moment. You must always be prepared. Never fail to be clean or to wear the fresh clothing I bring to you." His eyes returned to Sharon's face. "Do you understand this as well?"

Sharon swallowed. Another nod.

The smile appeared, gums and teeth. "Excellent, my bride. Our love shall have no end. You are mine for all eternity."

He turned and seemed to simply melt into darkness. Sharon heard bolts lock on the door. She was alone. Mercifully, she was alone.

Only after the burning within her chest became unbearable did Sharon remember to breathe. Inhaling in sporadic gasps, her exhales spewed in a wheeze that gradually became coughing from deep within her lungs. Candles cast dancing shadows on the walls. Her mind could not orientate nor could her eyes focus. The room felt as if it were tilting on its edge. Finally, her legs refused to support her body and Sharon crumpled, first to her knees and then, in total collapse, she lay prone. Coughing spasms continued, spittle oozed from her lips. Filth from the floor embedded in her palms as she found strength to lift herself and crawl. An empty stomach bubbled sour bile into her mouth. Grasping, her fingers felt the icy rim of her toilet as vomit erupted, splashing into the water, splattering onto the floor and soiling her gown.

Sharon allowed her cheek to rest on the lip of the toilet as she embraced the bowl. Lungs and throat rattled. Pitiful moans rose from her chest. As seconds passed, she calmed and her body wilted. She remained limp, head resting on the porcelain. How long had it been since she had seen daylight? The darkness felt heavy. Darkness was so very heavy. She could feel it pressing on her flesh.

As she rested, her mind wandered without focus, unable to hold a thought. Sharon could not even conjure an image of the despicable man who held her. She tried to think of her fiancé and her family who must be going insane with worry. They refused to come into her mind. They would not be with her in the darkness. She was alone. Again, she moaned. It was her loneliness, unimaginable loneliness that so tormented. Sharon listened to the sounds of her labored breath. She heard the silence of her room. Loneliness. More haunting than the wail of a wounded animal, Sharon Moore's mournful cries were not heard by another soul.

FIVE

Over one million years ago, volcanic activity created what is today Valles Caldera National Preserve, a thirteen-mile circular depression within the rugged mountains of Northern New Mexico. As eons passed, the hand of nature transformed ash and stone into a tapestry of artistic magnificence that has inspired a sense of awe and spiritual reverence to Native Americans for centuries.

Brad Walker sat beside Rio San Antonio, a stream within the heart of the Caldera. Temporarily ignoring his fly rod that lay unattended on the stream's grassy bank, he sat with his arms clasped about his knees, contemplating the land that surrounded him. Reaching to his shirt pocket underneath his waders, Brad touched the photograph of Sharon Moore and her girlfriends that Kurt had given to Sam and him at the time of their farewell. The story of Sharon Moore's abduction had affected Brad in a profound manner. Since riding their horses down from the mountains, thoughts of a young woman, so similar in age and appearance to his own daughter, having her life stolen away had left him terribly unsettled. Remembering that Valles Caldera seemed to exude a peace that served as a balm during past visits, Brad had decided to spend the final day of his fishing vacation within this enchanted jewel of New Mexico.

It had been the perfect decision. His day in the Caldera had allowed opportunity for contemplation of his unease and to also realize absolute solitude. A few trout had taken Brad's fly, sometimes by means of a subtle sip, sometimes with a jolt. In the magical moments that followed, time was measured in the heartbeats of a fish that seemed to miraculously harmonize with Brad's own heart. But in the end, each fish had been released, continuing to swim, wild and free. Marveling at their beauty, Brad had delicately rocked each fish beneath the surface, while pulsating gills inhaled oxygen to regain the strength that had been depleted in the struggle. Suddenly, with a flick of body and fin, the fish would be gone, disappearing into depth, sand and stone. There simply was nothing else quite like the solitude of nature and the magic of a fly rod and trout.

Afternoon light slanted in a manner that caused the rolling valleys of the Caldera to illuminate as if subterranean lights glowed from within the earth. "What is it about this place?" Brad whispered the question as he contemplated the vastness encompassed by the Caldera's encircling rim. It was amazing to Brad that, within the rugged peaks of the surrounding mountains, a landscape so gentle as the Caldera somehow existed. Idyllic meadows stretched endlessly and streams, such as Rio San Antonio, meandered with dispositions so delicate that, if one paid attention, the ages drifting within the water could be seen and felt.

Brad closed his eyes. The watchful presence of 11,254 ft. Redondo Peak, sacred for centuries to the Jemez Indians, sat at the edge of the Caldera. The mountain could be sensed even when not in view. Native Americans had lived within this mystique of nature for centuries. Dusty trails stirred by moccasin-clad feet formed a labyrinth of life and death, forever woven into the fabric of New Mexico's history. But Brad realized the story of this land did not end with the lives of early Native Americans. Particles of the very dust once trod upon by those ancient people had somehow been converted to unimaginable power of atomic destruction. Los Alamos, the modern city that overlooks Valles Caldera, had served as the womb and birthplace of that awesome energy.

Listening to the silence of the Caldera, Brad could feel time in the wind as surely as one can see sand pass through an hourglass. What messages were within the silence? What did the Caldera remember? Natives in moccasin feet or a mushroom of atomic death rising over New Mexico? Where was Sharon Moore? What was the fate of a young woman randomly victimized by demented human behavior? Could the same flaws of human nature that allow for the violation of an innocent Sharon Moore someday permit the nuclear destruction of civilization?

Brad gathered his fly rod and stood. Time to go. Casting a final, sweeping gaze over Valles Caldera and, with a sense of personal insignificance, Brad began the hike back to his truck.

———

After climbing up and out of the caldera valley, Brad drove the twisting Highway 4 until he cut north, making his route through Los Alamos before connecting with Highway 502.

Brad cruised through the city that had originally been erected in secrecy; a home for the unfathomable genius that was America's desperate hope for conclusion to World War II. Brad sat at a traffic light and watched high-end automobiles speed past in an endless stream. Teen-aged kids stood on a corner, transfixed with smartphones and ear buds. What would Robert Oppenheimer and the scientists who developed the atom bomb think or say about Los Alamos today? What would they think or say if they could hear or observe evening newscasts?

With Los Alamos behind him and heading east, Brad descended from the mesa. Final rays of sunlight settled in end-of-day flush over the valley and rocky cliffs that lay between Brad and the Sangre de Cristo Mountains. The view was both oceanic and desert-like. Fluid swells of evening's light washed over the valley's floor, submerging canyons in a watery glow of dusk while the mesa caps protruded like islands rising from the sea. Barren stone, sand and lonely junipers held the sun's final embers in magenta-fired eulogy to another day.

Once on the outskirts of Espanola and headed south toward Santa Fe, Brad began to arrange the next twenty-four hours in his mind. Juanita would be back in Albuquerque tomorrow night. He would certainly be there to greet her. In the meantime, however, he planned on spending the night in Santa Fe. He planned to treat himself to an enchilada dinner at the locals' favorite, La Choza. This would be followed by a good night's sleep and a sunrise walk through Santa Fe's historic plaza and Arts District. No matter how many times experienced, there was something magical and spiritual about the peace of first light in the shadow of St. Francis Cathedral. His morning excursion would be perfect before making a short one-hour drive to Albuquerque. He would have plenty of time to put away his camping and fishing gear, purchase a bouquet of flowers and prepare a special dinner for Juanita.

Brad had to smile. He recognized and welcomed the familiar change in heartbeat when thoughts of Juanita filled his mind. Santa Fe would be the perfect conclusion to the recent days of camping and fishing with old friends and once again wandering the Valles Caldera. Brad set his cruise control and tuned music into the cab of his truck. With Santa Fe in his sights and Juanita on his mind, all felt right with the world.

Brad had forgotten words that he had heard his parents often quote during his younger years: *Man makes plans and then God laughs.* The reality of this sage wisdom was about to hit home. Brad's cell phone vibrated. It was Kurt Riddle.

SIX

WITHIN THE SHADOWED catacombs of his mind, he sometimes realized that he had become delusional. For so long he had strategized a life of camouflage, pretense and deceit that he could no longer remember in which chamber he traveled or what turns lay ahead. His fantasy life had become a series of mirrors, allowing him to see only reflections of reflections. He had no idea of where reality ended or illusion began. However, what he did know for certain was that he had come to love the life he had chosen. A life of delusion and fantasy was far better than the other life that had held him captive for so many years. How he now lived was easily the best choice. He intended to enjoy it to the fullest.

Shrugging his shoulders, his loosened robe slid from his body and tumbled to the floor. Standing before a full-length mirror with crumpled folds of cloth about his feet, he savored the visual effect that he stood on a cloud, suspended, floating above all that lay below. With negligible but carefully choreographed maneuvers, he adjusted his nude body from one position to another, allowing examination from all angles.

He was pleased.

Sculpted definition outlined each muscle group that he could flex into rippling motion or freeze into chiseled hardness. His scrutiny shifted to the reflection that came from another mirror that was placed behind him. Lifting his arms into an arch over his head and then slowly lowering them, he was able to witness rope-like muscles of his neck and shoulders beneath the brown hair that hung well beyond the base of his neck.

Yes, he was quite pleased.

Lifting his feet from the material of his discarded robe, he turned and walked away from the mirror, only to see his reflection again and again from all imaginable angles. He made his way across the cavernous room, each step captured by the myriad of mirrors strategically positioned to reveal and repeat every movement. This was what he loved the most about his new life, the ability to view endless images of his body in a single glance. Yes, he truly was omnipotent. He was everywhere, all places at the same time, all things to all men.

He could not be more pleased.

Reaching the far wall of his domain, he looked into the abyss of a long, unlit corridor that obscured the door that held her. He could feel her presence behind the door. The soft compliance of her breast was a sensation that remained within his fingertips. The thought of her flesh within his hands was his promise of the erotic euphoria that awaited him. His breath quickened.

Diverting his gaze away from the hallway, he focused his attention to a shelf that was crudely affixed to the wall. Reaching up, he removed a bottle and twisted the cap to expose the contents. Holding the bottle within both hands as if he held a sepulcher, he lifted it to just beneath his nostrils. With a sharp breath, he inhaled fragrance from the cologne and held it deep, allowing seconds to pass. Finally, he tilted the contents into his hand and methodically saturated his face and neck, swiping his hand over and down his shoulder length hair. He continued to breathe the cologne's scent deep into his lungs, trapping it as if he were afraid the aroma could somehow escape.

He replaced the bottle onto the shelf and cast another longing glance into the darkness of the hallway. Selecting a different bottle from the shelving, he again poured the contents into his hand. In loving caresses, his oiled hands moved over chest and shoulders, lathering his body with moist slickness. His hands worked their way to his abdomen, hardened muscles glistening. Gradually, his hand lowered to his groin.

Extending his arms slightly outward and rotating his shoulders in a circular motion, he looked toward her door, thinking of her face, feeling and tasting her body within his mind. He eased his now slippery body onto the bench press machine. Two hundred-seventy pounds, light as a feather; up-down, up-down. Blood flowed within veins, the power of heart and strength of muscle together in harmony. With thoughts of her breast within his hand, he looked toward her door. Oh, how she wanted him. She would now be touching herself in anticipation of when he would come to her. Up-down, up-down – effortlessly he thrust the weight bar. Up-down, up-down. No resistance at all. Breath and blood rushing, he replaced the bar into its cradle and stood. His mirrored reflection looked back in endless images. Closing his eyes, he opened his mind to the visions of her passion as she thought of him. He saw the erotic movement of her hand between her legs, frantic with desire, longing for him to take her. His eyes now open and dilated, darting from mirror to mirror, he observed his ejaculation again and again.

SEVEN

AFTER DARKNESS IS BRUSHED from the New Mexico night sky, light of dawn bathes the adobe walls of Santa Fe in a morning ritual of beauty. Hues of orange, pink and gold may cause one to wonder if Santa Fe is indeed a gilded city.

Brad had left his room in the La Fonda Hotel well in advance of first light. He wanted plenty of time to reach the special place where he now stood so that he could witness the miracle of sunrise over Santa Fe. His trek had been well worth the effort. As the sun ascended into the sky, its fiery mass bringing light to mountains and desert, Brad filled his lungs with morning's crispness. He stood beneath the Cross of the Martyrs. He felt as though the cross held open its arms in a gesture of greeting, welcoming the sun and another day to the hills of Santa Fe.

While climbing the hillside in pre-dawn light to reach the cross, Brad had taken time to read the series of bronzed plaques lining the pathway. The plaques provided a sequential history of the birth of Santa Fe and its development. One in particular had captured his attention. It read:

"In the seventeenth century New Mexico was plagued by drought, conflicts between civil and church authorities, and extreme demands placed by the

Spanish settlers on the Native population. The latter situation caused a dete-rioration so severe that by 1680, the Pueblo Indians under the leadership of Pope' and others, revolted against the Spanish and succeeded in driving them completely out of New Mexico. During the revolt, 21 Franciscan priests and friars lost their lives. The monument on this hill commemorates their martyrdom."

Awed by the incredible expanse of land and space visible from his lofty perch, Brad looked south to the Sandia Mountains and west to the Jemez range. With the words of the plaque still in his mind, he whispered into the dawn, "Just who in hell were the martyrs here?" Was it the priests who died while forcing a new religion on Native peoples or was it the Pueblo Indians, struggling to maintain their hold onto a way of life that was being stolen away? Only because he had been raised in New Mexico and knew something of its history did Brad know the untold, and contradictory, second chapter to the story engraved on the plaque. Within the United States Capitol in Washington, DC, the National Statuary Hall holds marble or bronze statues of two persons from each state who are illustrious for their historic renown or for distinguished civic or military service. One of the two figures honored by New Mexico is that of Pope', leader of the revolt that took the lives of the priests and friars now memorialized on this hill over Santa Fe.

It was too much to take in all at once. New Mexico always delivered introspective emotions but, for the past couple of days, such feelings had been unusually keen. The brutal reality of Sharon Moore's abduction had triggered something in Brad and his nerves remained in a state of turmoil. He was unable to shake the feeling that her disappearance was every bit as alive in the winds about him as was the history of New Mexico. He had experienced such feelings before when handling investigations. In the wake of Kurt's surprise telephone call the previous afternoon that had delivered new information, something was stirring. Brad could not place a finger on exactly what he felt but something unknown held just beyond his senses.

No longer strolling, Brad picked up his pace and walked with purpose as he headed back to the La Fonda Hotel. Instead of returning to Albuquerque as he had planned, a two-hour drive in the opposite direction was ahead of him. He now had a noon meeting scheduled with the man Kurt Riddle had identified as the original owner of a stolen flashlight, the same model and make of the light recovered in Sharon Moore's vehicle. The man, a local rancher, had agreed to meet Brad at the Vietnam Veterans Memorial in Angel Fire. This was why Brad had needed a sunrise walk in Santa Fe. He was trying to sort out the sixth sense that told him somewhere within the Vietnam Memorial and the rancher's story of a stolen flashlight, a key to Sharon Moore's disappearance was likely to be found.

Hustling to make time, Brad took only moments to honor his tradition of standing before Saint Francis Cathedral and listening to her ringing bells. For no reason other than he had always done so, Brad spoke a silent good morning greeting to the statue of Kateri Tekakwitha, the first Native American woman of North America to be canonized by the Catholic Church. He then departed the tranquility of Saint Francis Cathedral for a quick pass by what he simply knew as 109 East Palace. This had been the address given to all incoming employees reporting for duty to the secret mission of the Manhattan Project in Los Alamos. Brad had walked here multiple times but never lost his sense of misplaced values in how this landmark of history had been forgotten. Surrounded by the prattle of commercial tourism, a barely visible plaque was the only remembrance to one of the most significant episodes of history.

Back inside the La Fonda Hotel, Brad headed straight for the restaurant situated within the hotel's historic lobby. He had time for coffee, a plate of huevos rancheros and a sopapilla before his trip north to Angel Fire. Because Robert Oppenheimer had dined in this very room with regularity during his days in Los Alamos, the restaurant held a sense of history for Brad. As he dined, Brad gave his mind freedom to imagine and fantasize. He kept one eye open for a tall, angular man with piercing blue eyes, a snap-brim hat and a pipe clinched within his teeth. How Brad would love to see that man take a seat at a nearby table. Brad savored the thought. What in the world would Robert Oppenheimer say if one could share a meal and have a discussion with him today?

It did not happen. The tall stranger of Santa Fe and mastermind of the atomic bomb must have been busy elsewhere. Perhaps he had been summoned to Washington for a conference in the White House with military planners, possibly even FDR himself. Brad unconsciously smiled and shook his head, amused at the folly of his fantasy. But he continued to scan the dining room in hopes of spotting the legendary figure. Heaven knows, stranger things had happened in this crazy old world.

EIGHT

Maintaining traditional military strategy, the Vietnam Veterans Memorial State Park in Angel Fire, New Mexico, holds the high ground. From its elevated vantage, the Memorial commands an encompassing view and perspective above the Moreno Valley. Having arrived early for his appointment, Brad parked his truck, crossed the lot and entered the Memorial. He had been here before with Elizabeth and their children but that had been years ago. Brad was thankful for the surprising turn of events that gave him an opportunity to once again visit the Memorial.

From the moment of entry, a sense of sorrow and loss was palpable. The tragedy of that war weighed heavy in the air and hushed reverence was intuitively expected. It was difficult for Brad to know how to navigate his way through so much history, so much tragedy, so many national and personal memories. He stood before a photograph of soldiers weeping over a fallen comrade. Another of men standing at attention on a lonely hill paying tribute to 98 pairs of empty boots.

Brad read the story of the Memorial and its founders, Jeanne and Dr. Victor Westphall. After losing their son in the Vietnam War, the New Mexico residents dedicated their lives to the construction of the Memorial. They sold all but five of the eight hundred acres of this very land that they had owned to fund the Memorial. Brad held his breath. The image of his own military son, Cody, crystal clear in his mind as he read the words of Dr. Westphall: "*When sons or daughters die in battle, parents are confronted with the choice of what they will do to honor the courage and sacrifice of that son or daughter. Following the death of our son, Victor David Westphall, on May 22, 1968 in Vietnam, we decided to build an enduring symbol of the tragedy and futility of war.*" With a silent whisper of "Oh, my God," Brad continued to learn of the story of the Memorial. He read how the Memorial welcomed home the "*Maimed in body and spirit…We must do what we can to encourage humankind to preserve rather than to destroy.*" Brad swallowed hard, unable to imagine the agony of the parents and families of 58,000 Americans slain and so many more broken bodies and spirits.

Brad thought of Cody in his Naval uniform. His other children, Meghan and Michael, entered his mind. They were so young and so eager for all that life held in store. Thoughts of Sharon Moore crept into Brad's consciousness. Was the tragedy of a young woman heartlessly abducted within miles of her home any less horrific than the death of a soldier, alone and in a strange land? Hoping that his prayer would reach a listening Deity, standing motionless and with his head bowed, Brad spoke to whatever God may listen. "Please, God, keep them safe. Let them be safe."

Leaving the hallowed atmosphere of the building, Brad introspectively walked the Memorial's grounds. A bronzed statute caught his eye, one he did not recall from his previous visit. Standing close, it took a careful examination to realize the significance of what the figure represented. It was a young soldier, an ammo box his only seat and using his helmet for backing, the soldier had begun a letter; "Dear Mom & Dad." Brad stood beside the statute for minutes. What could the young soldier possibly say to his parents about where he was or what he was doing?

Walking further, Brad stood before the graves of Dr. Victor Westphall and his wife Jeanne. The Memorial and all that it represented were so much more than just a building and manicured grounds. Brad had always considered the Moreno Valley a place of stunning beauty. Today, he was once again enamored. Looking north, nestled beneath the shadow of Wheeler Peak, New Mexico's highest, was Eagle Nest Reservoir. In mile after undulating mile, the valley floor rolled southward, vibrantly green and idyllically lush. The valley extended beneath the ski mountain of Angel Fire before finally being swallowed into the shadows of Taos Canyon.

As Brad inhaled and took in the view, the air was breathtakingly clear. Aspen forests shimmered. Still under the spell of the memorial, Brad could not imagine a more reflective setting for the grieving of lives lost or to honor the heroism of so many. He drifted his eyes over the valley in realization that he stood in a memorial created by both the hand of man and the hand of God. In Brad's mind, the entire Moreno Valley was the Vietnam Memorial Monument.

Slowly sauntering and still mesmerized by the valley, Brad made his way back to the parking area. He stood by his truck and cast a glance at his watch. He had timed things perfectly.

———

The pick-up truck that Kurt Riddle had described pulled into the parking area. Even without Kurt's description, it was easy to see that the vehicle would never be at home among the array of tourist cars, campers and motorhomes that populated the parking spaces of the Memorial. This was a real rancher's truck. Despite having never seen the vehicle prior to this moment, Brad understood that this truck was used to pull horse trailers, feed cattle, haul hay, fence posts and groceries. With a wash-job every once-in-a-while, it was also good for church, weddings and funerals.

Walking toward the truck, Brad observed a man exit the driver's door as a woman stepped from the passenger side. Both moved to the rear of the truck. "You must be Jim Price," Brad said as he extended his hand. "Hello, I'm Brad Walker. My friend, Kurt Riddle, asked that I meet you today. He said your ranch would be hard to find so thank you for driving here to meet me."

Jim Price stood at eye level with Brad's six-foot three-inch frame. He was of medium build, right around sixty years old and wore a Stetson that looked to have been fifty years old on the day Jim Price was born. "Yep, I'm Jim Price alright." His smile was brilliant beneath a face tanned by the New Mexico sun. His grip clearly told Brad that Jim Price could break bones if he wanted to. "For some reason, folks refuse to call me plain 'ole Jim. They insist on using my full name so Jim Price has simply become the only name I answer to."

"Okay by me," Brad replied, "Jim Price it is."

"First thing out of the chute, I want you to understand something. No matter what folks around here might say, I've never done anything to get you law boys after me. My eyes are bad, my knees hurt, I got a bad shoulder and I'm not very smart. But I've never broken any laws up there in Colorado, I promise." Jim Price allowed a few beats as he evaluated Brad. "When your friend told me you were FBI, I was hoping that meant you were a female brand inspector." The eyes of Jim Price brimmed with humor. "Just one more disappointment in life to contend with I suppose."

Brad wanted to laugh out loud but he was aware that the woman standing next to Jim Price was fidgeting and making faces with her eyes and mouth, clearly expressing that she had something to say.

Not sure what to do, Brad turned his attention to the woman. Before he could say anything, Jim Price put his arm around the woman's shoulder and brought her close. "Hope you don't mind but I brought along my wife." With a quick glance down into her face, Jim Price continued, "Not that I had a choice in the matter. She wasn't about to miss out on this adventure."

Pulling herself away from the embrace, the woman extended her hand to Brad. "Hello, I'm Margie." Gesturing her head toward her husband, she spoke. "I make this guy here call me Mrs. Price, but you feel free to call me Margie."

Grasping her hand, Brad felt a strength not all that different from that of her husband. "Hello Margie, I'm pleased to meet you and I'm glad that you are here."

Maintaining her grip on Brad's hand, Margie rolled her eyes and spoke with a sarcastic tone. "While Mr. Humble here was telling you about all of his ailments, he neglected a couple of the more important things you should know." Margie's voice retained a mocking edge as she continued. "You see, Brad, many years ago, right after we were married, one heck of a blizzard came rolling through and this brand-new husband of mine was out in a truck that he had somehow forgotten to gas up before leaving the house. He ended up walking home in a blizzard that was so bad he was lucky to even find his way back to the house where we lived."

Unsure of what was coming next, Brad simply grinned

Margie gave an even tighter squeeze onto Brad's hand. "Because of his meticulous attention to detail, you know, little things like putting gasoline into a truck, he managed to lose his right testicle and can only smell from the left nostril when the wind blows from the north." Refusing to release Brad's hand, Margie smiled.

Brad felt his silly grin grow but a quick-witted reply failed to materialize. After a moment of awkward silence, Margie let go of Brad's hand and leaned into her husband with affection. "Now, thirty years later, I don't care at all about what he can smell. He gave us two of the most handsome boys ever born in New Mexico."

Adoration for his wife was obvious in the laugh of Jim Price. Margie beamed with satisfaction at having caused a moment of embarrassment for the two men. Brad spoke directly to Margie, "Remind me to never tell you about some of the really dumb things I've done in my life. I don't think you are a keeper of secrets."

"It's my duty," Margie's laugh was infectious. "Who else is going to keep cowboys like my husband and FBI folks like you humble and in their proper place?"

Jim Price turned away and stepped to the cab of his truck. "Okay, now that we have been introduced and suffered proper humiliation at the hands of Mrs. Price, I'll show you something that may be of interest to you." He reached into the truck's cab and returned with a large, brown envelope that had been heavily taped. "When your friend from Colorado called, he explained that he had been notified by the local sheriff down here that we had filed a burglary report and had listed a special kind of pretty darned expensive flashlight among the items taken. I was surprised to hear from anybody about this because I know perfectly well who broke into my tool barn and took my stuff. I only filed a report out of trying to do the right thing. I sure never expect to see the jerk again or to get anything back that he took. I'm just glad to see him gone off to wherever the wind blows."

Brad nodded, waiting to hear more.

"Honestly, I don't care much about what happened to my stuff or the fancy light that was stolen. But, when your friend told me how there is a chance that there may be a connection to a crime against a young woman and my stolen flashlight, it was like a big loud bell went off in my head. I told your Colorado friend that there is no doubt that a guy who was my hired hand for a while broke into my barn. He's the one who took off with tools, a little camping gear and that light. I was angry with myself for being so stupid to ever hire the idiot to begin with." Jim Price lowered his head a fraction. "But once your friend told me about the case he was working on and how a girl had been abducted, I knew in a heartbeat that somehow all this is tied up together."

Brad shook his head in acknowledgement. "Kurt told me about the conversation he had with you. Since I was in the area, he asked me to meet up with you and go over everything. We've been friends for years and have worked a ton of investigations together. He has a tough one on his hands with the disappearance of a young lady. If you have something that may help, believe me, you have the undivided attention of both Kurt and me."

Jim Price lifted the bulky envelope that he had removed from the truck. "Here is a bunch of mail that came for the weirdo after he skipped the area with my stuff. I've not looked at it so I'm not sure what's here. I was just about to toss it in the trash, but your friend called, barely in the nick of time." He handed the envelope to Brad.

Stamping her foot in frustration, Margie interrupted the conversation with a snort. "Lord save me from the likes of you two! Just like a couple of men. Do you retards plan to stand here in the middle of a parking lot and talk your jaws off?" Pointing to a bench that offered a view overlooking Moreno Valley, Margie continued. "Any chance we could at least sit down while we talk?" Giving Jim Price and Brad a 'what the heck is wrong with you' look, she broke into a smile and spoke in a softer tone. "Come on guys. Let's go take a seat. We can enjoy God's beautiful creation and talk this over like civilized adults."

Jim Price's entire face was a lop-sided smile as he spoke to Brad. "Just so you understand what we're dealing with here, let me explain a little bit about my wife. When she isn't helping me work cattle, mow hay or cooking for half the county, she spends her time caring for the loves of her life." Jim Price winked. "Those loves happen to be two ornery and useless donkeys. On top of all that, she works as an assistant over there at the Angel Fire High School." Jim Price pointed across the valley in the direction of Angel Fire. "She is convinced that the entire school system would crumble into ruin without her oversight. Especially since the superintendent and principal just happen to be of the male gender."

Without even a moment for Brad to respond, Margie looked straight to Brad and pointed for emphasis. "My donkeys are not ornery or useless. I'm absolutely certain they are smarter than my husband here and far more likeable too." She hesitated a moment as her eyes evaluated Brad. "I'm still deciding about you."

Shuffling his feet, Brad spoke. "I'm happy to sit with you on the bench or anywhere else you suggest. My mother taught me better than to ever get between a woman, her husband and her donkeys. I'm way smarter than that." Brad extended his arm in a gesture indicating for Margie to lead the way.

Once seated, Jim Price placed an arm about Margie's shoulder and their facial expressions became serious. Jim Price's eyes now shadowed as he looked to Brad. "My brain tells me that I haven't done anything wrong, but yet I feel that carelessness on my part may have somehow enabled a tragedy." Jim Price tapped fingers on his knee. "If only I had paid more attention to my instincts, maybe we wouldn't be sitting here having this conversation."

Margie's hand reached for her husband's leg and gave a pat.

Uncertain of what to say, Brad leaned forward, placing elbows on his knees and twisting his body so that he held the eyes of both Margie and Jim Price. "Look, I know the gist of what you told Kurt Riddle on the phone. What you said certainly sounds like you may have some critical information about a really serious investigation, but that's it. From what I know, you sure as heck didn't do anything wrong or have any reason to feel guilty. Kurt just asked me to meet with you and go over details, face-to-face. It is important to be sure we have everything nailed down solid."

"Yeah, I understand and appreciate your words. But let me tell you, I knew that guy was a damned three-dollar bill from day one. I sure wish I had done things differently."

Brad gave a soft laugh. "I'm not sure what you're talking about but that's life. Everything we do is clear and simple in hindsight. Do me a favor and just go through the story you told Kurt but in more detail. Let me hear everything straight from you and then we can figure out what we have on our hands."

As if on cue, Margie and Jim Price nodded together. With a deep breath, Jim Price spoke. "Okay, fair enough. Let's get 'er done." Shifting his body and with a quick glance to Margie, Jim Price began. "It was right at the end of April. Snow was mostly melted into mud down low but there was still plenty of the white stuff to be had up high. You know how it is at the end of winter, things thaw out in daylight then they freeze solid again at night. But no matter the weather, it's always the time of year when all heck breaks loose on a ranch. There's about a zillion thing that need to all get done at once and yesterday is too late."

Brad nodded.

"Every day I get my ass up and head out the door long before daylight. I stumble around in nothing but freezing cold slush all day long. My poor old truck gets stuck in oozing holes of muck, my cows are pregnant, and my bulls are horny. Of course, they're all needing to be fed and have ice broke off their water tanks. I stay cold, wet and hungry all day long and wonder why the hell I don't go off and get me a job selling shoes. Painting pictures to sell in a fancy gallery somewhere sounds even better."

There was no way Brad could keep a straight face. Ducking his head, he scrutinized the ground and his running shoes. His shaking shoulders gave him away. Brad glanced up to see Jim Price simply staring at him, a half grin slowly developing. Brad shook his head as he now openly laughed. "You sound just like my dad. He used to get mad at something and he would rant and rave like a maniac. My brothers and I bit our tongues not to howl out loud at his antics."

"Yeah, well you just come spend a week with me next spring and we'll see who raves like a maniac." Jim Price's voice was dry as powder. "Be sure to bring your dress pants though. I just may be unveiling some mighty pretty pictures in a gallery somewhere."

Margie placed her hands over her face as she spoke in exasperation. "Maybe you two have time to sit on your biscuits all day and yap your jaws but I've got woman's work to do. Can we talk some business here? Please let me get busy before I have to stop everything and fix steak and gravy to feed a bunch of men who have done nothing but talk all day?"

Jim Price looked to Brad as he rolled his eyes. "As you can see, life ain't always easy walking in my boots." He shifted his body once again as he continued. "Okay, let's try this again. I was in bad need of a road to be built over a ridge that separates two pastures. With a road between the two, I figured I would save many a mile of driving every year by just cutting straight over the ridge instead of circling my ass to get to my elbow. But the ridge was darned near solid rock. I sure couldn't afford to hire it done. So, like a fool, I decided to add road building to my impressive resume of being a cowboy and husband to Margie the Magnificent here." Jim Price tilted his head in the direction of Margie. "I was smart enough to realize I needed some strong back muscle to get the job done. Both my boys were off in fancy college classrooms." Jim Price grinned. "You know, learning important stuff about some Greek warrior from ten thousand years ago who thought it would be really a neat thing to have an affair with his mother." Jim Price now smiled openly. "Or listening to some four-eyed goof, with elbow patches sewn on his jacket, talking about how cows on my ranch are melting the North Pole cause they like to fart every once in a while."

A sharp elbow jab from Margie made Jim Price's smile grow even more.

"Anyway, I sure as heck couldn't blast out rock and build a road by myself. I let it be known in our local community that I was looking to hire someone for a few weeks to help me out. I was thinking some kid who was a ski bum over in Angel Fire would jump at a chance to make a few bucks since the ski season was over." Jim Price shook his head. "I don't understand the world anymore. Over two weeks went by and not a single response. If kids ain't skiing down a silly mountain, they're planning trips to Tahiti or some such nonsense. Beats the hell out of me how they do it."

Moving her head slightly, Margie signaled her agreement and Brad again could not keep a smile from creeping across his face.

"So then one day out of nowhere this bright blue Jeep Wrangler, with Utah plates, pulls up to the house right at lunch time. Margie had just given me her usual crust of stale bread for me to gnaw on." Jim Price shook his head. "I don't eat a bite cause I see a mighty weird looking guy get out of the Jeep. He looks around a few seconds and then he walks up to the house and knocks on the door." Jim Price's eyes narrowed. "I kid you not, my jaw must have dropped clean down to my pecker when I first saw him up close. I had never seen anyone like him."

Margie was smiling and nodding her head.

"All kinds of thoughts went shooting through my old brain, and all at the same time. This guy ain't exactly dressed like what we're used to seeing around here. He was wearing big baggy pants that looked like they were made out of old flour sacks or something. His shirt just sort of hung off him like big curtains. I couldn't figure whether to look at his clothes or his head. He's got long brown hair hanging down to his shoulders but, believe me, it sure as heck wasn't scraggly looking hair. This guy could've been in one of those shampoo commercials. Up until that moment, I'd never seen hair that actually glistened. But by golly, his hair was shining like a baby pig's ass. I'm no style or fashion expert but I'll swear he must've brushed it for an hour. It was glistening and every damned one of his beautiful hairs was hanging there just perfect." Jim Price took a deep breath. "And, he had a beard that matched his hair. It was groomed and trimmed just as dandy and perfect as his hair."

"He's not exaggerating." Margie interjected. "I went to the door with Jim and was standing right there, not more than a few feet from the strangest man I think I'd ever seen. I had no idea if I was looking at a kid or a man."

With a forced laugh and shifting in his seat, Jim Price looked uncomfortable. His voice assumed an apologetic tone. "I sure don't mean to be irreverent, but you gotta believe me. For a second, I thought I was looking at none other than Jesus Christ himself. It was just like what we used to see in Sunday School days." He looked to Margie. "In fact, Margie told me later that she thought for sure the Lord had come to carry her off to the clouds of heaven. She had it figured that they was gonna float off together and leave me standing there with my mouth wide open. Left behind to suffer for all eternity. Just me and my sin-loving pals."

Throwing her head back in an out-loud laugh, Margie confirmed that her husband spoke the truth.

His tone becoming serious again, Jim Price continued speaking. "Even though his appearance was crazy, and no matter how baggy his clothes were, it was impossible not to notice that this guy was one strong dude." Jim Price removed his arm from around Margie and lifted both arms in front of his chest, imitating the pose of a muscle-man photograph. "There was no doubt, this guy spent time in a gym," he paused, "and probably chugged steroids instead of orange juice every morning."

Leaning back again, Jim Price was contemplative for a moment. Brad watched as Margie looked at her husband, giving a nod and an understanding look. She spoke softly, "Go ahead, you're doing fine."

"This is where I wish I could just turn back time and tell the guy to hit the road. But that's not what I did." Dropping his eyes for a moment, Jim Price paused before looking at Brad with regret clearly on his face. "I invited that crazy loon into my house. We sat down for a talk. He told me he had heard I was looking for help. He said he wanted work and could start immediately. We talked for a bit. I explained that building a road by hand was gonna be really tough-ass, hard work. He just shrugged his shoulders and said that was fine with him."

Taking a breath, Jim Price continued. "Even though it struck me that he was weird as hell, I honestly couldn't put my finger on anything specific. He was basically pretty nice. I thought he seemed sincere enough and I sure needed help. So, bottom line, I told him I would pay twenty dollars per hour and give him our bunkhouse for sleeping and cooking his own meals, except for lunch. I told him Margie here would feed us royally each day at noon sharp. Pay day would be every Saturday morning. The guy thought for a couple of seconds before answering, then looked right at me and said he would work for fifteen dollars an hour if I paid in cash."

Jim Price gave a guilty grin. "I have no idea how you feel, being a federal guy and all that stuff. I figured he just didn't want to pay taxes. I was absolutely good with that and told him his offer suited me just fine as could be." Jim Price looked to Brad, not sure what reaction might come his way.

With a chuckle and thumbs-up gesture, Brad gave his answer. "I'm on your side all the way. More power to you."

"Whew! I was afraid you might haul me off to the rock pile for twenty years hard labor."

Casting a serious glance to Margie, Brad moved his head from side to side as if in serious thought. "After answering to this woman all these years, the rock pile would be way too easy. I'm afraid your destiny is settled."

"Fair enough, I suppose, fair enough." Jim Price took a heavy breath before continuing. "Okay, so there I sit, not really comfortable with this guy. I'm so desperate for help that I decide to take a chance." Jim Price shifted in his seat. "Now, listen to this next part and tell me I shouldn't be locked up in the funny farm. Up to this point, I had not even asked him his name. Once we had agreed that he would work on a cash only basis and be paid weekly, I casually asked his name. He just looked at me for a few seconds and then, serious as hell, told me his name was Nazareth." Jim Price looked to Margie. "I suppose both of us must have looked like we weren't sure of what the heck he had just said. He said it again, calm and serious as could be, 'My name is Nazareth.'"

Stifling a laugh, Margie cut in. "I just sat there speechless. I mean, we are talking to a man who is a dead ringer for the Good Shepherd himself. With a straight face, he says his name is Nazareth." Margie now let herself go with laughter. "Nobody, I mean nobody, could make this up."

Joining Margie, Brad's face was a mixture of mirth and disbelief. "What in the world did you say?"

The somber tone of Jim Price's voice quickly caused the brief moment of humor to evaporate. "Oh, yeah, I would be laughing my head off if I didn't think it pretty darned likely that this whacko did something awful to a young woman in Colorado." Shrugging his shoulders, he looked at Brad. "I think we must have just stared at him without saying anything. He finally spoke just like it was nothing more than answering someone who asked for the time of day. He said his parents had been devoutly religious and named him Nazareth as a way of honoring the Lord. That's it. That was his reply and no more. I started to press him but then realized since I had agreed to pay cash for his work, I really didn't have to know a last name or anything more." Jim Price looked to Margie and back to Brad. "How in the hell could I have been so damned stupid not to tell that weirdo to keep on trucking?"

Margie reached for his hand and softly spoke. "I didn't say anything that day either. Please, don't be too hard on yourself." Jim and Margie Price sat quietly, fingers intertwined.

Brad sensed that it was time for him to speak. "Look, I'm no cowboy or rancher. I was raised around cowboys and ranchers. I understand perfectly well how hard you work. Finding help is tough as the dickens. Don't beat yourself up with twenty-twenty hindsight." Brad paused a moment. "Here's how I think we need to look at this. If it turns out that this Nazareth guy is in fact the person who abducted the woman in

Kurt's case, then it's going to be a huge break that your paths crossed. You are good people who are taking time to do the right thing and help out."

Brad leaned so that he brought his face closer to Margie and Jim Price. "Instead of beating yourselves up, why don't we say his knock on your door may turn out to be a huge blessing? Let's get through your story and see what we have." Leaning back, Brad signaled that it was time for Jim Price to continue.

Speaking softly and with a thoughtful nod, Jim Price spoke. "Thank you for saying that. Maybe what you say is a better way to think about this whole deal."

Margie nodded her approval as Jim Price continued. "To cut to the chase here, I put on my boots and walked Nazareth down to the bunkhouse. I showed him the lay of the place and we agreed that he could settle in immediately. We agreed to begin work at eight o'clock the next morning. He pulled his jeep down to the bunkhouse, unloaded a few bags from the back, went inside and that was it. We saw a light in the window during early evening, but the place was dark not long after sunset." Jim Price smiled at his wife. "We don't usually bother to lock our doors after dark, but that night Miss Margie here made sure every door was locked and all windows were shut tight. Hell, for all I know, she may have plugged up the damned chimney."

"Smart woman." Brad pointed to his head as he smiled.

"Okay, so next morning we went to work. The weather was perfect and I mean we worked like slaves. We dynamited into solid rock. Then we had to move boulders the size of Volkswagens with nothing but our hands. We had to work a couple of days like that before I could get my tractor and a blade close enough to help out." Jim Price looked hard at Brad to add emphasis to his next words. "I'm telling you, Nazareth was a hard worker. And holy shit, he was one strong son-of-a-buck! That guy could lift rocks that were bigger than a damned cow and just toss 'em like they were nothing."

Shaking his head in amazement, Jim Price continued. "We worked hard as hell. I was starting to feel bad for ever questioning the guy. He wore regular work jeans, kept his hair in a ponytail and never complained about a thing. We headed back to the house every day for lunch and Margie fed him like a king. He was quiet, very mannerly and scarfed up every crumb. He always thanked Margie for her wonderful cooking." Jim Price turned to Margie. "Why don't you tell him the next part, where things got weird?"

"Humph! Weird, eerie or plain old scary. I'm not sure which to call it." Margie gazed across the Moreno Valley as she gathered her thoughts. "After a string of almost two weeks with perfect weather, it all came unraveled on a stormy afternoon. It was one of our New Mexico mountain storms that came rolling in about mid-afternoon. Long before the worst of it actually hit, there was no doubt that all heck was about to cut loose. All any fool had to do was take a look at the sky. Jim and Nazareth came scootin' home early and made it to the house as rain was barely beginning to fall. Lightning was just getting warmed up. Jim headed to the shower, and I was cooking supper when the skies opened up. Rain got serious and lightning started sizzling like it meant business. In fact, the lightning got so bad, and was striking so close, that I ran back to the bathroom. I told Jim to get his buns out of the shower before he got himself fried up." Margie grinned at her husband and then turned back to Brad. "Now, don't you even start to think that I used that lightning as an excuse just to sneak a peek at this handsome cowboy in the shower." Margie tossed her head as she laughed. "I truly was afraid of something bad happening and I wanted him out of that water pronto."

"Yeah, right." Tilting his hat back on his head, Jim Price slowly drawled, "It's awful, Brad. I can't even shower after a day's work without this woman wanting to jump in there with me."

Loving the scene playing out before him, Brad just chuckled and kept his eyes on Margie and Jim Price.

"Oh, for heaven's sake! If only half your dreams ever came true ...." Margie let her thoughts go unspoken and turned back to Brad. "As I was trying to tell you, I had supper cooking and sure wasn't thinking about any afternoon romance silliness. I got back into my kitchen and by now rain was coming down in buckets. Lightning was nonstop and the whole house was shaking like a leaf. Thunder sounded like it might blow the walls out. I went to the sink to run water in a pan and happened to glance out the window in the direction of the bunkhouse." Margie's eyes widened and the tone of her voice altered as she continued. "I almost dropped the pan right into the sink. Out beside the bunkhouse, standing in the middle of one heck of a storm, was Nazareth." Margie leaned her body for emphasis. "That fool was outside in the middle of one of the most gosh-awful storms you've ever seen. He was walking back and forth in front of the bunkhouse while lightning was popping everywhere. The crazy loon was holding his arms up above his head and it looked like he was shouting up into the sky, just having a wonderful conversation with himself or the Lord. Who knows? Good heavens, I started screaming for Jim to come quick." With a toss of her head, Margie let loose with a laugh. "I scared poor 'ole Jim half to death. He came running with nothing but a towel around his waist and dripping water all over the floor."

Shaking his head and grinning, Jim Price looked to Brad. "I didn't even take time to put my hat on and that just don't happen."

"Now, try to picture this, Brad." Margie was half serious and half laughing as she continued. "Nazareth is wearing some sort of robe or gown. He's strutting around like a rooster, arms up high over his head and we can see that he is singing, shouting or something right up at the sky. Lightning is everywhere, wind is howling. Rain is blowing in sheets and it sure looked to us like Nazareth was either having the time of his life or was in some sort of trance."

Listening to Margie tell her story and watching the look on both their faces, Brad had to laugh. "I'd give anything to have been a fly on the wall just to hear the two of you while this was going on."

Margie and Jim Price exchanged a quick glance. "Oh, Brad, we haven't even gotten to the good part yet." Margie placed her hand over her face in a gesture of mock embarrassment. "Maybe Jim better tell you what happened next."

"I'll be glad to take over and tell this my way from here on. You coulda been a fly on the wall but you wouldn't have heard a thing cause we weren't saying a word. What could we say, for crying out loud? We were absolutely speechless. Then, just about the time I'm beginning to get my brain accustomed to what the heck my eyes are looking at, off comes the robe! That crazy bastard is now standing in the rain, screaming up to heaven and he's naked as a gol-derned jay bird. That long hair of his is plastered all wet down to his shoulders while he keeps on holding his arms up to the sky and talking straight to heaven. And every second all this is going on, he's getting more excited." Jim Price gave Brad a questioning look. "Do you understand what the hell I'm saying to you? When I say he was excited, he was, you know what I mean," Jim Price hesitated, "aroused."

Brad quietly uttered the only words that seemed to even come close to an appropriate response, "You've got to be shitting me!"

"Shitting you I am not, my friend. I speak the bare-naked truth." Jim Price smiled at his own joke. "Of course, with what was taking place out by my bunkhouse, I quickly became concerned for the modesty of my bride." Jim Price turned to Margie and, with humor in his voice, continued. "I told her to avert her gaze from the awful spectacle that was taking place right before her innocent eyes."

All three shared a laugh at the vivid image Jim Price had created. Once humor had subsided, Jim Price looked to Margie and asked, "Okay, Margie, is all this story, everything we've told, word-for-word, the Bible-swearing truth?"

"You bet it is. Everything you've told is just the way it happened." Margie patted her husband's forearm. "You done good, sweetheart."

The moment seemed a perfect time for everyone to take a break and let the details of the story of Nazareth settle. After a few moments had passed, Brad spoke. "Well, Kurt only told me that you were pretty sure that this guy had stolen some stuff from your tool barn. He certainly didn't have all the details of what I've just heard in your story."

"No. When your friend called yesterday, he explained about his interest in the burglary report of my heavy-duty flashlight. We talked just enough for him to tell me a little bit about the kidnapping of that girl up in Colorado. He said that a light like mine had been found at the scene. Once I heard that, my gut sank like a rock. Sometimes a man just gets a feeling. You know something without knowing what it is you know." Jim Price grinned. "Understand what I mean?"

"You bet I understand. I'm a big-time believer in those feelings."

"Well, anyway, Kurt didn't try to get all the details. He said he had a good friend who was nearby. He preferred that I talk to someone in person. So, here we are."

"What happened after the nudie show in the storm? How did you handle the guy after being witness to something that crazy?"

Rubbing his chin, Jim Price spoke matter-of-factly. "I didn't handle anything. Everything handled itself. Once he finally picked up his robe from off the ground, he took his naked ass back into the bunkhouse.

Lights were out by the time darkness fell. Margie was having a fit that she would not live another day on the ranch as long as Nazareth was anywhere near our property. She went all through the house, sealing it up tight as a drum. It was just like she had done on the first night he first showed up. She said if I wanted to have a wife for another day, Nazareth had to be gone first thing after sun-up."

Margie sat rigidly on the bench, clearly re-living the memory of what had happened. Brad could only imagine how she would have looked and behaved immediately after watching such insanity.

Laughing lightly, Jim Price continued. "Margie was raising so much hell, I couldn't get a word in sideways. I sure as heck intended to fire him. I just didn't think I wanted to take a walk down to the bunkhouse at that very moment. It was pouring rain. Lightning was a killer and the ground was a muddy mess." His eyes twinkled. "It just didn't seem to be the perfect time for me to saunter down to have a talk with a naked-ass man, with a big 'ole hard-on, about how he might should be planning for his future."

Jim Price now laughed. "Especially since I'd seen him toss boulders around that weighed twice as much as my stiff old bones. We were scheduled to work the next morning. I knew it would be way too muddy. I told Margie that I was going to see him first thing the next morning, pay him for every day's work that I owed, and then kick his ass off the ranch. All this was gonna happen before she had the coffee pot fired up."

Margie now sat with her arms clinched about her body, not even a trace of a smile on her face. With a look in her eyes and a tone in her voice that let the world know she was not a woman to be taken lightly, Margie spoke in words that came out more of a hiss than an ordinary statement. "I wanted to go down there and set that damned old bunkhouse on fire. It's no good for anything anyway. I would've burned the whole building and that naked weenie of his in one big campfire!"

Her statement was not intended to be humorous. Brad was almost certain that he saw a shudder ripple through Margie's body as she finished speaking.

Jim Price continued with the story telling. "Lord all mighty! Later that night, when I finally convinced Margie that we had to go to bed, she refused to put on her nightgown. She got my hunting rifle out of the closet and lay on top of the bed all night, fully dressed and ready to blast away. Hell fire and Mother Mary. I was afraid that she was likely to shoot me in the kneecaps by accident. We both spent the night without sleeping hardly at all."

His eyes shifting from Margie to Jim Price, Brad asked the obvious. "What the heck happened?"

"Next morning, first light, I hopped out of bed, pulled on my jeans and boots and was ready to do what had to be done. But when I walked to the kitchen, I looked out the window to the bunkhouse. His Jeep was gone. I knew right away that Nazareth had skipped the territory. Just to settle things in my head, I walked on down to the bunkhouse. Sure as the dickens, he was gone to the wind. The bunkhouse was empty except for a few empty soup cans and some dirty paper plates on the floor. I saw that he had took our pillows and blankets from the bed. Other than that, the place was fine." Jim Price gave a quick laugh. "Hell, I had a wad of cash in my pocket that I had intended to pay for all of his work. I wasn't at all that upset about a couple of old blankets." Turning to Margie, he continued. "And that just about wraps up the story of Jim Price, Margie and Nazareth."

"Thank the good Lord up in heaven!" Margie still was not smiling.

"Later that day, I happened to go for some of my tools out in the barn. That's when I realized that the jackass had cleaned me out of a bunch of tools, some camping gear and that fancy light you boys are interested in. I was a whole lot more pissed about my tools than the blankets. That's why I decided to file a report."

Brad lifted the large envelope Jim Price had given him earlier. "What about this?"

"A few days after he started working for me, an envelope just like that came in the mail. It was addressed to our ranch address. The words 'Attention Nazareth' were written across the front. When I gave it to him, he wasn't surprised. He took it like he was used to getting his mail like that. I remembered that he had asked me for our address so he could get mail, so I didn't think much about it." Nodding to the bulging envelope, Jim Price continued. "That one there came right after he skipped. Not sure why, but I hung on to it. Glad I did. Maybe something in there will help you."

Brad nodded, deciding to wait until he was alone before opening the envelope. "Alright, folks, what a story. I thank you from the bottom of my heart for taking time to talk with me." He looked questioningly to Margie and Jim Price. "By any chance can you give me the tag number from his Jeep? During his time on your ranch, did you happen to take any photos of Nazareth or his vehicle?"

Regretful expressions and a shake of their heads gave Brad his answer.

Pulling a pen and paper from his pocket, Brad leaned over his knees. "I'm going to ask for all the descriptions about Nazareth, his car and all kinds of details that you can think of. But while we do this, it is important to keep in mind that even though this guy sounds looney, there is nothing at all to solidly connect him with what happened in Colorado. Kurt is following up on other reports of the same type of light that have been stolen in burglaries in Arizona, Kansas and all kinds of places. We'll do our best to figure Nazareth out but it's possible that there may be no connection whatsoever."

Without hesitation, Margie came right back with ice in her voice. "You can sit there and talk all you want about proof and high fallutin' legal stuff." Margie's eyes narrowed as she hurled her words and jabbed a finger in Brad's direction. "That man did it. He took that girl and don't you doubt it for a second." She relaxed a fraction as a tiny smile appeared. "Sometimes we ranch women know a whole bunch more than policemen and FBI guys all put together."

"Margie, I would follow you to the gates of hell if your instinct said that's what needed to be done." Brad spoke with sincerity. "I take every word you say straight to heart. Women just know things. I absolutely believe in your intuition, Margie, I promise I do." Brad held Margie's eyes. "But I'm asking for you to believe in me long enough to track all this down and put a case together the way it has to be done. Police investigations have to be based on hard evidence."

Margie's eyes never wavered as she slowly moved her head up and down. "You've got it, Brad, you've got it. I do believe in you. My instinct tells me that Nazareth has evil in his heart and has done something terrible." She held her breath a moment, her face intense as she lowered her voice to speak again. "My instinct also tells me that you are not going to let this go. I am looking into your heart. I can see you are a good man." Her gaze still piercing, Margie slowly shook her head. "Yes, you are going to find him, I'm sure of that." But dropping her eyes in doubt, Margie spoke even more softly. "What I don't know is if you are going to find him in time to help that poor girl."

All of the preceding conversation, serious and humorous, was suddenly encapsulated within Margie's final words. There was nothing more to say. Margie and Jim Price answered Brad's questions in subdued voices while he scribbled notes for the details that he needed. When finished, Brad put his pen away and all three sat in silence, looking over the Moreno Valley. "What a beautiful but sad place," Brad spoke reverently.

Margie stood. Turning her head toward the Memorial and then back to the Moreno Valley, a tear appeared on her cheek. Jim Price also stood and brought his wife close to him by placing an arm about her shoulder. "Margie lost a brother in Vietnam, Brad. We come here quite often. We knew the Westphall family, the folks who lost their son and then created this memorial in honor of all who served in Vietnam."

"I'm so sorry." Brad's words were a whisper.

Turning to Brad, Margie gave a smile. "Sometimes I come here and find sadness. Sometimes I come here and find happiness. I recall the days of our growing up and what a cut-up my brother was. How much fun we had." Margie dropped her voice. "Other times, I come here and just cry." She moved her head from side to side and tears now flowed. "Why? For what reason did my brother have to pick up a gun and go to the other side of the world? For what reason did he die, so far from this beautiful valley where he was raised and that he loved so much?"

Jim Price hugged his wife. Brad felt that he had become an intruder, that he should not be a part of Margie's grief. He stood without moving or speaking.

Margie and Jim Price seemed to both sense Brad's discomfort. Relaxing his embrace of Margie, Jim Price spoke. "There is always sadness when we come here but we feel lucky to have this memorial so close by. It is sad but it is also a balm. Lots of people carry the same grief that we carry. Sadly, many aren't so fortunate to have this incredible tribute for visiting and remembering."

"Jim is right. We are lucky." Turning to Brad, Margie wiped tears and smiled. "Don't you worry for a second about being with me during my little spell of emotion. I come here every once-in-a-while with family and friends. I think it's good to share grief. Somehow, it makes what I've lost seem not so lonely."

Not sure of what to say, Brad looked out over the Moreno Valley as he spoke. "Before you arrived here today, I walked through the Memorial. I asked myself the same question you ask, Margie. Why? In the name of heaven why do we keep sending young people off to die?" Brad hesitated. "I sure don't have an answer. In my many years of law enforcement, I've had to ask similar questions. Why do demented minds cause some people to abduct young women?" Brad pointed to the horizon. "Why was there a need for all that took place in Los Alamos just down the road? Why, why, why?"

No one spoke for a few moments. Finally, Margie broke the silence. "You know, Brad, my grandfather was a carpenter at Los Alamos during its heyday. Believe it or not, he actually became friends with Robert Oppenheimer, the man himself, the man behind the atomic bomb."

"No kidding."

"Yes, it's incredible. One day Oppenheimer needed to get down off the hill to Santa Fe for some super urgent meeting with a bunch of hotshots. The car that was supposed to take him broke down just as they were leaving the laboratory gate. Everybody got all excited and had no idea what to do. Oppenheimer very calmly looked around and spotted my grandfather just sitting in a government truck smoking a cigarette. So, he runs over, hops in the truck and says, 'Get me down off this damned mountain to Santa Fe and do it fast!'"

Laughing as she talked, Margie told her story. "My grandfather was quite a character. He drove Oppenheimer down that hill like a dog chasing a rabbit. The two of them got to smoking and joking about government nonsense and what they thought of all the pretty women going to waste in Santa Fe." Margie paused and winked at Brad. "From what I hear through family conversations that took place after too much whiskey, my grandfather was one horny coot. Anyway, Oppenheimer had so much fun with my grandfather that every so often he would order an underling to go find 'that crazy carpenter' just so the two of them could drive to Santa Fe together." Margie raised her right hand. "God's honest truth. My grandfather and the man who led us into the Atomic Age, they became pals. They laughed, fantasized about women and had themselves the time of their lives." Margie grinned and shook her head in amazement. "And all their nonsense was going on while the fate of the world hung in the balance of what was going right over there." Margie pointed in the direction of Los Alamos.

"What a great story." Clapping his hands together and laughing as he spoke, Brad turned to Jim Price. "The way I see it, you have a tough act to follow."

Jim Price threw his head back and laughed. "Oh, don't you worry. I gave up trying to follow that man's antics years ago. Her grandfather's preferred manner of death was to be shot dead crawling out a window while running away from a pissed-off husband."

Knowing that the time had come, Margie, Jim Price and Brad poised to say farewell. The handshake of Jim Price was even more firm than when they had initially met. Years of life and experiences streamed through their silent and prolonged contact. Brad turned to Margie. There was no thought of shaking hands. Without hesitation and with no hint of awkwardness, they hugged. Brad intuitively knew that Margie and Jim Price were his kind of people. Just like his parents and the many others who had helped to raise him, they were everything that was right in a world gone terribly wrong.

NINE

TELL GENERAL HOWARD I know his heart. What he told me before I have in my heart. I am tired of fighting. Our Chiefs are killed. Looking Glass is dead. Too-hull-hul-sote is dead. The old men are all dead. It is the young men who say yes or no. He who led on the young men is dead. It is cold and we have no blankets. The little children are freezing to death. My people, some of them have run away to the hills, and have no blankets, no food; no one knows where they are — perhaps freezing to death. I want to have time to look for my children and see how many of them I can find. Maybe I shall find them among the dead. Hear me, my chiefs. I am tired; my heart is sick and sad. From where the sun now stands, I will fight no more forever.

(Words of Chief Joseph of the Nez Percé at the time of his surrender to General Oliver Howard, Eagle Creek, Montana, October 5th, 1877)

If atomic bombs are to be added to the arsenals of a warring world, or to the arsenals of nations preparing for war, then a time will come when mankind will curse the names of Los Alamos and Hiroshima. The people of the world must unite or they will perish.

• • •

(From a speech given by Robert Oppenheimer on October 16, 1945 at Los Alamos, New Mexico)

Peace brings riches; riches bring pride; pride brings anger; anger brings war; war brings poverty; poverty brings humanity; humanity brings peace; and so, the world's affairs go around.

(Words of the Italian historian, Luigi da Porto and displayed in the Vietnam Memorial, Angel Fire, New Mexico)

TEN

Back in his truck and sitting quietly, Brad contemplated the bizarre story he had just heard. A ton of craziness had been related in the words of Margie and Jim Price, but nothing to give rock solid connection to Kurt's case. He recalled Margie's face and words as she had pronounced her intuition that Nazareth was in fact evil and responsible for the Colorado abduction. Brad acknowledged that an inner voice was speaking to him as well, whispering that Nazareth was the key to finding out what had happened to Sharon Moore. But sadly, intuition and inner voices were woefully insufficient. Not only was conclusive evidence lacking to connect Nazareth to the crime, there was no hint as to where Nazareth may have fled after leaving the Price ranch.

Holding the large envelope, Brad thought about how to proceed. Any sort of successful fingerprint or forensic analysis on the envelope was highly unlikely. More importantly, there was no time for the bureaucratic process that would be involved. If there was any chance of resolving the disappearance of Sharon Moore before it was too late, things had to happen at light speed. Brad absently thumped the envelope against his thigh. With an exhaled breath of "Screw it," and knowing that legal technicalities were involved, Brad opened the large envelope.

It was what he had expected; a variety of letters that had been sent through the U.S. Mail. Quickly shuffling through envelopes of assorted sizes, he saw that each item had been mailed to Madrid, New Mexico, in care of a Post Office box in Cerrillos, New Mexico. All were addressed to Onias Phillips. The envelopes appeared to be an assortment of junk mail, so Brad decided to leave them sealed and unopened for the time being. The only items not individually sealed were a magazine and a single sheet of lined paper that bore a handwritten note addressed to Onias.

Feeling his heart accelerate, Brad placed everything else aside and read the words that had been neatly written in pencil:

Dear Onias,

This is the mail that has come for you in recent days. I don't think it amounts to much except for the magazine that you always request. I hope that you will find some comfort in it. You know how my heart aches for you. I begin each day and end each day with a hope that you will find whatever it is that you seek and that the demon living within you can be slain. You have suffered more than God should ever allow one of his children to suffer. I beg you to come back and allow me to help you. If you do not free your mind and heart of the devil that has taken you, I fear for your life. If I lose you, I don't know what I will do. Please come home.

My love forever,

Anna

After reading the letter twice, Brad reached for the magazine that had been included within the larger envelope. The professionally colored and designed cover bore the name, '*Ensign*' and in small print over the magazine's name were the words:

The Ensign of the Church of Jesus Christ of Latter Day Saints

• • •

Brad realized the magazine was a publication of the Mormon faith, published and distributed out of Salt Lake City. An assortment of religious articles, ranging from living a life of overall spirituality to very specific advocacy for Mormon beliefs, filled its pages. He closed the magazine knowing it surely held significance but, exactly what, he had no way of knowing.

His mind racing, Brad whispered, "First things first." He called Kurt Riddle. When he heard Kurt's voicemail, he disconnected without leaving a message and punched in a text message for Kurt to call ASAP. With so many thoughts rolling through his head, Brad could not possibly just sit idly and wait. He had to move. Stepping out of his truck, Brad stretched his arms over his head and began to walk. Within seconds, his phone beeped. He read Kurt's message, "Gimme 10."

Knowing he had a few minutes to kill, Brad decided to again walk the grounds of the Memorial. Perhaps that would be a way to settle his mind. After a few minutes, Kurt's call came through but, before Brad could begin to relay the details of his time with Margie and Jim Price, Kurt's excited voice took control of the conversation. "My friend, I sure want to hear what you have to say. But I gotta tell you first about a call I just had from a police officer in Cheyenne, Wyoming. I think there may be a ray of hope for Sharon Moore."

Catching his breath in a mid-inhale, Brad uttered, "Oh, my God! Please, let me hear it."

"Ain't nothing for sure here but it's the first bit of good news I've had since we got back from our fishing trip. We've been flooding cyberspace and every law enforcement agency in the country with pleas for help on anything similar to what happened with Sharon Moore. That's a pretty general scenario so I haven't been too optimistic. Just when you were calling and texting a few minutes ago, I was on the line with an investigator up in Cheyenne. Holy shit, Brad, if his case is related to ours, and I think it probably is, we just might have ourselves a ray of hope that Sharon Moore is still okay."

"Oh, good heavens, Kurt, talk to me. What I have to report is nowhere close to this important. Keep talking."

"Okay, here we go. A little less than two years ago, they had a girl go missing in Cheyenne. Just like in our case, she had been out with friends in a restaurant and bar type place. At the end of the evening, she said she was going straight home because she had an early shift the next morning as a nurse in the Cheyenne hospital. Poof! The girl is gonzo. No word, no sign. After she failed to show for her shift at the hospital, her roommates and friends became concerned and called the police. This girl was sharing a house with other nurses out on the edge of Cheyenne. It was a on a pretty desolate dirt road but still within the city limits of Cheyenne. So, the police cruised what would have been her logical route home. Sure enough, they spotted her car sitting on the dirt road a short distance from her house. The engine was still running and lights were on. The only difference from our case is that all doors of the car were shut."

"Jesus."

"Just like our case, her purse and belongings were left in the car. Nothing else taken. Oh, and by the way, she was a very attractive blonde. Same age and general physical appearance as Sharon Moore." Kurt took a breath and was quiet, waiting for Brad to speak.

"So far, it sounds like the same scenario but I'm guessing this one had a happy ending because you seem pretty excited and optimistic."

"Well, it isn't exactly what I would call happy, but the ending is pretty remarkable. At least was not tragic. Here's what happened. The guy who took this girl hauled her to a public storage unit. He tied a rope around her legs and arms and then used a rope to attach her to the wall. He gagged her and left her locked up in a ten-by-ten cubicle. She had a mattress to lie on but could hardly move because she was tied so tightly. Twice a day the guy came to see her. He brought food, untied her and provided a big bucket for her to relieve herself. He turned his back for her only sense of privacy. Then the asshole carried away the bucket and brought a fresh one each time."

"Good Lord Almighty."

"Yep, what can ya say except Good Lord Almighty? The girl said he complained a bunch about having to carry away her bucket and told her that God wanted her to be clean. The guy repeatedly told her that he was waiting for a sign from God."

"This is unreal."

"The good part is that this girl is one tough cookie. Wyoming born and raised. On the third day of being held captive she realizes that the guy had done a crappy job of re-tying her to the wall after his last visit.

Her hands are tied but she can reach the wall. With her fingers and a bunch of struggling, she somehow managed to free herself. She had to roll across the floor to the door where she starts kicking like hell on the metal door of the storage unit. Someone finally hears her, calls for help and that's the happy part. She was rescued. She is alive, and unbelievably, was not molested."

"She was one lucky girl."

Taking a deep breath, Kurt continued. "What really gives me hope is that if it is indeed the same bad guy in both cases, then maybe Sharon Moore is still alive and unharmed. Hopefully, the shithead is just holding her somewhere while he waits for his friggin' sign."

"That's more hope than I ever expected."

"There's all kinds of really strange stuff here. Just as we predicted a couple of nights ago around our campfire, the Wyoming bastard used a police traffic stop as a ruse. It's weird as hell but, thank goodness, the guy did not molest the girl in any way. He just took her directly to the storage unit, tied her up and left her. Every time he came back to the storage place to see her, he babbled about Jesus and God and how he was waiting for a sign from God. The victim said the guy seemed very unsure of himself and was making his decisions on the fly. It's her opinion that he didn't really have a plan or know what the heck he was doing, other than waiting for whatever the hell damned sign he was looking for."

"Any idea who the guy is?"

"Nope, not a clue. The storage unit was rented by means of identification that turned out to have been stolen out of a fancy health club in Salt Lake City. He paid in cash for three months in advance. We've got the victim's description of the guy and his vehicle but that's it. Forensics in the storage locker and on all the paper documents that were signed came up with a big goose egg."

"Man alive! Now that I've heard this story, it might be that what I have to report is more significant than what I initially was thinking. How did the Wyoming girl describe the guy? Anything on his vehicle?"

"The girl thinks that the vehicle he used in the ruse traffic stop was an SUV-type vehicle, dark in color. When he grabbed her, she was blinded by his lights and never got a good look at what he was driving. Whatever it was, it had a back seat cause he shoved her into the back. He pulled a covering of some sort over her head and tied her up in a flash.

She had several good looks at him later when he was with her in the storage locker. He was a white male and she puts the guy at about six feet tall, around mid-thirties, give or take. Medium build but strong as hell. Even though he was always wearing a long-sleeved shirt and stocking cap, she got a definite impression that he had the look of a serious body-builder. When he first grabbed her out of her car, she said she tried to fight back but he was incredibly strong. She had no chance at all."

"Did she get a look at his hair?"

"Afraid not. It was summer and hot as the dickens, but he always kept a stocking cap on his head when in her presence. But, this girl was astute enough to observe that his hair had to be cut fairly short because the cap fit over his head nice and tight."

Brad was quiet for a moment as he formulated his thoughts. "Kurt, give me a listen for a minute. I'm not sure but I think we might have a break from that theft report of the flashlight from down here in New Mexico." Brad related the details of his talk with Margie and Jim Price. He related the critical discovery of the name Onias Phillips that had been obtained from mail sent to the Price ranch.

Except for an occasional "Holy shit" or laugh, Kurt let Brad tell his story without interruption. When Brad became silent, Kurt took a breath and offered his response. "Well, it ain't enough to go asking a judge for a warrant but I've gotta think we're looking at the same bozo in both cases. You agree?"

"Absolutely. I agree both ways. We're nowhere near the warrant level but the physical strength of the guy and using a name like Nazareth, along with religious mumbo jumbo are too much to be coincidence. Plus, the ranch folks in New Mexico say their guy drove a vehicle with Utah tags. The Wyoming case has a guy who stole identification from a Salt Lake City health club. That's just one more piece."

"Yep, I think you're right." Kurt's voice was energized. "I'll hop on finding out if this guy Onias Phillips has a record or driver's license. Maybe we can get our hands on a photograph that the Wyoming folks could show their victim. Wouldn't that be a break?"

"Good gosh, yes."

"You're a New Mexico boy. Know anything about these Madrid or Cerrillos places?"

"Yeah, I do. Madrid is spelled like the city in Spain and some people pronounce it the same. But many of the people who live around there call it 'Mad-Rid.' It's an old mining town that's now become a unique little spot that attracts all kinds of artists and kindred souls that are pretty independent-minded. It has a bunch of galleries and sees quite a tourist trade. I was there a couple of times with Elizabeth. It's been several years. We enjoyed the place. Cerrillos is a bit larger town, right next door. My guess is that Cerrillos would be the Post Office location for people who live in Madrid."

"Where in the world is it?"

"It's between Albuquerque and Santa Fe but on the opposite side of the mountains from the interstate. There's a two-lane road that gets you there. It's called The Turquoise Highway. The area is classic Northern New Mexico territory, both desert and forest. Beautiful scenery is all around. It's laid back like Taos but much smaller and a different feel entirely."

"Sounds like it's pretty remote."

"Getting there is no problem, maybe forty-five minutes from Albuquerque. About the same from Santa Fe. Not a lot of people around if that's what you mean. I can't think what county it's in, so I don't know who the responding law enforcement agency would be."

Kurt was silent but Brad could hear him thinking. Finally, Kurt spoke with ideas and words forming together. "Okay, here's the way I see it. There is a chance that Sharon Moore is still alive and maybe not harmed. But that sure as hell isn't going to be the case indefinitely."

"I'm with you."

"Bottom line, time is critical. If I screw around and go through channels to find the name and address that goes with the Post Office box, then figure out who the proper agency is to contact, and then wait God knows how long for someone to find the time to get in a unit and drive to this Mad-Rid..." Kurt paused without finishing his thoughts. "Get my drift, Knucklehead?"

Brad tried to think of a clever retort, but a sarcastic laugh involuntarily erupted before words could form. "You know something, Kurt? Those horses we rode a couple of days ago were a whole lot more subtle than you ever dreamed of being. I'm pretty sure they were smarter too."

Brad took a breath. "Yes, I get your drift and yes, I agree. There really is no choice but to move as quickly as possible."

"How long will it take for you to get your bony ass down there?"

"Three hours or so, I suppose. But it's up to you to come up with an address that belongs to the Post Office box. I don't have the juice to do that anymore."

"You just start driving and leave the police work to me. I've got an old pal with Postal Inspectors named Greg Freeman. He's a salty guy and will know exactly what to do and who to call. He can track this down in no time. I'll call you back or text you with a name and an address."

"This is just peachy, Kurt. Here I go again, supposed to be retired, getting myself into heaven knows what. Juanita just happens to be on an airplane as we speak. She's flying back to Albuquerque and is expecting flowers, music, dinner and a handsome lover, not an empty house."

"Well, one thing is for certain. Your ugly ass not being in Albuquerque sure as hell don't make any difference in the handsome lover part of the equation."

"Lord in heaven, I'm glad I don't have to deal with you very often. I'm rolling in a matter of minutes. Just get me that address."

"You'll have it, Brad. Adios. And, no shit, I do appreciate this. I'm dying to get this resolved."

"I'm dying right along with you so no problem. I'll call Juanita and she wouldn't have it any other way."

By the time Brad had disconnected from Kurt, he had made his way back to his truck. Before entering, he took one last gaze over the Moreno Valley. He turned for a final look at the Vietnam Memorial. His mind was racing in so many ways. Could the next few hours be key to saving Sharon Moore? Was the entire Moreno Valley large enough to hold the grief and tragedy of the stories that lay within the walls and grounds of the Memorial? Brad looked to the south where, within the tranquility of Valles Caldera, centuries of life sifted each day in streams and meadows. He held his eyes in the direction of Los Alamos, contemplating the scientific prowess that had been conceived there by Robert Oppenheimer and the most brilliant minds of the ages. Is it all connected? Do the voices of the past still speak in the wind over Valles Caldera and Los Alamos? Is there actually some master with all-knowing eyes or caring hands that shaped Valles Caldera and watched over her native peoples?

What did those eyes see when thousands died in Vietnam? When the mushroom cloud of Los Alamos erupted over New Mexico? Where was that master's caring hands or seeing eyes on the dark and stormy night when Sharon Moore was stolen away?

Shaking his head in frustration, Brad climbed into his truck and headed back toward Santa Fe and the village of Madrid.

ELEVEN

MAKING a turn from Paseo de Peralta, Brad navigated through Santa Fe's narrow streets toward the Plaza. After parking his truck, he gratefully stretched his body in a stroll to The Plaza Café. Had it really been only that very morning that he had begun his day with a pre-dawn walk to Cross of the Martyrs? It seemed a lifetime ago.

The Plaza Café was just what he needed for both a physical and mental respite before searching for answers in Madrid. The café had somehow managed to avoid the glitzy sheen of high-end shops of the Santa Fe Plaza. It retained a down-home character that Brad and many Santa Fe locals loved. With a cold Santa Fe Pale Ale and blue corn enchiladas on order, Brad called Juanita. He had already left her a message while she was on her flight home, but he desperately wanted to hear her speak. The voice he heard was frustratingly that of her recording, "Please leave a message." Brad suspected that she was out for a jog, undoubtedly going nuts after days in a hotel, a boring conference, and a cramped flight home. After telling Juanita the short version of what he was doing to help Kurt, Brad promised that he would be with her in Albuquerque as soon as possible.

Earlier, while Brad was driving, Kurt had relayed all of the latest information developed so far. He had found no criminal record for a person named Onias Phillips but a New Mexico driver's license with a photograph had been located. Wyoming investigators planned to show the photo to their victim. The holder of the Post Office Box in Cerrillos was Anna Carter, a white female, fifty years old. Her physical address was in the town of Madrid. She had no criminal record. A ten-year-old Subaru was registered to Anna Carter and she had a New Mexico driver's license. Kurt was still checking for records in Utah.

Brad scrutinized the New Mexico Driver's license photos of Anna Carter and Onias Phillips. The image of Anna Carter was of poor quality. Brad squinted in concentration, as if his efforts could bring her face to life. He wanted to look into her eyes, examine her face and feel her body language. It did not happen. Whatever story or secrets Anna Carter held would have to wait until he found her and, hopefully, talked with her.

The photograph of Onias was a clear image of a man, around thirty, short hair and lean face. It should be adequate for the Wyoming victim to say yes or no if he had been her abductor.

———

After exiting Interstate 25, Brad began his drive south on Highway 14, the Turquoise Highway. Wisps of evening's scattered clouds began to join forces. Becoming darker by the second, they gathered and, within the distance of only a few miles, towered into the sky. Shimmers of lightning flashed within the dark canyons of the clouds and volleys of thunder launched over piñon forests. Then came rain. With ferocious power, sheets of water were flung from the sky, cascading over thirsty land. Within the cab of Brad's truck, sounds of nature's fury were deafening and wiper blades became helpless against the onslaught. Brad was driving blind. Gripping his wheel and slowing to a crawl, Brad thought of Sharon Moore. What incredible terror she must have felt if she had experienced similar conditions on the night of her abduction. What was she experiencing at this moment?

In only minutes, it was over. As quickly as it had begun, the rain and bluster transformed into nothing more than scampering puffs of vapor. Sunshine beamed in cylindrical shafts through the prism of dissolving clouds. The effect was magical. A ballet of celestial light caressed the high-desert landscape. Brad loved it. Then, as an encore, a rainbow arched, one foot anchored on the eastern horizon, another in the west, vibrant and beautiful. Brad saw it as the doorway to heaven. The fading storm transformed into the soft breath of evening and an amber glow settled over the Turquoise Highway. Brad drove, thanking whoever or whatever was up above for creating the land and sky that made New Mexico so spectacular.

———

With Madrid only minutes away, Brad had no idea what to expect. Who was Anna Carter? What would cause a fifty-year-old woman to compose a letter expressing both love and concern to a man many years younger? Surely, if Anna was his mother, she would have signed it, 'Love Mother,' or some affectionate phrase other than using her given name. Who or what was the demon that she mentioned? What did she mean when she wrote about the devil that had taken him? Why did she fear for his life?

With no answers and no idea of what he was going say to Anna Carter if he even found her, Brad entered the village of Madrid. The sky had darkened into a violet dome. Brad knew that night's first stars were only minutes away. His uncertainty over Anna Carter and her relation-ship with Onias, Nazareth, or whatever the hell the guy's name might be, delivered an increasing sense of unease.

Brad had felt unsettled during his drive. Was what had happened in Wyoming reason for hope? He was certain that each passing hour cast shadows on hope for Sharon Moore. As an encounter with Anna Carter drew near, nervousness tightened within his chest. He drew a breath and whispered, "One thing at a time, Brad, one thing at a time."

Driving slowly through Madrid's only main street, Brad managed a stem-to-stern look at the old mining settlement. He pulled to the side of the road and once again read Anna Carter's hand-written letter. Making a U-turn and again passing through Madrid, Brad drove with windows down, seeking the mood of the tiny town. Unique galleries, shops and boutique cafés were the lifeblood of Madrid on a beautiful summer's evening. In the descending darkness, Brad was lucky to spot the sign that identified the street where Anna Carter lived. He made the turn and as he did so, perspiration gathered within his palms. What was the sense of omen that he felt over meeting with this woman?

His truck moving at idle speed, Brad felt eerily alone as he strained to see his surroundings. A row of simple houses lined both sides of the street. Tiny yards, crumbling fences, rickety porches and tired old dogs all seemed to say farewell to the last embers of light. There were no street lights, but Brad recognized the house when his headlights illuminated a rusted Subaru parked to the side. Once his eyes fell on the vehicle and house, he knew he had found what he was looking for. He also could feel that Anna Carter had found him. She was watching. Brad just knew it.

A silhouette, a shadow within a shadow, was all that he saw but Brad knew it was Anna Carter. She sat, barely moving, in a rocking chair on the front porch. The house appeared miniature beneath the open sky. Brad brought his truck to a halt and killed the engine and lights. Even though his windows were still down, not a sound was to be heard. The street, the house and everything around him seemed to hold a collective breath. The woman on the porch halted the motion of her rocking. Brad sat in his truck. Evening had become night and darkness cast a void between Brad's truck and the figure on the porch.

The woman did not move. Not a word had been uttered nor a muscle twitched in the space that separated them. But the woman and Brad heard each other. Unspoken communication was clear and undeniable; Anna Carter knew exactly why a strange vehicle, with an unknown man driving, had just parked in front of her house. With equal certainty, Brad knew that the woman in the rocking chair was the woman who had written the letter to Nazareth. He also knew with inexplicable certainty that the key to finding Sharon Moore was only a few feet away, shrouded in the night.

Gulping a breath and opening his door, Brad prayed to find the proper words. He prayed not to botch what may be Sharon Moore's best, or only, chance. Following a brief moment of light from the cab as he stepped out, he again saw nothing more than the outline of the woman and her chair in darkness. It was impossible to see her face, but Brad felt her eyes. He sensed the scrutiny she gave to the stranger who was as much a shadow to her as she was to him.

Without moving, Brad spoke into the darkness. "Good evening, Ms. Carter. I don't mean to intrude. My name is Brad Walker." He hesitated a beat. "I would appreciate a few minutes of your time. I want to ask you about Onias." Another beat. "I think Onias may be in trouble. I'm hoping you can help me, Ms. Carter." Brad held his breath. "If you will help me, I think we may both be able to help Onias."

The shadow began a slow rock, forward, back – forward, back. Somewhere on the street, a dog barked. Forward, back – forward, back. A voice came from the darkness. The voice was soft, but what else was it? Confident? Sorrowful? "I've been expecting you, Mr. Walker." Forward, back. "At least you didn't come to my house in a police car with all sorts of lights flashing. I thank you for that." The rocking ceased. "It is my hope that your subdued manner means good news and not bad." The shadow stood. "Please, Mr. Walker, come in. I know we need to talk." Appearing to glide as she moved to the doorway, Brad watched in fascination as the shadow moved silently but ever so gracefully. Hinges of a screen door groaned. A light appeared within the house.

Her back still to him, and nothing more than contour against the light, Brad was startled by her stature. She was well over six feet tall. Slender in build and, even in silhouette, she exuded elegance as she moved. Simply because it felt like the right thing to do, Brad crossed her tiny yard, stepped onto the porch and approached her door as softly as if he were entering a church. His running shoes were almost silent on the weathered wood. He hesitated upon reaching the doorway. The woman had moved further inside, her back still the only view available.

Sensing that Brad had halted outside, the woman turned to face the doorway. Waving her arm and hand she spoke, "Please, please, come in, Mr. Walker. I do not snarl or bite, I promise."

Upon opening the screen door and crossing the threshold, Brad saw Anna Carter's face for the first time. He stood before a fifty-year-old woman, her grey hair swept back and held behind her head with a silver and turquoise barrette. Wrinkles about her eyes and mouth were testament to years of life. Proud cheekbones and a captivating smile defied age. Obviously, a complete stranger to cosmetics or make-up, Anna dressed unpretentiously in loose-fitting jeans and an oversized shirt. Brad was immediately taken with her natural beauty. But there was something more, something deeper. There was more to Anna Carter than just an attractive woman. Had it been her voice, the manner in which she softly articulated each word? Or was it how she moved her body, as if she floated, totally without effort? Holding her posture perfectly erect, which called attention to her height, Anna extended her hand. "Mr. Walker, it seems you already know my name but let me introduce myself anyway. I'm Anna Carter, welcome to my home."

Her hand within his, Brad felt rough skin, the texture of sandpaper. Her firm grip delivered strength. Brad also felt a warmth that conveyed inner character. With their hands clasped and their eyes engaged, Brad saw a face of mystery. Anna exuded grace, dignity and charisma. That was undeniable. With her hand still within his, Brad found her unnerving.

Evaluating Brad with deep blue eyes, Anna smiled the knowing smile of a woman accustomed to having a profound effect upon people. Removing her hand from Brad's, Anna twisted her body as she swept an arm across the landscape of the room. "This is pretty much it, my home, all right here. What you see is what you get." She again turned to Brad, expectancy on her face. It was his turn.

Grateful for an opportunity to look somewhere other than into Anna's face, Brad gazed about his surroundings. Anna had spoken truthfully. The room where they stood was quite small and it served as kitchen, studio and bedroom, all in one. A sink sat below a window that looked outside to where Brad's truck was parked. Next to the sink stood a wooden table that held a camping stove and a cubed-shaped refrigerator made for the smallest of spaces. Her few dishes and cooking utensils were neatly arranged on a shelf beneath the table top. A television or computer were not to be seen. A small radio stood near the camp stove.

The back wall, opposite the front door and kitchen area, held a couch with a neatly folded blanket and pillow. A smattering of clothing hung from a wall bracket at the foot of the couch. It was apparent that this portion of the room and the couch served Anna both as a bedroom and closet. Peering into a darkened hallway, Brad saw a bathroom and another door that was closed. That was the extent of Anna's house: tiny, sparse and austere. But Brad felt a warmth within the room that was similar to what he sensed in Anna. This small house and single living room was a place where life was lived.

Bringing his attention back into the center of the room, Brad spotted a table that he had scarcely noticed in his initial observation. A hodge-podge of jars, bowls and odd-looking artifacts cluttered the table's surface. Rags of various sizes and colors were scattered about. A body-length apron hung from a simple coat tree. Then he saw it. Partially obscured by the coat tree and the array of materials on the table was a potter's wheel. Realization settled that much of what he saw on Anna's table were pieces of pottery in various phases of completion.

Understanding flickered across Brad's face as his eyes and mind absorbed how Anna lived. He allowed a few additional moments of observation before he finally spoke. "First, thank you for inviting me into your home. I appreciate your kindness to my unannounced appearance."

With a slight smile, Anna nodded her head.

"I am absolutely fascinated by this," Brad pointed to the potter's wheel. "I'm sure that I could never develop the skill or the finesse to do what you do, but I absolutely love the art of pottery. In my mind, it represents much of what is so special about New Mexico. Pottery and potters are the fabric of a soul that simply doesn't exist in most places."

Lifting her hands to shoulder height, Anna spread her fingers and rotated her wrists, showing stained palms and fingernails worn to nubs. "These hands have been molding Mother Earth's clay for many years." She shrugged. "I'm not great but I sell a few pieces here and there. Once in a while I get commission orders." Lowering her arms, she continued. "I make enough to live in this house and keep gas in that old Subaru out there." Anna smiled. "The housekeeper, yard crew, personal limousine driver, private pilot and my investment banker are also very well compensated."

With Brad's laugh at Anna's humor, the atmosphere eased a bit. Brad grinned. "I'm not bad with a lawnmower so, maybe one of these days, we can trade lawn mowing for pottery lessons." Their eyes held, both still evaluating. "Cutting grass is the best I can do. You probably wouldn't like my housekeeping skills. People tell me that I'm a terrible driver, my eyesight is no good for flying, and I think stocks are bunches of cows."

Now it was Anna's turn to laugh. "Let's keep that possibility in mind. Someday we may strike the perfect business arrangement." Anna's gaze intensified. "Now, Mr. Walker, you did not show up here tonight to talk about pottery or apply for a job as a grass cutter for a woman with no yard." She paused, her eyes never leaving Brad's face. "You are a policeman of some sort. You want to talk with me about Onias. As I said earlier, I've been expecting this visit." She hesitated. "Maybe I should say I've been dreading this visit." Anna paused and glanced about the room.

"My options to you are limited. I have two rockers on the porch, but it's pretty dark out there. I'm guessing you prefer the other option, which is to talk here, inside and under lights. That is how you will keep your eyes on me. Evaluate my body language. You want to decide whether or not I'm speaking the truth. You wish to be able to watch my every move and facial expression. I think you will be looking for signs of deception." A heartbeat passed. "Am I correct, Mr. Walker?"

Brad did not rush his response, letting Anna know that he had paid attention to her comments. When he finally spoke, he did so in a soft but straightforward tone. "Yes, Ms. Carter, you are correct that I am some sort of policeman. But you are not being fair with the rest of your assumptions. I was being honest with you when I said I think Onias is in trouble. The difficult aspect of the trouble that Onias faces is that, in all likelihood, his trouble is also placing other people in danger." Brad looked straight into Anna's eyes. "I am not here tonight to judge you, Ms. Carter. I'm in no position to do that. I am simply here to ask your assistance, straight and simple. I am not holding anything under the table." Brad allowed a moment for Anna to contemplate his words. "I have no hidden agenda, Ms. Carter. I need your help. We can sit wherever you wish. On your porch or in this room." Brad met Anna's eyes head on.

Seconds passed as Anna evaluated Brad's response. Without speaking, she turned and walked to the table beside her kitchen sink. From behind the table, she extracted two folding chairs, carried them toward the potter's wheel and placed them to face each other. Indicating for Brad to be seated, she finally replied. "Forgive me, Mr. Walker. I should not have spoken to you that way. I was very wrong and very rude. I allowed pre-conceived bias to cloud my manners. That is unacceptable. Please, take a seat and let's talk."

Nodding in gratitude but with no further words, Brad sat down. Anna followed. There was nothing between them. No desk or table providing a psychological barrier. No place to rest hands or arms, no surface on which to fidget fingers or manipulate a pencil. Anna had positioned the chairs so that their knees practically touched. She now looked directly into Brad's face, expectancy in her expression.

Brad's mind raced. He had never met a woman who exuded such intrigue. A trace of panic stirred. It entered his mind that he stood a good chance of making a terrible mess of things. With this sobering real-ization, Brad sought to slow his heart and calm his mind. There was not going to be a second chance with Anna Carter.

For lingering moments that stretched to borderline discomfort, Anna and Brad faced each other. Uncertainty tinged with anticipation hung in the space between them. Adjusting his body within the chair, Brad finally began. "Ms. Carter, I don't know for sure what is the right way or the right place for me to begin. Please bear with me. About a week ago, a young woman in Colorado was taken from her car on a remote moun-tain road. She has not been seen or heard from since. Evidence recovered from the scene of her abduction led the Colorado investigation to a man who calls himself Nazareth. I suspect you can figure how a link between Nazareth and you developed."

Brad stopped speaking. Anna's body was rigid but Brad thought he detected something in her eyes. Perhaps desperation. Possibly sadness. Whatever it was, it had not been there when he first entered her home and shook her hand.

A drop of perspiration oozed from Brad's armpit. An icy trickle trickled down his ribs. Continuing, he leaned forward slightly. "I'm not a police officer, Ms. Carter. I am a former FBI Agent. I worked for years with the Colorado investigator who is in charge of this matter. We are very good friends. He is feeling tremendous pressure to resolve the disap-pearance of this young woman. He desperately wants to keep her from harm. We both think that every minute is critical. By pure luck I happened to be traveling close by and my friend asked me to find you. He thinks that if he took time to notify local police agencies down here and follow a traditional chain of command, the delay could have tragic consequences for the abducted woman."

Brad took a deep breath as he looked to Anna. "That is why I'm here tonight. I have no idea what your relationship might be with Onias - or Nazareth - but the clock is ticking for an innocent young woman in Colorado." Brad held his words for a moment. "Ms. Carter, I am asking that you talk to me. I am pleading on behalf of that young woman. And also for the good of Onias. I ask that you talk with me and tell me how we may find Onias. Anything you can do to help find him immediately is critical. I am asking that you talk with me and tell me the truth about what you know about this man and how to find him." With an extended exhale of relief, Brad leaned back in his chair and looked to Anna.

From somewhere in the room, a clock made the only sound. Anna remained ramrod straight in her chair. Her face assumed a distant expression. Eyes staring vacantly, it appeared that her body and mind had become detached.

Gradually, Anna's eyes again registered. Her shoulders and body sagged just a bit. Anna's voice was noticeably different as she began to speak. "The truth, Mr. Walker, is that what you wish to hear? The truth?" She moved her head from side to side. "The truth will set you free. How many times have I heard that? Let me tell you what the Bible has to say about the truth. The book of John, Chapter eight, Verse thirty-two, reads like this: 'And you will know the truth, and the truth will set you free.' " Anna looked to Brad and gave a sad smile. "I know the Bible, Mr. Walker. I know it exceptionally well. It was drilled into me from the time I left my mother's womb. I have heard people quote the Scriptures. I have heard about the virtues of truth, how it is truth that sets one free." Anna's voice hardened. "People who spew those Scriptures know absolutely nothing about the truth. They know nothing about the truth outside of their safe and protected world."

With a slight movement of his head and a puzzled expression, Brad remained quiet.

"The truth did not set me free, Mr. Walker. The truth is my prison. It is truth that torments me every day of my life." Anna dropped her gaze for a hesitating moment before looking to Brad with pain in her eyes. "Perhaps it is the truth that is responsible for that woman's abduction." She leveled her eyes directly onto Brad, seeking his reaction.

"I'm sorry, Ms. Carter, I don't understand."

Anna's spirit seemed to wilt as she leaned forward. Brad could not recall ever seeing such agony in another person's face. Her voice became fragile as she again spoke. "You have asked me for the truth. I am going to tell you the truth. But I promise you, Mr. Walker, when I am finished with what I have to say, neither one of us will be free. You are about to step into a dungeon. I am going to take you into the darkness where I have spent much of my life. It is where many women are forced to live every day." Anna closed her eyes briefly before continuing. "Alright, Mr. Walker, you seek the truth. I am going to give you what you have asked for." Anna paused. "Come with me, Mr. Walker. Listen closely. Follow me into the dungeon of truth."

Brad simply looked at Anna. There was nothing to say.

"Please, Mr. Walker, tell me. Have you heard about the radical hold-outs of the Mormon Church? Those people who follow the teachings of Joseph Smith and his commandment that men should have many wives and father as many children as they possibly can? They are called Fundamentalists. Do you know what I'm talking about?"

"A little bit, yes. I've done some reading but I don't know much."

Moving her head in understanding, Anna replied. "You and millions of others. You know a little bit, but not much. Keep a safe distance, Mr. Walker, that's what works best. Keep a safe distance. Very few people really want to know the truth of that world. The truth of that world is an ugly, ugly truth." Bitterness coated Anna's words. "That is where I come from, Mr. Walker. I am a victim of that truth." She leaned forward, her face only inches from Brad. "When I was thirteen years old, a mere child of thirteen, I was given to a forty-one-year-old man to be his fourth wife." Anna let her words settle.

Brad swallowed hard.

Looking directly at Brad but staring through him as if he did not exist, Anna continued. "I gave birth to a daughter when I was fourteen. My only daughter, my only child. I was fourteen, Mr. Walker, fourteen years old."

Brad did not blink or move.

With a deep breath, Anna became quiet as she pondered how to proceed. "My husband was not satisfied with a daughter. He wanted a son. I became pregnant once more, but I miscarried. This happened again and again. With each miscarriage, my husband became increasingly angry and more demanding. He told me the miscarriages were my fault. He said they happened because on the inside I was a wicked person. He said my heart was not pure in the sight of God." Venom radiated as she delivered her next words. "The Mormons who follow that despicable life will tell you that holy commandments teach that a woman's body is only to be taken when she is clean, when she is fertile." Anna paused. "Here is another Bible verse for you. This one from the book of Leviticus: 'If a man lie with a woman during her menstrual period and uncovers her nakedness, he has made naked her fountain, and uncovered the fountain of her blood.'" Anna spat the words. "The truth, Mr. Walker, the truth! The blood of my miscarriage was still fresh and he was on top of me. Fat. Grunting. Sweating. Emptying his every drop into me." With the speed of a blinking eye, Anna twisted her body and viciously hurled spittle from her mouth onto the floor. She then leaned forward, elbows on knees, and covered her face with her potter's hands. Her body rocked.

Stunned, Brad sat with no idea what to do or say. He remained silent. The only sound came from the clock.

Straightening her body, Anna looked at Brad. "Now, you have heard a tiny part of the truth. Truth from the Scriptures is not always the complete truth. Truth from the Scriptures is true when interpreted by men, of course. Men who claim to be recipients of holy wisdom that is beyond the grasp or understanding of a lowly woman." Her eyes on fire with anger, Anna continued. "From the book of Timothy, Mr. Walker: 'Let the woman learn in silence with all subjugation. But suffer not a woman to teach, nor to usurp authority over the man, but to be in silence. For Adam was first formed, then Eve, and Adam was not deceived, but the woman being deceived was in the transgression. Notwithstanding, she shall be saved in childbearing.'"

Her breath now heavy, Anna forced her body to calm and fell silent. Her eyes closed and her fingers flexed, squeezing into fists of outrage. Seconds passed.

Brad did not move.

Bringing a long, deep breath into her lungs, Anna again spoke. "I'm sure you must be wondering what my life as a child bride has to do with Onias." She looked at Brad and her voice softened in sadness. "There is so much more truth to tell. The truth goes on and on. I lived with that repugnant man for twelve years. The only way that I survived those horrible days was because of my daughter. Every time I was forced to lie beneath his hideous body, every time I felt his thrusts violate my very being and had no choice but to listen to him grunting like a hog, I closed my eyes and transformed hatred for that animal into love for my daughter. She was my life, the only thing I lived for."

"I can only imagine." Brad's words were slightly more than a whisper.

"I had no schooling after marriage. My only friend was a woman who was ten years older. She lived close by and was one of three wives. She also had only one child. She had grown too old for her husband's desires. He wanted nothing to do with her. He preferred his other wives who were still in their teens. My friend's name was Sarah. Thankfully, Sarah took me under her wing and helped me through those terrible days. Her one child, Mr. Walker, her one and only son was Onias, the man you are looking for. He was the same age as my daughter. Onias and my daughter grew up together in that hideous, oppressive world of holy commandments, intolerance and abuse."

Brad thought Anna was going to spit again but it did not happen. Instead, she surprised him with a twisted smile. "Onias is a name from some prophet or holy man after Joseph Smith, who knows. Half the men who live in that upside-down world think they talk directly with God and have Divine authority to tell others, especially women, how to conduct their lives." Anna's face softened but her voice was strained. "I try not to hate. I think hate is a poison that fouls the human heart. It destroys the soul." She leaned closer to Brad. "But make no mistake. I hate the man who claimed me as his property. I hate him and every person who stood idly by and allowed it to happen. I hate. I hate with all my being the people who support the evil of that despicable religion. I hate them all." Anna leaned back and looked at Brad.

"I have no words to say to you other than I am so sorry. I am so sorry, and I agree with you."

"Thank you, Mr. Walker, but there is much more to tell. I am not yet finished. You need to hear more of the truth. We lived on the Utah - Arizona line. Really cold weather before December or January was unusual. One year, it was only November, a spell of bitter cold came through that froze water on several ponds in the area. My daughter and other children were delighted and, of course, immediately began playing on the ice. The unthinkable happened one awful morning. The ice was too thin. It cracked right beneath my daughter. She went straight down into that freezing water. Everyone out there on that shattered ice just stood and screamed. Not a soul did anything to help. They simply stood, doing nothing as my daughter was dying." Anna halted for a moment, closing her eyes to the memory.

When her eyes again opened, Anna looked directly to Brad. "Who do you think had the courage and strength to throw his body into that death trap and save my little girl?" Anna did not wait for an answer. Her voice cracked and she continued. "It was Onias, Mr. Walker, it was Onias. He was always large and strong, even at that early age. He flung his body into the pond and somehow lifted her up onto solid ice. Onias saved her life. Had it not been for him, my daughter would have died a horrible death."

Sounds from the clock and stark silence filled the room. Anna and Brad sat with their eyes locked.

"Someway, somehow, that young boy managed to stay afloat and kick his way up onto ice that held long enough for him to crawl to safety." Anna crossed her legs, folded her hands into her lap and was quiet as she looked to Brad.

Shaking his head from side to side, Brad's voice was soft. "What an incredible story, Ms. Carter. I cannot begin to imagine what you have endured. However, let me tell you something. I too have children. I have three. I know something of the love you have for your daughter." Brad shifted his weight and leaned forward. "Ms. Carter, the story of you and your daughter did not end on that icy pond. There is more to tell. Please, I want to know."

"Oh no, you are absolutely right. The story does not end on the pond. In fact, in some ways the pond is just the beginning of the story." Anna sighed. "After the event on the pond had settled and I had time to think about how close I had come to losing my daughter, a realization began to develop. I realized that as long as we lived in the manner that we were living, my daughter and I were both drowning. We were drowning in false religion and pretensions of edicts from God and make-believe holiness. This was a fate far worse than falling through ice."

Brad moved his head in silent agreement.

"I became obsessed with escape. I knew that if my daughter were to ever have a chance for a real life, I had to get her away from the horrible trap of where and how she was living. In addition to what I realized about her future, I recognized that my own life was on the brink. I could not continue any longer. I too had to escape." Anna crossed her arms and gave a false laugh. "Sounds logical and easy doesn't it? Leave, go away, begin a new life." She brought her body forward, placing arms on her knees, her face once again only inches from Brad. "It's that ugly truth again, Mr. Walker. The truth. I had no money. No car. Nowhere to go.

My own parents thought it was God's will that I be subservient to my husband forever. They would never have allowed me back into their home." Anna's voice became mocking. She gave Brad a real smile. "God in heaven and his chosen one, Joseph Smith, would not approve of such haughtiness."

Happy for Anna's sliver of humor, even though made sarcastically, Brad gave an understanding chuckle.

Anna actually laughed before continuing. "So, my ticket to salvation came from my friend, Sarah, the mother of Onias. She had some money she was willing to give. More importantly, she had an uncle who despised the life and people of our world. He had been raised in the fundamentalist ways but rejected everything they espoused. He walked away from it all as a young man. So, through my friend, Sarah, I had money for a bus ticket to what at the time sounded like another world, Albuquerque, New Mexico. Sarah's uncle agreed to find us a house, help me with a job and get me on my feet with my daughter." Anna now smiled openly. "But there was a catch. All of this was available only if I agreed that Sarah and Onias could run away with us." Anna again laughed. "Life's choices should always be that easy. I was thrilled!"

"I admire your determination to leave for a better life. The courage to do something that drastic, with children involved, that was a big deal."

Nodding her head in agreement, Anna spoke with a mischievous laugh. "When children are involved, it makes decisions more difficult. But I can't lie to you, we also had some fun. Sarah basically stole her husband's car and we drove to the bus depot that was about thirty miles away. We left the car for whoever found it and hopped a bus to Albuquerque. For all of us, it was the happiest day of our lives. We laughed for the first hundred miles of our trip."

"Wow!"

"Sarah's uncle was an incredible man. He found an apartment for us. He helped us get our children enrolled in school. He was generous beyond words. I found work as a waitress. My daughter loved her school. We were truly happy." Anna's voice dropped. "My friend, Sarah, was a different story. She never was able to adjust. She hated the man who had claimed her as his wife. She detested everything about her old world. But yet, she could not shake her feelings of guilt. She thought that she had violated some sacred bond and that God would doom her to hell. I tried talking with her. It did no good. One day she was just gone. She left a note saying that she was going back to face her husband and God." Anna moved her head in disbelief. "I cannot even think about what torment must have been inside of her." Anna looked hard at Brad as she spoke her next words with a tone of incredulity. "Sarah went back to that hell, but she left Onias with me."

Brad dropped his head and massaged a hand over his brow. "Oh, my God."

"Sarah's uncle found out a few months later that, shortly after her return, she committed suicide. Sarah's body was found hanging inside her own home."

Another "Oh, my God" was all that Brad could say.

"You asked for the truth. I have given it to you, Mr. Walker. You have asked me to me tell you about Onias and to help you find him. Now, it is my turn to ask something of you. Let's think about this a moment. Onias saved my daughter's life. My daughter was my strength to escape from a life of religious fanaticism and abuse. So, if I am fair, I must say that Onias also saved my life. He saved both our lives." An accusatory tone crept. "You show up at my house, knowing nothing about me or my life. You know nothing of Onias and his life. And all in the name of truth, you think I should open to you the wounds and scars of our lives so that you can find the person who saved me and my daughter from a fate worse than hell itself. Is this what you are asking of me, Mr. Walker?"

Their gazes remained interlocked with growing intensity. Anna leaned forward, bringing her body and face so close to Brad he could see the pores of her skin. "Tell me something. How would you define the word betrayal? That's an ugly word. Betrayal." She paused. "After Judas betrayed the Lord Jesus, he had the common decency to slip away and hang himself in solitude." Anna shook her head slowly. "I don't believe in betrayal. I think betrayal is a sin. I'm not prepared to hang myself for either the truth or betrayal, Mr. Walker. I know that is not what you wish to hear but that's the way it is. I'm sorry." Anna leaned back in her chair and, crossing her arms over her chest, directed a silent, challenging stare at Brad.

Chills prickled Brad's body. He felt the cloth of his shirt to now be obscenely soaked beneath his arms. He knew that the words he spoke in the next few seconds would likely determine the fate of Sharon Moore. Somewhere in his desperation for a proper response, Brad managed a silent, "Oh, God, please help me," as it was now his turn to lean close to Anna.

Seconds ticked. Anna waited.

"Ms. Carter, you said a couple of things early on in our conversation that struck me. You said that your story would be the truth, but would not set either one of us free." Brad shook his head from side to side. "You were so very accurate with that one. After listening to all that you have told me, I feel like someone just held my head under muddy water for several minutes. I understand what you meant when you said that the truth is your prison." Brad hesitated. "I also understand that the memories of a person's life are not a collection of physical things that can be swept up like broken glass and tossed into the trash. Memories are for life. They are not simply forgotten or discarded."

Anna scarcely moved her head. It was enough to acknowledge that she was listening.

"You also said when I first arrived that you had been expecting this visit. That tells me there is yet another chapter to your story. Something has been left unsaid. I'm guessing that somewhere within what you have not said is the part that you see as crossing a line into betrayal."

Brad took a deep breath as he saw another barely perceptible nod from Anna.

"The only way I know to approach this is to be honest with you. Yes, I am asking you to tell me about Onias. I need to know anything and everything you can tell me about who and what he is inside. I need to know what makes him get up in the morning, what makes him happy and what makes him angry. Most importantly, I need to know where Onias is right now." Brad held for a moment, letting his words take hold. "The way I see things, there is another ugly truth with us in this room right now. This ugly truth is that, like it or not, you have no choice but to betray someone tonight. Time and events have passed in a manner that leave no alternative but for you to make a decision about betrayal. You are going to betray someone tonight, Ms. Carter. The only choice you now have is who are you going to betray."

A flicker of bewilderment appeared within Anna's eyes.

"I ask that you go back to the repugnance you felt when your husband abused you as a young girl. Think about the hopeless desperation you felt that was so overwhelming, a life that was so unbearable, that you decided to turn away from everything you and your daughter had."

Anna's eyes narrowed.

"Ms. Carter, this is a terrible thing to ask but I'm going to do it. I want you to remember those horrible moments, feel them, smell them, breathe them all over again. And then, I ask another terrible thing of you. I want you to think of your daughter when she fell through the ice. I want you to try to feel how she must have felt as her body sank. Dark, murky water, icy cold burning straight through her lungs. Would she have closed her eyes? Or did they remain open as she descended? What were her thoughts? Did she think of you as she felt life ebbing from her body?"

The clock ticked.

"Now, I ask that you be absolutely honest and tell me something. Is there any difference in how you felt with your husband's unwanted body smothering the very life from your soul or how your daughter felt as she sank into a grave of dark icy water? Think of those things and tell me if there is a difference in how an innocent young woman would feel when the hands of a stranger molest her body? What do you think that young woman in Colorado felt when alien hands plucked her from the life she had known? Does that woman think of her parents and family as she is dragged away? What does she feel when an unknown body presses his weight against her defenseless flesh?"

Noise of the clock, nothing else.

"Ms. Carter, this is an awful situation. I understand that perfectly. But when I walk out of your house this evening," Brad pointed to Anna's front door, "a betrayal will have occurred. You no longer have a choice. Your fate is sealed. If you choose to not help find Onias, you will have betrayed an innocent woman. A young woman whose destiny may very well rest entirely within your hands." Brad moved his head in a gesture of sadness. "There is no way to know how many other destinies hang in the balance, depending on whether or not Onias is found quickly. Please. I beg you. Consider which betrayal you choose. One betrayal may lead to life and hope. The other betrayal almost certainly leads to further pain and darkness." Brad straightened but his shoulders sagged in a deep exhale.

The clock sounded like gunfire in the silence.

After tortuous moments with neither Brad nor Anna speaking, Brad again leaned toward Anna. Reaching for the photograph of Sharon Moore that was within his shirt pocket, he held it in his fingers.

"Everything you have heard about the woman in Colorado has been impersonal. You have no idea of her name. What she looks like. What are her plans for life? It's easy to allow one's thinking to conjure an image that is not really human. When you see someone with a face, a heart or a life, it becomes painful." Extending the photograph and pointing to Sharon, Brad continued. "This is her, Ms. Carter. This is the woman I'm talking about. This smiling, beautiful woman is somewhere tonight, taken from her family, taken from the man she planned to marry. What do you think she is feeling? Is she drowning in an icy pond as we speak?" Brad paused. "What do you think this woman would say about betrayal? Do you think she feels betrayed tonight?" Brad held the photograph before Anna's face and remained silent.

Anna gazed at the photograph for several seconds. Brad struggled to read what was happening behind her agonized eyes. Suddenly, Anna startled. Seemingly panicked, she reached for the photograph, snatched it from Brad's hand and brought it close to her face. Her eyes widened and her expression contorted into something Brad could not define. Time seemed frozen. Anna stared at what she held in her hand, her body rigid. Slowly, she then extended her hand to Brad, returning the photograph.

Without speaking but obviously shaken, Anna stood and walked to her kitchen sink. Placing her hands on the rim, she leaned her body toward the window, looking out into the night. Anna opened the faucet handle, and bringing water into her cupped hands, drenched her face repeatedly. She turned, again facing Brad. Water dripping onto her shirt went unnoticed.

Their eyes held; Brad's pleading while agony brimmed within Anna's.

Still not speaking and appearing to be in a state of shock that she had not shown earlier, Anna returned to her chair, seated herself and looked at Brad.

Sounds of the clock persisted.

Something had happened, Brad was certain, but exactly what he did not know. He decided not to speak and to give Anna time.

Defeat sounding in her voice, Anna finally spoke. "I loved and raised Onias as if he were my flesh and blood. His last name at birth was Phillips but he has used my name, Carter, just as frequently." Pain in every word, she looked straight at Brad. "I vowed that Onias and my daughter would have what they needed to put their past behind them. Move on to decent and happy lives. I did the same for myself. I felt I had been given a second chance in life. I was not going to let it slip by. Sarah's uncle continued to help with finances so, after work, I enrolled in night school for adults. I hired private tutors and read everything I could get my hands on. I even managed to find a job working in the University of New Mexico library. I was passionate about surrounding myself with knowledge and people of stature. My oath to God in heaven was that I would raise my daughter and Onias with love and opportunity. I vowed to become educated, speak properly and conduct myself with dignity. That became the goal for my life."

Brad smiled and looked directly to Anna's face. "Ms. Carter, you are the epitome of dignity. I've known you for less than an hour but there is no doubt about your intellect or dignity. You have made your life's goal a reality."

A trace of a smile appeared on Anna's face. "Even when I spit on my own floor?"

"That was the most dignified spit I've ever seen, absolutely!"

Tension eased as Anna and Brad smiled at each other.

"Everything rolled along just fine for several years. My daughter and Onias graduated from high school. My daughter went straight into college. She did great and today is a nurse. She has a husband and a child. She is exactly what I hoped for." Anna dropped her eyes for a second. "I don't know for sure why, but things never worked out that way for Onias. He was always angry. He hated school and his temper was only a heartbeat away. At times, he could be loving and compassionate. But, when the switch flipped, it was terrifying what a completely different person he became."

Anna stopped speaking for a few moments and gazed into empty space. Brad was certain that he could see memories swirling behind her blue eyes.

"When Onias was about fourteen or so, he asked for a pet. I thought it would be good for him. I found a dog at a rescue place and took it home to Onias as a surprise. For a while, they were the best of friends, practically inseparable. But, as time went by and the dark moods came over Onias, he became negligent. I ended up caring for the dog most of the time." Anna sighed. "Negligence was only the beginning. I discovered that anytime he could do so without my knowledge, Onias would take food away from the dog and torment him by holding food close but not allowing the dog to actually eat. Then the abuse progressed to physical torment. Onias would savagely kick or hit the dog just for fun and verbally terrify the poor animal."

Tears etched tiny rivers down Anna's cheek. "The dog ran away. I'm quite certain that the only sorrow Onias felt was that he had lost a form of amusement by no longer having a means to inflict suffering."

Unconsciously, Brad failed to exhale. Finally, his lungs burned and his escaping breath was the only sound. Anna had once again fallen silent.

"After he grew older, Onias moved to his own apartment and became more and more restless. He was almost always angry. He went back to using the last name of Phillips again. I have no idea why. At the same time, he developed an obsession for religion and physical fitness. When he wasn't in a gymnasium lifting weights, he was reading the Bible. He spent hours devouring all kinds of religious teachings about Mormonism, both traditional and fundamentalist. He also spent hours listening to those crazy television preachers. At times, he talked of returning to Salt Lake City to join the traditional LDS Church. A few days later, he would spew hatred for anything even remotely related to the Mormon faith. He was all over the place. He desperately wanted female companionship but, after a date or two, he was always rejected. Even my daughter, who felt tremendous loyalty to Onias, found him to be creepy. She warned me several times that something had gone badly haywire with him."

Lifting her head to peer at the ceiling, Anna sighed and shook her head. "I just don't know what happened but somewhere along the way, something snapped. He grew his hair to his shoulders and wanted to be called Samson. I thought he was absolutely ridiculous and told him so. But then, Samson sounded like a good idea after he began to preach to people on the streets of Albuquerque. He then insisted that he be called Nazareth."

Anna seemed to speak to herself. "This went on for some time. Onias would come to visit and we would talk. At times, he returned to his old self, cut his hair and lived peacefully. But he always went back to darkness. Spending days alone, he grew his hair and studied Mormonism or read the Bible for hours. What really hurts, Mr. Walker, is that he recognized he was troubled. He admitted that he had issues that seemed beyond his control. He even said that he wanted help. I had all kinds of friends at the university who offered to intervene or recommend professional counseling. Onias went so far as to schedule appointments with a therapist on a few occasions, but he never would follow through. He always returned to the gymnasium, body building and street preaching."

Turning her hand so that the backside of her wrist touched her cheeks, Anna wiped tears from her eyes. "I have spent hours talking with Onias, begging that he seek help. He knows something is wrong. He has told me that something terrible, a sort of demon, is living inside his body."

"I am so sorry, Ms. Carter. I am so very sorry."

"I believe you, Mr. Walker. I'm a decent judge of character and I think you truly do have compassion. Thank you."

The clock was the only voice for a few seconds.

"Sarah's uncle passed." Anna smiled. "We called him Uncle Pops because he was half uncle and half father to us. Uncle Pops left a substantial sum of money to me." Anna twisted her lips with a strange contortion, part smile, part sneer. "I simply didn't want it. I was tired of city life in Albuquerque and wanted to return to something more simple, closer to the earth." Anna looked at Brad. "Do you know what I mean? Sometimes a person has to step backwards in order to move forward. Does that make any sense to you?"

"It makes perfect sense. It is easy to spend our lives just waiting for something to happen, waiting for opportunity to come knocking. When a person simply waits for life to happen, the multitude of choices that may be available are seldom seen. It's possible that those choices and opportunities pass right by. We never know they even existed." Brad folded his arms over his chest and contemplated Anna for a moment. "I've learned enough about you in the past few minutes to know that you are certainly not that kind of person. You don't wait. You step outside of yourself and look for choice and opportunity. I admire you hugely for what you have done."

"You are very kind. Thank you." With a sigh, Anna continued. "Right or wrong, I gave practically all of the money that I inherited from Uncle Pops to my daughter and Onias. My daughter has been wise with her portion. I'm not so sure about Onias. As for me, I moved to this tiny house and this small village. I have learned to love the heart of small-town people and discovered the beauty of pottery. It is art from the very body and soul of Mother Earth. I am happy with who I am."

"I understand."

"My daughter visits frequently. Onias has been in and out. I have no idea if he will ever be here again or if he has left me for good. In the past, when he has been here, he lives in the one bedroom I have." Anna pointed to the back side of her home. "I hold it for him to use and I am content to sleep on that couch." Anna turned her head to look at the darkened hallway and her solitary couch. When she turned her gaze back to Brad, a strange look had come over her face. Anna moved her head slowly. "I will never go into that room again. That is something that I cannot do."

Not certain about what to think of Anna's obviously strong feelings about the room, Brad spoke cautiously. "Thank you for telling me these things. There are all kinds of details that will become important if this matter goes on. The critical thing at this point is simple. Do you know where Onias is right now? Do you know how to find him?"

Before answering, Anna rocked her upper body up and down in what Brad hoped was an affirmative gesture, but uncertainty clouded her face. "I can answer your question, but only partially. I cannot give you the specific details you are hoping for."

"I will take anything you can offer. It may lead to something useful."

"Long before Onias drifted into the unknown of whatever lurks within his mind, Uncle Pops gave him a terrific opportunity for summer employment. You see, Uncle Pops was a master furniture craftsman. He was an extraordinary artisan with his hands, especially wood and leather. People from all over the Southwest came to him with requests for his unique style and vision in furniture. It was Uncle Pops who inspired me to become a potter. He caused me to realize that working with clay is a very special type of art."

Brad nodded. "There is no better way to live than by using one's own hands. But very few are blessed with such talent."

"Oh, I completely agree." Anna's face and smile was beautiful again. "Uncle Pops was a one in a million. I'm so lucky to have had him in my life. What he did for Onias was to connect him with one of his furniture clients up in northern New Mexico. The guy was a wealthy man who had Uncle Pops build all kinds of incredibly special furniture for his ranch home. It was somewhere near a place called Folsom. Uncle Pops was able to arrange for Onias to work on this man's ranch for a full month during every summer vacation from school. Onias learned the rural lifestyle, worked like a slave every day and slept like a rock at night. Onias slept in a make-shift bedroom that was attached to the barn.

Several years ago, the ranch sold to one of those huge conglomerates based down in Texas. The man who had been such a good client to Uncle Pops had become all crippled up with arthritis. After selling his ranch, he retired and moved away. After that, everything changed. The new Texas owner very seldom showed up on the ranch. The hired hand's house and barn was simply abandoned."

Brad's eyes narrowed.

"I was mortified when Onias first told me that he occasionally went back to Folsom and basically squatted on the property where he used to work." Anna snorted. "You can go to the bank with the fact that Onias paid no attention to me or my concerns. How often he's been there, how long he stays or what he does to conceal his presence there, I have no idea. I just know that the Folsom ranch offers him seclusion. It seems to be a place that holds significance for him. It is where he likes to go when he is particularly troubled. He once told me that there was a small water-fall above the barn where he slept. Onias said the waterfall was a holy place and its waters sacred. That's all I know. He only lets me know about his visits there after he leaves. He has been very secretive about Folsom."

"Do you have any specifics on where the ranch is located other than close to Folsom?"

Shaking her head, Anna replied. "No, not at all. During the periods that Onias used to work there, all communication was handled through

Uncle Pops. I never had a phone contact or a mailing address. I never even knew the rancher's name. It was a deal totally handled by Uncle Pops."

"And you think Onias is there now?"

With a shrug, Anna replied. "I think that is where he is very likely to be. I'm sorry, I can't be sure. If he is not there, then I have no idea where he might be. I have no way to contact him. From time to time he borrows a phone and calls me with an address to forward his mail. Beyond that, I've never known how to reach him. He and my daughter ceased all communication about two years ago. She refuses to have anything to do with him." Anna released a sigh of despondence. "I have to sit on that porch out there," Anna pointed with her chin. "All I can do is rock and wait. Rock and wait."

Rubbing his brow, Brad sensed Anna's exhaustion. She was emotionally drained. He needed to wrap this up as quickly as possible. "Just a couple more questions, Ms. Carter, and I'll leave you in peace. To the best of your knowledge, has Onias ever lived in Wyoming?"

Alarm flashed over Anna's face. "Did something bad happen in Wyoming? What makes you ask that question?" Without waiting for a reply, she continued, "Yes, he lived in Cheyenne many months ago. It's been well over a year, maybe even two. All I know is that I sent some mail to a Post Office box in Cheyenne. I have no memory of the specifics." Anna halted and her voice dropped. "Was another person hurt?"

"A girl was taken, yes. But she is okay. She managed to escape. We're not sure, Ms. Carter, but we're looking into it."

Dropping her gaze to the floor, Anna closed her eyes and massaged the bridge of her nose. She spoke no further words.

"What kind of vehicle do you think he's driving? Do you have any photographs of Onias or his vehicle?"

"He drives a dark blue Jeep. It's a big, rugged vehicle for rough roads or mountain areas. He bought it with money from Uncle Pops. Onias loves that Jeep. I'm sure he still has it."

"What about a photograph?"

Apparently choosing not to respond to Brad's question, Anna stood and stretched her lean body for a moment. She again walked to the sink. Reaching under the table where her utensils were stored, she retrieved a key. Moving back to Brad, she held it out for him to take. As Brad's fingers clasped the key, Anna indicated with her head the direction of the darkened hallway. "This is the key to his room, Mr. Walker. You will find more pictures and more photographs than you ever imagined. You are about to enter the dungeon of truth."

Anna turned and walked away. Without another word, she stepped onto her porch.

Finding himself suddenly alone, Brad stared at the key in his hand. He listened to the clock.

———

Anticipating a squeaking hinge after he turned the key and gave a gentle shove, Brad was surprised when the door swung open in silence. The first thing to strike his senses was the pungent odor of neglect. Air within the forsaken room stirred groggily, wary of unexpected intrusion. Brad felt vulnerable and silhouetted standing in the doorway. Something between dread and an unexplained fear tightened in his stomach. Hesitantly, he entered the room and, with light from his cell phone, located the light switch. A naked bulb of inadequate wattage hung from the ceiling and cast an aura of stagnation about the room.

What in the name of heaven had he entered? Brad's eyes darted, frantic in their search on where to focus. More importantly, what to avoid. He stepped onto a wood floor, neglected and dust covered. Discarded cans of opened food. A bare mattress, filthy with stain. A collage of garbage filled Brad's vision. With passing seconds, the stench of spoilage seeped into his nostrils.

Brad held his breath as his eyes continued to move. The reality of the room slowly registered. Photos of naked bodies, women, legs spread, pubic hair, lustful faces. He exhaled, sucked hard and again held the pressure in his chest. Along with the exposed bodies, images of Jesus Christ were everywhere. An indecipherable collage of photographs of naked women and Jesus Christ covered the walls. Lungs on fire, Brad finally exhaled in a slow release. His dazed scan finally came to rest against the far wall. Small tree trunks or large branches, he wasn't sure which, were crudely strapped together by rope and, reaching almost to the ceiling, stood as a cross. It had been deliberately positioned as if the room were a cathedral. Its towering presence dominated the room and held Brad motionless.

As his eyes adjusted and his senses absorbed all that was before him, chills erupted on Brad's skin. He was looking at a menagerie of the bizarre. Pornographic photographs and magazine foldouts of nude women plastered one entire wall. It took a few moments before Brad realized that the photographs depicted only women with blonde hair. The opposite wall held posters and photographs of various sizes, each depicting traditional images of Jesus Christ. Practically every square inch of the room was littered with piles of books, magazines and loose papers. Discarded food bags, socks, batteries, water bottles and unimaginable junk was strewn in chaotic disarray. But, after taking time to evaluate all that the room contained, the most startling by far was the life-sized cross. For a symbol of holiness to hover in protective vigilance over such clutter and vulgarity reeked of obscene sacrilege.

Within seconds, Brad understood that he had entered the domain of a mad man. He also intuitively recognized that, at some point, this room may very well be the subject of an extended crime scene analysis. There was no way to predict what clues may lie buried within this trash heap. Evidence relevant to crimes committed miles away or months removed may very well be within this room.

Brad's first instinct was to depart. Touch nothing and leave everything undisturbed. But that thought quickly evaporated when he considered that if Sharon Moore had any hope at all, it was dependent on finding Onias very quickly. Clues to his whereabouts may lie buried within the accumulated garbage of the room.

Praying that he was gambling correctly, Brad first utilized his cell phone to photograph the room from where he stood. He then gingerly made his way over the garbage-strewn floor, approaching the cross. Candles, with their wicks burned to nubs, had been arranged in a half-circle pattern at the base. To the left of the cross, and neatly positioned within the half-circle of candles, was a large book. Brad leaned to get a closer look. The dark cover was inscribed in gold letters:

Folsom
1888 – 1988

Then and Now

Shifting his eyes to the right, Brad saw a paper that had apparently been torn from a magazine or book. This too, was within the circular alignment of candles. It had been weighted on each corner with round stones. A smattering of dried flower petals lay on the paper. Brad had to drop to his knees, bringing his phone light close, before he was able to read the paper:

The dead lay as they had fallen, in every conceivable shape, some grasping their guns as though they were in the act of firing, while others, with a cartridge in their icy grasp, were in the act of loading. Some of the countenances wore a peaceful glad smile, while on others rested a fiendish look of hate. It looked as though each countenance was the exact counterpart of the thoughts that were passing through the mind when the death messenger laid them low. Perhaps that noble-looking youth, with his smiling up-turned face, with his glossy ringlets matted with his own life-blood, felt a mother's prayer stealing over his senses as his young life went out. Near him lay a young husband with a prayer for his wife and little one yet lingering on his lips. Youth and age, virtue and evil, were represented on those ghastly countenances. Before us lay the charred and blackened remains of some who had been burned alive. They were wounded too badly to move and the fierce elements consumed them.

Brad gulped as he whispered. "What in the name of God?" He went back to the Folsom book. Lifting it gently, he looked for markers that would indicate special passages but saw nothing. He quickly flipped the pages but saw no more than a detailed historical story of the town and the areas surrounding it.

After photographing all that lay at the foot of the cross, Brad stood and turned to the wall of commercial pornography for additional photographs. Next, he shifted his attention to the wall holding photographs of Christ. Some were poster sized while others looked to have been ripped from the pages of a Bible or religious magazine. They were the classical images of Jesus and his life: tending sheep, feeding the multitudes at the Sermon on the Mount, in the Garden of Gethsemane, on the cross, ascending into heaven.

Brad abruptly ceased his examination of the Christ-related art and caught his breath. His heart accelerated. He looked more closely at the wall. He was stunned all over again. "Oh, my God," escaped his lips and hung in the stagnant air. He had initially missed it but, with his gaze transfixed on the wall, Brad now understood the strange reaction he had witnessed a few minutes earlier when Anna had viewed the photograph of Sharon Moore.

Inserted within the collage of images depicting Jesus Christ were photographs that were obviously self-made. Brad looked at a multitude of 'selfies' of a man who bore an uncanny resemblance to the images of Christ that covered the wall. "Oh, my God," again seemed to echo as Brad repeated himself again and again. Reaching into his shirt pocket, Brad extracted the group photograph of Sharon Moore and her friends. The only thing Brad had ever paid any attention to was the group of young girls, especially Sharon Moore. But now, he looked at other aspects of the photograph.

There he was, clear as day, a patron in the bar. Seated directly behind the smiling young women, his face turned directly into the camera and his eyes focused on Sharon Moore was Onias Phillips. Nazareth. The same face, the same man that was now looking at Brad from the Jesus Christ wall.

———

Sickness rumbling within his stomach, Brad closed and locked the door. He wanted to forever seal the door that led to a chamber of depravity. He quietly walked through Anna's small home. The room was empty and hauntingly quiet. Brad moved to the doorway, turned out the light and stepped onto the darkened porch. The sound of Anna's rocking told of her location. Brad stood beside Anna, allowing time to pass, unsure of what to do or say.

Anna continued to rock. Her body was scarcely visible in the darkness. Brad remained beside her, not speaking. What must she be feeling right now? Her world had just irrevocably changed. There was no turning back. How much could one woman be expected to suffer? Brad wanted to say something. He desperately yearned to touch her, put his arms around her. Brad yearned tell her the deep sorrow he felt for her tragedy. Words would not come.

Anna rocked. The night air was warm. Crickets made music.

Timidly, Brad placed his fingertips on Anna's shoulder, allowing them to linger. After moments, Brad felt the course skin of her potter's hand grasp his fingers. She squeezed. "Thank you, Mr. Walker. This could have been much worse. I appreciate what you did, how you handled everything."

Their hands still touching, Brad spoke, scarcely above a whisper. "I'm leaving now. You have endured enough for one night. I may need to call you tomorrow or sometime soon. Other people may contact you fairly soon, I'm just not certain." Brad was quiet. "But no more tonight. No more tonight. Thank you, Ms. Carter." Brad placed the key in her lap.

Pressure again from her hand. A desperate cling about his fingers. A silent response that spoke more than words.

Brad walked to his truck. Sitting in the stillness of his cab, he breathed deeply, trying to summon calmness as his mind continued to spin. With a final look to the rocking shadow on the porch, Brad drove away.

TWELVE

AND IT SHALL COME to pass that I, the Lord God, will send one mighty and strong, holding the scepter of power in his hand, clothed with light for a covering, whose mouth shall utter words, eternal words; while his bowels shall be a fountain of truth, to set in order the house of God.

———

If any man espouse a virgin, and desire to espouse another, and the first give her consent, and if he espouse the second, and they are virgins, and have vowed to no other man, then is he justified; he cannot commit adultery for they are given unto him; for he cannot commit adultery with that that belongeth to him and to no one else.

And if he have ten virgins given unto him by this law, he cannot commit adultery, for they belong to him, and they are given unto him; therefore he is justified.

The Doctrine and Covenants, Sections 85 and 132
    Revealed to Joseph Smith in 1832

THIRTEEN

Blackness of the night was oppressive. Leaving Madrid, retracing his way back toward Santa Fe on the Turquoise Highway, Brad was desperate for the companionship of Juanita. Following his heart-wrenching conversation with Anna and the sickening experience in the room of Onias, he needed to hold the woman he loved. He longed for her touch, to hear her voice. He wanted to talk with Juanita of their good fortune to have found each other and the happy life they shared.

However, instead of heading to Juanita and their home in Albuquerque, he was driving in the opposite direction. Distance between them grew with each mile. There was no choice. It was possible that enough had been learned through Anna to locate Onias.

As badly as Brad wanted to be with Juanita, he realized that words in a telephone conversation could never convey what he had just experienced in Anna's home. It was too complicated. Even more so, he could not bring himself to draw Juanita into the repugnance of what he had just experienced. After pulling to the side of the road and pecking out a text, Brad continued to drive. Folsom and any hope for Sharon Moore was five hours to the north.

After clearing Cerrillos, the highway was deserted. Brad knew he had to talk with Kurt but he also had to find a way to settle his heart and his mind. Pulling off the road, Brad killed his engine and headlights.

Windows lowered and sitting quietly, he listened to the night for a few peaceful moments.

Dreading to break the tranquility of the silence, Brad forced himself back into the reality of what had to be done. Activating his phone, he forwarded the photographs of Onias Phillips that had occupied the bedroom wall. He also transmitted the remaining photographs he had taken that depicted the entire room and the cross. In Brad's mind, the photographed images failed to carry an adequate sense of the repugnance he had felt while within the room. The eye of a camera could never replicate what his eyes had just seen.

Giving time for Kurt to receive and digest the photographs, Brad sat in the quiet of the night. He was haunted by the words of Anna and the images he had seen. He wanted to forget it all, erase it from his memory. Impossible. Brad punched in Kurt's number. He knew his friend well enough to recognize by the somber greeting that the depravity of the evening had arrived in Kurt's phone. When Brad explained the shocking discovery that the photograph of Sharon Moore clearly depicted Onias in the background, haunting silence followed.

"Unbelievable!" Kurt's only response echoed in Brad's ear.

The men exchanged ideas about the need for a search warrant for the bedroom. They agreed that a search was secondary in importance to moving quickly to locate Onias. Brad conveyed his conviction that the room would remain secure. Anna realized that the world of Onias had crumbled. His life, as well as hers, was now opened to scrutinizing eyes of the outside world.

After sorting through the significance of all that they had learned, Kurt and Brad agreed on a plan of action.

"What about the Wyoming victim? Did she make an identification from the driver's license photo of Onias?" Hope tinged Brad's voice.

"The Wyoming guys tried but their victim is off backpacking somewhere in the Wind River Mountains. She's out of the picture for a few days. Nothing to do but wait on that one."

"Got ya. Thanks, Kurt, sorry to bother you so late at night."

"Gimme a break. This is the best call I've had in days. You get busy with your plan. I'm going to turn things upside down everywhere possible for records on this creep. I'll check using names of both Onias Phillips and Onias Carter. Then I'll try variations with names using

Nazareth. There's gotta be a parking ticket, a phone bill, electric bill, credit card activity or something, somewhere, that gives a hint as to where this goofball is hanging his hat."

"I sure hope so, Kurt. I sure as hell hope so. We'll talk in a few hours, my friend."

With a sigh, Brad leaned his head against the seat of his truck and sat for moment. The image of Anna's tormented face remained in his memory. Her story of abuse echoed again within his mind. His own children and Elizabeth seemed to join him in his truck. Each of them shared the night's pain. The unconditional love that had existed among Elizabeth, Brad and their children made the story of Anna's abuse impossible to comprehend.

The night was deathly silent. Brad was desperate for Juanita. "To hell with this," Brad muttered as he opened the door, stepped out and then slammed his door with such force it sounded like an explosion in the night. "My ass hurts from sitting all day, my head feels like it's going to explode. I need a beer. I miss my family. I want Juanita to be with me." Brad's words were heard only by grass, scattered trees, an empty highway and the black of night. He kicked at the ground as he moved to the front of his truck. Leaning against the hood, he placed his face into his hands, speaking to himself. "What a day. What a fucked-up world." He received the same response as from his first outburst: a silent night and shimmering sky.

Pacing in the darkness, Brad re-lived his hours since leaving the mountain campfire he had shared with Sam and Kurt. Valles Caldera seemed a century ago. Surely, a full week must have passed since his sunrise walk in Santa Fe. Was it really only this morning that he had stood at the Cross of the Martyrs, marveling at the beauty of a rising sun on Santa Fe's adobe?

Recalling the solemn sadness of the Vietnam Memorial and the Moreno Valley, Brad closed his eyes. Did all of these unexplained tragedies emerge from the womb of Mother Earth? Where was she, this Mother Earth? Would any caring mother ever allow something as terrible as the Vietnam War? How could any kind of mother allow the atrocities that Anna Carter had endured? Where was this so-called mother when Sharon Moore had been abducted?

A coyote howled. Another answered.

Brad's chest tightened with thoughts of Anna. What an incredible woman. How many thirteen-year-old girls, at this very moment, were suffering the same unspeakable fate that Anna had endured? Brad recalled from his Bureau days how an exhausting manhunt had taken place to locate and arrest Warren Jeffs, a cult leader of the Fundamentalist Mormon Church. Jeffs was believed to have had over seventy wives and fifty children. He was ultimately convicted for having forced marriage and sex with girls as young as twelve. He arranged marriage and sex for his family members to under-aged girls. "How in the name of God can that still be happening in this country?" Brad once again spoke out loud into the void. Once again, no reply.

As he paced, Brad felt ill. Where was Sharon Moore tonight? What was she feeling? What did her family and loved ones feel? He thought of Anna's daughter, her body sinking into freezing water.

Slowly sauntering and recalling his incredible recent hours, Brad finally found solace in conjuring an image of Margie and Jim Price. He smiled to himself when he thought of their love and unconditional respect for each other.

Back at his truck and resting his body against the hood, he looked to the sky, the marvelous New Mexico sky. Brad sought answers to questions for which there are no answers, solutions to riddles for which there are no solutions. Gazing at the stars, shimmering like icy glitter in a sky of black, Brad felt a trace of peace somewhere inside. The Milky Way, a river of light, mysterious and of unknown depth, flowed north to south. "I wonder if angels fish that river?" Brad's whisper drifted. "Hope they catch beautiful trout on dry flies for all eternity."

As Brad settled his mind, Juanita's presence came. She stood close. Her skin warm, her breath soft. He allowed his time of fantasy to work its magic. Juanita had been mystical and other-worldly from the first moments her image had appeared after he had been assaulted and lay unconscious. Thank God Juanita was no longer a dream. She was real flesh and blood who now shared his life.

Shoving his body away from the truck, Brad knew just what he needed to center his spirit and his brain. Hoisting his body up onto the hood, he leaned against the windscreen for a comfortable view of the sky. Flicking his thumb, Brad scrolled through the music stored on his cell phone. He found what he wanted. This was how he needed to conclude this incredible day.

Brad looked to the sky. Galaxies unknown, worlds beyond human grasp, unimagined cosmic forces whirling. Finally settled, he gazed into the heavens as he listened to the graveled voice of Louis Armstrong:

I see trees of green, red roses too
  I see them bloom for me and you
  And I think to myself what a wonderful world

I see skies of blue and clouds of white
  The bright blessed day, the dark sacred night
  And I think to myself what a wonderful world

The colors of the rainbow so pretty in the sky
  Are also on the faces of people going by
  I see friends shaking hands saying how do you do
  They're really saying I love you

I hear babies crying, I watch them grow
  They'll learn much more than I'll ever know
  And I think to myself what a wonderful world
  Yes I think to myself what a wonderful world

Forty minutes later, Brad was in a motel on the outskirts of Santa Fe. All he needed was a couple hours of sleep. Time was critical and he was ready to go.

FOURTEEN

DRIVING NORTHBOUND on Interstate 25 in pre-dawn darkness, Brad cleared the historic New Mexico settlement of Las Vegas. The first rays of light tinged the sky as he approached Wagon Mound, a small ranching settlement. Chuckling to himself, Brad spoke out loud as he punched numbers into his phone, "Gonna piss him off, but he'll get over it." Stifling a laugh when the groggy voice of Bob Lance answered, Brad immediately became obnoxious as possible. Sounding in his best Irish accent, Brad virtually shouted at his old partner. "Bobbie me boy, how in the world are ye on this glorious morning?"

Moments of silence followed. "My aching ass. Walker, you shit, don't you ever sleep?"

"Of course, I sleep. I snooze like a little puppy. But I do my sleeping at night. The sun has been up for at least ten minutes. Life is passing you by. Rise and shine."

"What the hell is so frigging important and what in God's name makes you so damned happy at this hour?"

Laughing out loud and loving every second, Brad realized how much he missed his old friend. Brad and Bob Lance had worked cases and flown airplanes together for years in the Bureau. After leaving the Bureau, Lance had purchased an airplane and remained an active flyer.

Delighting in tormenting his friend, Brad continued speaking louder than was necessary into the telephone. "It's your lucky day, Lance. It's going to be just like the old days. Dè-já-vu all over again!"

"You smoking dope, Walker?"

"Nope, I'm serious. Wanna do some flying today? Look for a bad guy? It's going to be just like the old days, back when you were young and had me as your partner."

Brad knew that his boisterous manner was getting through. He could hear Lance's wife grumbling for him to get out of the bedroom and leave her alone. Gripping his cell phone tightly to keep from laughing, Brad listened to the sounds of Lance stumbling through his house, muttering about needing a cup of coffee. After seconds, Lance practically shouted into the phone. "What the heck you talking about, Walker? I always want to fly. Looking for bad guys? We gave that up a while back. Or have you gone totally senile?" A pause. "Hold on a minute. I'm going to put the phone down. I've gotta fire up my coffee machine."

After seconds of listening to clattering and grumbling, Brad heard the sound of what he was pretty certain was that of a coffee cup dropped onto the floor. The outburst of swearing that followed confirmed his suspicion.

"Damn you, Walker! This is no way to begin a day. I just broke my favorite coffee mug and you're talking to me in tongues. You're making absolutely no sense at all. How 'bout we forget this call ever happened and we try again around noon or so?"

Now laughing openly, Brad managed to speak. "Come on, Lance, you can do this. Take a deep breath and move your body real slow. You're gonna be fine."

"I'll be fine when your lips are on my ass. Now, start over again. Try to talk in American."

Wiping tears from his eyes, Brad settled enough to give Lance a synopsis of the past few days and what he proposed for the two of them to do.

After hearing Brad's story, any hint of drowsiness had disappeared from Lance's voice. "Okay, so what are we looking at? How much territory are you talking about?"

"Oh, heavens, well over a hundred square miles, I'm sure. That's big-ass country out there but it's about as sparsely populated as the moon.

Lots of land but very few people. If we get that airplane of yours up high for a bird's eye view, we can spot every ranch, farm and outbuilding pretty easy. Then we just take 'em one by one and look for a blue jeep or a place that might have a small waterfall close by. If he's parked his rig in a garage or barn, we may have wasted our time. But I have to do this, Lance. I think the lady in Madrid is spot on that this is where he's going to be hiding. I think there's a chance he's got the girl with him and she just might still be alive."

"Oh, hell yes! You gotta do it and I'm gonna help you. Here's the deal. I've leased my airplane out to a guy and he's flying in from Arizona this morning. I won't have my bird until noon or so. By the time I fuel up and get down to Raton to meet with you, we're looking at three o'clock, best case."

"I'll take it."

"But listen up, I think weather might be blowing in by evening. The plane is leased again tomorrow morning, so I can't hang around for cocktails and caviar. I'll have to shoot on back soon as we handle our mission."

"I owe you big time, Lance. I have another call to make so let me run. I'll be waiting for you at the airport."

Sunlight always made Brad feel better. As the morning's sky brightened, he felt a sense of renewal stream through his body. Still, he was desperate for a mug of coffee. Santa Fe had been dark and closed up tight when he and his truck had headed north. Brad knew of a cafe that would be convenient to the highway once he made Raton. That was half hour further. Just enough time for his next call.

———

Ron Slater had spent years working with the FBI's behavioral science and criminal profiling program. Brad knew just enough about these fascinating fields to get himself in trouble. As he made his way toward Raton and a cup of hot coffee, he entered a telephone number into his cell and held his breath, hoping Ron would answer. Slater enjoyed an excellent reputation for analysis of criminal minds. He understood how they thought and the details of what made them tick.

Slater had developed profiles of criminals with uncanny accuracy. He was often spot on when describing the lifestyle and personality traits of people with disturbed minds. Brad took it as a good omen when he heard Ron's familiar voice. This was two out of two for the morning.

Following a summary of Sharon Moore's abduction, Brad continued with details of the similar incident in Wyoming. He related the story of Anna Carter and Onias, as well as the experiences of Margie and Jim Price. When telling the part of Nazareth dancing in the rain with a hard-on, Ron Slater interrupted. "I'd say this guy has real potential for a management position in the FBI. You agree?"

"Oh, heck yes. Get his ass to Washington, DC, as fast as possible. He'll have a corner office with a view overlooking Pennsylvania Avenue in no time." After a good laugh and agreement that the world was screwed up, Brad wrapped up with details of his conversation with Anna Carter and the bizarre bedroom he had visited. Slater followed with a few questions and was then quietly thoughtful.

"That's one hell of a story. Reminds me of the old saying that truth is stranger than fiction. What a perfect example."

"Absofrigginlutely!" Brad's reply was curt.

Speaking slowly, Slater formulated his thoughts as he spoke. "I'll throw a few observations or ideas at you, for whatever they may be worth. But first, I have to qualify what I'm going to say by telling you that I'm violating the cardinal rule of attempting to get inside the head of a bad guy. That rule is to make no judgement, diagnosis or attempt a profile until every fact, detail or scrap of information has been examined and thoroughly scrutinized. Relying on a third hand account from Wyoming is not perfect. Without going through this guy's bedroom with a fine-toothed comb and learning every possible detail, my perceptions are going to be general. We're not dealing with an ideal set of facts here."

"Of course. I understand perfectly where you're coming from. I would just appreciate your initial gut perspective. We're pretty much flying blind on this entire deal. So if, and I do mean if, we are lucky enough to find this guy, here are my primary questions: What are the chances that the girl is still alive? Do you think he would keep her close by so that if we find him, we also find her? If he wants separation, would he hold her captive somewhere far away or would he want to have her close by for control or to check on her? If we happen to locate him, should we go charging in like wild men, or should we be sneaky and try to watch him for a while?"

Pausing for a moment, Brad gathered his thoughts. "If he spots a surveillance, would that trigger him doing something to his victim? What about suicide? Worse, what about homicide and then suicide? That's the kind of stuff that I'm trying to sort out. All of this is unfolding as we go and any help you can offer is a bonus."

"You're dead-ass on target with your questions. That's the important stuff for what you're facing right now." Slater gave a sigh. "Okay, I'm going to give it the best shot I can with what I know. First, let's begin with what this guy was exposed to as a young boy. During the first years of his life, he was immersed in a world where women are really nothing more than sexual property for the use and satisfaction of men. To make matters worse, this way of thinking is supposedly based upon commandments from God, or hocus-pocus from so-called prophets of God. Holy cow, this craziness could really screw up a young man's head."

"No shit."

"So, based on what he was taught at an early age, how he abused his dog and his inability to develop lasting relationships with women, my guess is that he will have little concern for the safety or comfort of his victim. I sure think he will want to exert control. If I'm accurate in this prediction, my money says he will keep his victim very close by." Slater paused. "I'm going out on a limb here but I'm giving you my gut feeling. I say if you find the guy, then I think you'll find the girl."

"Got ya." Slater's assessment was exactly what Brad had hoped to hear.

"However, what the guy is going to do or how he will react if he spots surveillance or is confronted, I have no idea. Sorry, Brad, but I don't have an answer at all."

"Okay. I understand. If we find him, we'll just have to make a call at the time."

"Now, before we get to your other questions and talk about what you saw in the guy's bedroom, which, by the way, is very scary stuff, I'm going to hit you with a bit of pure speculation." Slater laughed. "Remember how through the years we liked to refer to WAG and SWAG, wild-assed-guess or scientific-wild–assed–guess?"

"WAGs and SWAGs are how I've lived my life, for heaven's sake." Brad laughed with Slater.

"What I'm about to tell you would just maybe qualify only as a WAG."

"I'm listening."

"My gut tells me that if the guy in Wyoming is the same guy that you're looking at in Colorado, I say he's had more victims between Wyoming and your current case in Colorado. You just don't know about them yet."

"Sounds reasonable but tell me why you think that."

"From what I'm hearing, the deal in Wyoming sounds poorly planned. I'd say this guy has fantasized about taking a girl captive for a long time, months to maybe even years. Usually, these clowns are satisfied with only fantasy for a while. But pressure builds and the fantasies becomes more intense. At some point, they cross the line from fantasy to reality. Probably, Wyoming was his first attempt. His erotic fantasies of holding a woman captive for an extended period simply didn't include having to empty her waste bucket. That ain't sexy to most folks, even screwballs. Also, back and forth trips to a storage locker would be a pain in the ass. Not to mention creating risk of somebody seeing something and becoming suspicious."

"I hear you. Makes sense."

"If Wyoming happened around two years ago, it's possible that the guy spent months doing nothing but planning his next episode. I consider that unlikely. Once the leap is made from fantasy to the real thing, fantasy no longer satisfies. I say your boy would have been impatient to try again. I'll lay you money that somewhere out there, maybe local or maybe many states removed, there's been at least an attempt or two that match what you're looking at."

"I suspected you might see it like that."

"Who knows? Could be unsuccessful attempts or possibly other actual abductions. Until these things happen several times and patterns can be discerned, connecting all the dots is mighty tough. Especially if the events are geographically scattered. Whichever the case may be, each time the guy will plan and execute his actions better. Every attempt teaches the bad guy how to be more prepared and to pull it off with fewer and fewer mistakes."

Grasping the significance of what Slater suggested, Brad replied. "So, chances are good that we're dealing with a guy who has either considerable experience in abduction and holding his victim in captivity, or a guy who has planned his actions with great care and detail over the span of many months."

"Yeah, I think that's correct. And that means two things. First, he's certainly going to be harder to catch. Detailed planning for control of the victim and a thoughtful game plan to avoid detection makes for a tough case. Second, as these guys progress in both fantasy and then the actual fulfillment of their fantasy, their urges grow and become more intense. What begins as a simple mental fantasy for control and fondling, combined with masturbation, matures into need for actual physical contact. This usually means rape, sometimes infliction of pain, and right on up the ladder. If these guys go on long enough, murder of the victim may very well be the ultimate outcome."

"Holy Jesus. These are certainly things that I've thought about but hearing it come from you, in the manner you've laid out, it ain't a real pretty picture."

"Sorry, Brad, but that's the way I see it. Now, once again, there's always deviation from the norm. Sometimes our predictions and analysis are just plain ole back-asswards. The fundamental religious stuff this guy was exposed to could certainly throw him out of the normal patterns of expectancy."

Releasing a despondent sigh, Brad spoke a bit more softly. "I understand the qualifiers. I've been around long enough to agree with how you see it."

Giving a laugh into the phone, Slater continued. "Hate to do this to you, Brad, but how about after this cheery assessment I've laid out so far, I give you the bad news?"

"What the hell. Sure, go ahead, Slater. Show me just how much gloom and doom you can deliver in a single conversation."

"I hate like heck to tell you this but, just in case your tour of that bedroom went over your head, you are dealing with one sick fucker. The signs of a severely disturbed mind are screaming from all kinds of directions. Once again, I have to go back to how the guy spent his early and formative years. When people from the outside look at the crazy, cult mentality of religious extremism, like this brand of Fundamentalist

Mormonism stuff, most people just can't comprehend or relate to their way of thinking. Normal folks simply shake their heads and say the only thing they can think of to say: 'those folks are frigging nuts.' But we forget that most of the misfits, like the guy you're dealing with here, are born and raised in that world. From the time they're at their mother's breast, that crazy stuff is what they see and hear. That's how they are taught from day one. And, possibly the most powerful influencing factor of all, they are brainwashed into believing that the behavior is divinely directed and inspired." Slater took a pause. "Can you imagine being raised in the screwed-up world that the lady in Madrid described to you?"

"Nope, you are so right. I can't imagine it from the male or female perspective."

"It's creepy shit. But then take it a step further. What happens when a young boy is suddenly removed from that world and is thrust into an almost entirely opposite culture and manner of thinking? Talk about wires going in all directions! It sounds like this is exactly what happened to your guy. He was thrown from one world into another. Keep in mind that things like this happen more frequently than we realize. By no means do confusing signals in youth necessarily result in deviant or criminal behavior. In fact, most of the time, the human brain sorts it all out pretty darned efficiently and these folks ultimately live a normal life. But, when things go wrong, they can go really wrong."

"Understood."

"Before I get to the cross and candles, I'll talk about the obvious. With photos of naked women plastered all over a wall of his room, and all of them blonde, it sure looks like he has a thing for blondes. There may be reasons for why blonde and not brunette or something else. I don't know. Perhaps his mother was a blonde. Maybe he had a teenaged girlfriend, real or imagined, who was a blonde and dumped him. It's anybody's guess with what we know up to this point. What I think is significant is this, he probably has a sexual attraction for blondes but, at the same time and for whatever reason, he harbors extreme hatred for blondes. It's a crazy but fairly common phenomena."

Brad spoke as Slater paused. "Lord only knows how many photos of naked women were in that room, and every damned one was of a blonde. It was impossible to miss."

"Oh, yeah. I hear you. The Wyoming girl was blonde and the Colorado victim was blonde." Slater gave a short laugh. "My sophisticated training and years of experience tell me that it don't pay to be an attractive blonde and go on a date with your good pal, Onias."

Joining Slater in a moment of wry humor, Brad fired back, "Damn, you're smart."

"Flattery works wonders, keep it up." Slater's voice took on a grave tone. "There are any number of things in the guy's room that hold all kinds of mysteries. Especially that stuff around the cross. I need to know more about your boy before I would feel comfortable in trying to analyze how all that stuff relates to what's inside his head."

"No argument from me on that one."

"There are a couple of things that I sure do think need to be considered. There has to be a reason why he would have a book on this place called Folsom situated within the ring of candles at the foot of the cross. There's something about the town or the place that carries weight with your boy. Is it a place where he felt secure as a young man? Did he have a romantic experience there that stays with him? Who the hell knows, but something about that place is significant and Anna's story confirms this."

"I agree completely. When I was in the bedroom last night and looking at the Folsom book, I specifically looked for a bookmark or underlined passage but didn't see anything. I thought about taking the darned thing but, for some reason, I was thinking a search team might very well be back in that room fairly soon. I wanted to leave everything just as I found it."

"You probably did right. What's important to your boy could be anything and may be obscure as hell. Who knows?"

"What else about the cross bothers you?"

"Well, the book being so carefully positioned within the candles shouts out for attention. So does the paper that was weighted down beneath the cross. But this one scares the hell out of me."

"Keep talking, I'm listening."

"I happen to be familiar with that particular passage. It's from Civil War writings that have been compiled by historians. You know, it never ceases to amaze me how those Civil War soldiers, young boys, teenagers mostly, farmers turned warrior, could write with such eloquence."

"Isn't that the truth. I've marveled at that very thing a million times."

"Sadly, though, eloquence is not the point this time. That passage is a grim assessment of the horrible realities of a battlefield. How death takes much more than the life of a single person. The ripple effect of lives taken in war flows endlessly. It devastates wives, children, parents, future brides and children who will never be born. God-Almighty, it doesn't end."

In a flashing instant, Brad again stood in the Vietnam Memorial: Los Alamos, mushroom clouds, the Moreno Valley, lives lost, futures that never happen. Brad held his private thoughts, allowing moments of silence before offering his reply. "I hear you, believe me I do." He spoke softly.

"Beauty of the written word and esoteric thoughts on war are not even close to what we're talking about this time. I say your guy is obsessed with death. Especially sacrificial death. I think he looks to the cross as a symbol of sacrifice. This printed passage he included under the cross, it screams of sacrifice. How that may translate specifically to his victims, I don't know. Hopefully, he is still in the fantasy stage concerning death and his victims. But at some point, that line will likely be crossed. There is a strong possibility that Onias will move from fantasy to reality, both in delusional sexual behavior and in his fascination with death."

Brad gulped. So far, Slater had not said anything that Brad had not already known and considered to some degree. But the sobering reality of Slater's final observations had a haunting effect.

A new passenger suddenly rode in the truck with Brad, a sneering skeleton. Holding a cross and images of women stripped naked, the skeleton stared straight ahead. Brad chilled.

Neither man spoke for a moment. Struggling for words, Brad finally managed a reply. "Okay, Slater, thanks for your time."

"I hope I'm wrong on all this. I told you the way I see it. No sugar coating."

"That's exactly why I called and what I wanted. I appreciate your time and expertise."

"No problem."

"Adios, amigo."

The truck was silent, just Brad and his new passenger.

Brad passed the exit for Highway 64, the road to Cimarron and Taos. The outline of Raton appeared on the horizon. Only a few more minutes to coffee.

FIFTEEN

Loaded with biscuits, bacon, eggs, hot coffee, and a full tank of gas, Brad left Raton. He didn't have a bunch of time before meeting Bob Lance at 3:00 but he calculated it was enough to make a circular drive through Folsom for a quick scouting run of the territory.

Taking Highway 72 East, Brad dropped down into a canyon of heavy brush and vegetation. Following a twisting, ascending climb, he topped out onto Johnson Mesa. An entirely different world took shape. Two thousand feet above the surrounding valleys, Brad felt he and his truck had somehow flown onto an island in the sky. Driving the narrow road, Brad enjoyed the sensation of soaring. It was absolute exhilaration. Realizing what an incredible environment he had entered, he pulled to the roadside, parked and stepped out of his truck. Sheer majesty. The air was at peace and immense silence lay over the land. No vehicles, no people, no buildings. Only endless rolling miles of grass-covered hills, cattle and oceans of sunflowers. A hawk circled. Thermal currents hoisted his streamlined body above the landscape. Late-morning sun, illuminating through ninety-three million miles of void, seemed no further than the vast distances surrounding Brad. To the north, he saw southern fringes of Colorado, the Rocky Mountains rose in the distance. In all other directions, it was nothing short of infinity. Rangeland extended until time and space converged into imagination of the planet's birth: volcanic mountains, mounds, cones, plugs and vents. The ancestral skeletons of a boiling planet. Brad breathed, held the air, whispering as he released, "I've got to bring Juanita here. She will love it."

Moving again with his windows opened, Brad no longer felt the presence of the macabre passenger from earlier in the morning.

Judging distance in the immensity of the incredible landscape was difficult. Brad spotted the church on the horizon but lost perspective as mile after mile passed while he gradually drew nearer. Brad expected to find ruins of a long-forgotten chapel, remnants of pioneer life faded into obscurity. But, after pulling into the short pathway leading to the church, he saw that he had been mistaken. Even though it was quite old, the stone and mason structure was obviously well cared for. Positioned atop the elevated heights of Johnson Mesa in a world of stark beauty and solitude, St. John's Methodist Episcopal Church was the only vestige of human habitation for miles. A small patch of green and trimmed grass around the church indicated regular guardianship, a labor of love speaking to the sacredness of the building and its location. Brad parked and gazed at the church. "I've gotta see this," he murmured as he exited his truck.

With a gentle twist on the handle and slight shove, the door opened. Of course, it would be open. No locks here. This was a place of refuge, always open to those who seek. Brad's eyes moved slowly over straight-back wooden pews, a plank floor, white walls and a simple podium flanked by two wooden chairs. Front and center, a cross hung behind the podium. To his left, an upright piano. Three tear-drop shaped windows lined walls on both sides, each offering views to the miles of open land.

What did he feel? Was it nostolgia for his past or reverence of the present moment? How many hours of his life had been spent in churches so very similar to this? Brad looked to the piano. Its aged keys held their own life and memories. They could surely tell forgotten stories of people, labor, marriages and funerals. Closing his eyes, Brad's mind summoned music from the aged piano: *The Old Rugged Cross, Amazing Grace,* and his favorite, *I Come to the Garden Alone.* Reluctant to make a sound or disturb the atmosphere of the church, he reverently walked the aisle. Stepping between the pews, he moved slowly, his fingertips caressing the wood of each one as he passed.

Reaching the podium near the front of the church, Brad halted and remained still. He looked through the windows, taking in the vastness that engulfed the church. He listened to silence and felt solace. There was not a religious bone in Brad's body but the faith and strength of the people who had built this church over one hundred years ago endured. A spiritual presence filled the tiny chapel. Brad felt the sacredness of the moment. He took a seat on the first pew, only feet from the podium and cross. Eyes again closed, Brad spoke to Elizabeth. He thanked her for their children and the life they had shared. He reached for Juanita, thanking her for the new life she had given him. Lifting his head to gaze at the cross, Brad felt his chest tighten. He appealed to the power within the old church and the arms of the cross. Please, protect Sharon Moore.

In his truck again and remaining captivated by the beauty of Johnson Mesa, Brad continued his drive toward Folsom. Reality of how expansive an area he was facing in his search for Onias began to register. It was a sobering long shot but he could not think of a better plan. If Lance and he could circle somewhere between three thousand to five thousand feet above the ground, there was a chance that they could do a fairly quick survey of the ranches and farms in the area. Unless he heard something solid from Kurt to send him in a different direction, Lance's airplane was the best option he had.

Finally, the road made a curving descent from the plateau of Johnson Mesa into lower land of fields and meadows. Pick-up trucks, ranch homes and farm equipment began to appear. The isolation and solitude Brad had felt while high upon the plateau faded with images that spoke to the fact that people and routines of life were again close by.

Entering Folsom was a step back in time. Small houses comprised the village. Some were neglected and junk-littered. Others were pristine, their tended flower gardens brilliant with hollyhocks. Tall trees offered canopies of shade. An occasional rooster darted across the road as if daring a confrontation with Brad's truck. "This is amazing," Brad spoke softly to himself.

A well-cared-for building, that almost certainly at one time had served as the community's general store, was labeled "Folsom Museum." Parking his truck in front of the museum, Brad was immediately taken by the old-fashioned covered porch that extended the length of the building. Two men, seated on wooden benches, carried on in easy conversation and raised a hand in greeting to all who happened to pass by.

Feeling that he was in a place and time long-past, Brad entered the museum. It was everything he anticipated: antiquated farming and mining tools, along with Native American relics of pottery, arrowheads and spear points. Photographs of early settlers, famous lawmen and notorious outlaws of the Old West were overseen by mounted trophies of wild animals indigenous to the area. The building held the smell of history.

After wandering the museum, Brad tossed a five-dollar bill into the contribution bucket and was about to exit when he spotted it: the same blue and gold book that had been beneath the cross in the bedroom of Onias.

Folsom
1888-1988
Then and Now

Obviously a popular-selling item, multiple copies were stacked near the doorway. Without hesitation, Brad paid for the book and went immediately to his truck. A soft breeze moved through his cab as he remained parked in the shaded front of the museum. Having no idea what he should be looking for but thankful for an opportunity to review the book in a calm setting, Brad began flipping through pages. It was possible that something would jump out as an obvious clue to why Onias was so attracted to Folsom. What should he look for? Page after page: early settlers, the land, railroad construction. It went on forever and would take hours to thoroughly scrutinize.

Two things made an impression on Brad even though they probably bore no relevance to Onias. Regardless, they were fascinating stories. Brad read in detail the story of a deadly flood in 1908 that had taken many lives from Folsom. He was captivated by the heroism of a tele-phone operator, Sarah Rooke, who saved lives with her own sacrifice by warning others to flee while she refused to leave her post. Also, Brad loved the story of a black cowboy, George McJunkin, and how his discovery of bison bones subsequent to the 1908 disaster turned out to be one of the most significant archeological developments in North American history.

Closing the book, Brad sat quietly. With new awareness of the history around him, he savored the feel of Folsom. Glancing at his watch, he decided to make his way back to Raton for his meeting with Bob Lance and the airplane. However, instead of back-tracking over Johnson Mesa, he opted for a route that would take him past Capulin Mountain. This was the place where Brad had lived the most terrifying experience of his life in an encounter with a pedophile who traded sex with young girls for stolen Native American artifacts. He still suffered periodic nightmares of that terrible day. Brad hoped that driving through the area once again might, in some manner, help cleanse his mind of those haunting memories.

Leaving Folsom and reaching the crest of a hill, the profile of Capulin Mountain came into view. Feeling the terror of his last time near the mountain, Brad began to second guess the wisdom of his decision to take this route. Just as thoughts of turning around entered his mind, something caught his attention. The Folsom cemetery, a field of tombstones and markers just off the pavement, seemed to beckon. Giving in to impulse, Brad abruptly made the necessary turn from the pavement onto a rutted trail that led to the graveyard. Parking his truck, Brad saw that the area was enclosed by a wire fence with a permanently opened metal gate that wearily sagged on worn-out hinges.

Strolling toward the gate, Brad took in the land, mountains and unfathomable sky that expanded in all directions. Exquisite beauty but extreme loneliness would be eternal companions to those laid to rest in this tiny patch of New Mexico soil. Wind stirred as he stepped through the entrance. In a ripple over the prairie, sunflowers and grasses rolled like ocean waves. Headstones appeared to rise and fall as though they floated.

At first, it was just something black, possibly a stone, a part of the landscape. But after a few seconds, the stone moved and was more clearly seen. Brad momentarily halted a few feet inside the cemetery. A black dog stood, watching intently as Brad again moved. Standing in the swaying grass of the cemetery, the dog remained motionless. Brad stopped. He and the dog made long distance eye contact, neither sure what to do. Cautiously, Brad moved his feet, one step toward the dog, then another, and another, closing the distance that separated them in tiny increments. The dog held his position. More steps and Brad could easily see that the creature was pathetically thin. Still standing on the gravestone where he had been lying, the dog's eyes were wary and uncertain. They focused on Brad with uncanny intensity. Brad dared to move closer. The dog reluctantly backed away, moving off of the gravestone in hesitant backward steps. Brad could sense that the animal was curious but certainly prepared to run if danger was perceived. Brad inched closer. He could now see the dog's ribs clearly outlined beneath short, black hair. Brad calculated that the dog should have weighed thirty pounds but, in its pitiful state, he was no more than twenty. The dog took another wary step backwards. Brad again halted. Each held their position. Brad squatted, never taking his eyes from the dog.

What did he see? Starvation for sure. But there was more. Staring back at this intruder were brown eyes that, despite intense hunger, seemed to see not only Brad but all the space about him in a single, focused gaze. Brad was captivated by the dog's eyes. They were unsettlingly intense.

Standing slowly and retreating one step at a time, Brad finally turned and walked back to his truck. He recalled that he had an entire bacon, egg and cheese sandwich in his truck, uneaten and still wrapped. Grabbing the sandwich, Brad again entered the cemetery. The dog had not moved. Making his way to where he had previously squatted, Brad again lowered his body. Man and beast. Alone together in a desolate New Mexico cemetery. Each interested but uncertain and cautious. Brad extended his arm, holding the sandwich. The dog stared, ears alert and nose twitching. Warily, the creature circled toward the offered food, slouching till his belly drug over the dirt. The animal crept, its tongue hanging in desperation, fear – hope? Following every movement, Brad never let his eyes leave those of the dog.

Now slinking over the ground, the heartbreaking waltz continued. With front paws clawing into dirt, the dog pulled his emaciated body toward Brad's outstretched arm. Pitiful desperation now filled the brown eyes that focused on the food in Brad's hand. Guttural whimpers seeped from his throat and his nostrils quivered. Brad felt his own heart breaking. He observed shivers ripple through the dog's deprived body. Regardless of starvation, fear dominated. The dog would come no closer. Brad could no longer withhold the food, to do so was absolute torture to the poor creature.

With a slight flick of his wrist, Brad tossed the sandwich. Faster than Brad could ever remember seeing an animal move, the dog snatched what had been given, scooping it from the ground and bolting in a single blurred motion of blinding speed. In the time it took Brad to blink, the dog was yards away and devouring his gift from a stranger.

Brad watched as the dog remained where he had eaten. Flashes of a pink tongue cleaned the fur about his mouth. Taking a breath and heartsick that he did not have more food to offer, Brad moved to where the dog had been lying. His eyes widened as the gravestone that had served as a resting place to the dog came into view:

George McJunkin
1856-1922

Brad was stunned. This was the grave of the black cowboy he had just read about. The man whose discovery had shredded scientific theories and assumptions about early man in North America. "Absolutely amazing!" Brad's whispered words drifted, carried on the wind.

Standing beside the grave of George McJunkin, Brad turned to survey more of the cemetery. It was not a large parcel, maybe two acres. Most gravestones were flush with the ground. Many were completely overgrown with years of creeping neglect. On the backside of the burial ground, Brad saw a tall stone marker that was clearly different from the rest of the memorials. Curious, he sauntered toward the monument, reading as he walked. Words engraved on stone after stone, etched names, dates of birth, dates of death, all that remained of so many lives. Reaching the large marker that had garnered his attention, Brad again felt the wonderment of incredible coincidence. This was the grave of Sarah Rooke, the telephone operator who had died in the flood of 1908 while attempting to warn others of impending danger. Etched in a bronze plaque were words memorializing her heroism. Brad silently mouthed the words as he read the inscription:

In Honored Memory of
SARAH J. ROOKE
Telephone Operator

Who perished in the flood waters
Of the Dry Cimarron at Folsom, N.M.
August 27, 1908
While at her switchboard warning
Others of their danger
With heroic devotion she glorified
Her calling by sacrificing her own
Life that others might live
"Greater love hath no man than this."
Erected by her fellow workers

Feelings similar to what he had experienced in the Vietnam Memorial ran through Brad's mind. He considered how not only soldiers, but ordinary people, cowboys or telephone operators, can be thrust into extraordinary situations and their actions alter history.

Wind blew over the cemetery with slightly more force than when he had arrived. To Brad, it was eerily forlorn. Within the enormity of this huge land and sky, wind moving over the bodies of what had been families, love, hope, labor and dreams, seemed mournful. A reminder of the frailty and fickle nature of life.

Walking away from the grave of Sarah Rooke, Brad looked to the front edge of the cemetery. There he was. The dog was once again on the gravestone of George McJunkin. Lying perfectly still, the dog's eyes watched Brad's every move. Uncertain of what was the best thing to do, Brad walked a wide circle, giving significant separation so that he would not alarm the poor creature that had apparently been abandoned. When Brad reached his truck, the dog stood. It was the only acknowledgement that the person who had fed him was apparently about to leave him alone. Another abandonment? Across the distance, Brad saw the piercing brown eyes once again. Bewilderment. Fading hope. Sorrow.

SIXTEEN

Within the barn that he now considered to be his home, Onias Phillips wandered contemplatively. He loved this special place. Examining every detail, he walked slowly, brushing his fingers over the walls and gazing up into to the ceiling. The array of speakers he had placed along the rafters would deliver sound as if coming straight from heaven. This was just as it should be. The barn's opened doors allowed light onto the decaying floor and the years of dust that had gathered along every joint and the ceiling beams. Onias walked among the multitude of full-length mirrors, choreographed so that reflections of reflections tracked every movement as he walked through the maze. He halted frequently, standing before a mirror to stroke his hair and examine his face from multiple angles. At times, he would loosen the ties of his robe, let it drop to the floor and admire the reflection of his nude body. After seconds, he covered himself again and moved on.

Reaching a wall where a crude closet had been constructed, Onias slid his hands over the assortment of clothing that hung from a rusted pipe he used as closet bar. He caressed each one as an object of adoration. He knew the exact placement of every garment. In his mind, Onias visualized the appearance that each piece of clothing would render when worn. Textures of velvet and satin stimulated his exploring fingers. Onias lifted a purple robe from its suspension. Enthralled with the richness of the material, fullness of color and the padded lapels that exuded a sense of royalty, he held it next to his body and stroked it lovingly. Onias placed the robe upon a nearby table. his senses tingled with anticipation. It was almost time. This would be his special robe, the one to be worn later tonight.

Again, his fingers traced the collection of clothes. He knew precisely the single garment he desired and where it hung. He caressed the fabric before lifting it from the rack and raising it high for scrutiny. Onias smiled. This was it, the special gown, the one that he had selected to be her wedding dress. How beautiful she would be, lying on their marriage altar. He envisioned her appearance, folds of the cloth flowing about her body. Onias placed the wedding gown next to the purple robe.

Once again standing within the maze of mirrors, Onias opened boxes of candles that had been placed on the floor. With painstaking precision, he arranged a half circle pattern of candles before each mirror. When finished, he walked to where he had a view down the hallway to her room. Onias looked to the bolted door. He thought of her, waiting on the other side. Familiar pressure swelled within his groin. He wanted to touch himself. This was not the time. Not now. He refused his desire. Everything must wait. Ecstasy was in store.

Leaving the barn, Onias shut the doors, knowing the total blackness that he sealed within. Everything was ready. He would return soon. It would be time to bathe his body and then give her special water and fragrance with which to bathe. After darkness arrived and the candles were lit, their wedding ceremony would begin. This was the night. The long-awaited sign from God was coming. He was certain.

However, one more task remained to be completed before commencement of this holy night. Onias went to his blue jeep and checked the contents of the rear compartment. Satisfied with what he saw, he entered the vehicle and drove away.

SEVENTEEN

The Raton, New Mexico, airport sits 6,350 feet above sea level and has intersecting runways, the longest of which is 7,620 feet in length. On hot summer days, at this elevation, over a mile of asphalt was not a luxury but a necessity for aircraft to operate in the thin air. While waiting for Bob Lance, Brad sipped coffee and examined a map of Folsom and the surrounding area. Only twenty or so miles from the airport, Folsom and the country around it was expansive. With very few roads to serve the meager population, Brad was cautiously optimistic that Lance and he could give this long shot idea a fair shake.

He had talked with Kurt while waiting but nothing more of significance had been learned. Kurt had searched data banks using all conceivable combinations of names and nicknames known to be affiliated with Onias, Samson or Nazareth. His efforts had been to no avail. He had fired off communications to law enforcement agencies all over the nation, asking for help in identifying similar cases. There was always hope, but nothing yet. They had ended their conversation with a promise from Brad to call the minute Lance and he completed their aerial search.

———

Watching the red and white Cessna 182 taxi to the fuel pumps, Brad's mind was taken back to the countless missions Lance and he had flown together. It felt just like the old days. Lance's profile in the left seat was unmistakable. Brad stepped outside and gave a wave to his old partner. A big thumbs-up flashed back from the cockpit. After Lance had killed the engine and given instructions to the fueling crew, he exited the aircraft and began walking toward Brad. At the half-way point to the doorway where Brad waited, Lance hunched his shoulders, grabbed his crotch with both hands, looked to Brad and mouthed the words, "I gotta pee." He then sprinted to the building, blasting past Brad without further acknowledgement or a word of greeting.

Brad was still laughing when a relaxed Bob Lance reappeared. Extending his hand and, with his trademark lop-sided grin of ornery humor, he addressed the situation, "Holy shit, that was a close one!" Laughing together, words were unnecessary to unearth memories of the times they had consumed coffee before flying a mission and, hours later, paid for their indulgence in sheer agony.

With perfunctory small talk kept to a minimum, Lance and Brad got to their business. Lance unfolded an aviation sectional map that corresponded with the regular road map that Brad had been studying. Together, they familiarized themselves with the territory they would soon fly over. Lance stood as he folded the aviation sectional and, with his usual tone of light-hearted determination, spoke all that needed to be said. "Okeydokey, let's get 'er done. I'll pay the fuel bill and let's launch." Lance grinned again and looked at Brad with mock seriousness. "I suggest you handle the first thing on our check list for every flight. Drain that dainty little radiator of yours before buckling up."

"Check." Brad's one-word reply initiated another round of laughter.

With business handled and while walking to the airplane, Lance tossed a ring of keys to Brad. "Left seat, compadre, this is your mission."

Grabbing the keys in mid-air, Brad gave Lance a 'you gotta be shitting' me look. "What the hell's wrong with you? I haven't flown in years."

"Bicycle, bicycle, you old goat. Flying an airplane is just like riding a bicycle. Only difference is bicycles are a hell of a' lot more difficult. A person can get hurt peddling around on a bicycle."

"Are you frigging nuts?"

"Unlax, Brad, unlax. Have you forgotten that in addition to being the most handsome and highly decorated flyer the United States Navy ever produced, I am also a C-F-I." Lance drug out the letters slowly. "With your advanced age, I suspect that you've forgotten this technical term of aviators so, let me help you out. It means I am a certified flight instructor. And, as the holder of that exalted title, I hereby designate you as my student pilot for the day." Lance flashed his smile and spoke in an exaggerated sing-song voice, "Come on, big boy, take me for a spin."

Secretly thrilled with the opportunity, Brad shook his head with a soft mutter, "This ain't gonna be pretty."

Once within the aircraft, a flood of emotions surged. Pure nostalgia. Anticipation. The contour of the seat, safety harness secured, rudder pedals beneath his feet, yoke in his hand. The smell. Headset in place. Nostalgia.

No need to prime. The engine was warm. Feet locked on brakes. Master switch on. Gyroscope spinning. Initial rotations of propeller. The machine shuddered before quickly settling into comfortable vibration. Gauges awakened, oil pressure green, radio set. Nostalgia.

Brad felt his heart racing. Taxi, feet steering, hold at end of runway, set brake, throttle 1700, mag check, compass alignment, control check. Cowl flaps. Carb heat. Flaps set. Trim adjusted. Radio call. Nose centered on runway. Throttle forward. Power. Acceleration. Speed, Right rudder. The craft yearned to fly, more comfortable in air than on the ground.

Brad could not help himself, he had to do it. Instead of applying a hint of back pressure on the yoke to allow a gradual ascent from the runway, he forced it forward, holding the craft just above the runway to gain speed in ground effect. Then, releasing pressure on the yoke, the craft catapulted upward. Sheer exhilaration for the two men in the cockpit. Inwardly, both men were convinced that the airplane itself felt the same thrill.

"You goofy shit. You'll never grow up." Lance threw his head back and laughed as the earth fell away beneath the airplane.

Upon reaching 1,000 feet above the ground, Brad brought the airplane into a gentle bank and continued their climb as they headed toward Folsom. Lance and Brad had decided to begin the search by orbiting directly over the village itself. Then, in a widening circular pattern, their flight would expand the amount of territory surveyed and display the land in a variety of angles. Within minutes, they were soaring close to the volcanic cone of Mt. Capulin. Brad shuddered as he recalled the day he had peered into the mouth of the extinct beast. He had almost died that day. He would much prefer to actually die rather than to live the experience of that day again.

Folsom was straight ahead. After clearing Capulin Mountain, Brad established a flight pattern at 3,000 feet above the ground. From this altitude, Lance and he knew they were high enough for expansive views but could still discern objects and details. If their flight ultimately took them over Johnson Mesa or back toward Capulin Mountain, a significant altitude adjustment would be necessary, both for safety and to maintain visual perspective.

Once power and control settings had been established, Brad became more relaxed and savored the joy of flight. With the familiar vibration of the aircraft and the landscape drifting below, he felt as if he had reconnected with an old friend.

Approaching Folsom, Brad spotted the cemetery just southwest of the village. "Hand me the spotting scope, Bob, I need to see something." Left rudder applied, and in a banking left turn, Brad held the scope to his eye. The stabilized device allowed for magnification of objects on the ground without the debilitating effects of motion sickness. In one sense, Brad expected it. But yet he felt an element of surprise as he peered through the scope. The dog was still there. He was easy to see, still lying on the gravestone of George McJunkin. "Wow," was all Brad could say as he lowered the scope. He related to Lance his experience from earlier in the day and the lingering turmoil he felt for leaving the dog.

"Shithead. Only a total shithead could abandon a creature like that."

"Yep, you're right. But, that ain't making me feel any better. After today, I feel like I'm the one who abandoned him."

"You gonna go back? You could take the poor critter to a shelter or give him a home yourself maybe?"

Shaking his head, Brad had to think before replying. "I've sure as hell thought about it. I'm just not sure I could ever convince him to come to me. He was one skittish animal. If I somehow coaxed him close and grabbed him, I think he would be terrified half to death. Maybe take a hunk out of my hide. He's starving and I'm sure he has been abused in the past. No telling how he might react."

"Shitheads, the world is crawling with shitheads. Wish I could line 'em all up, arm this little bird of mine and strafe every damned one of them straight to hell."

"Let me know. I'll keep your gun loaded up as fast as you can mow 'em down."

"Roger that, amigo. Roger that."

Brad dropped ten degrees of flaps and eased back on the throttle, banking into a turn over Folsom. Their mission underway, each man assumed his duty as they had done hundreds of times before. It took only minutes for Brad to scrutinize the few blocks that comprised the village.

Satisfied with what he had seen, Brad leveled the wings in preparation to begin the expanding search pattern. He spoke into his headset. "I didn't really expect to spot anything right here in the village. I think he's going to be out in ranchland somewhere. The only reason he would be in town is if he's spotted himself another cute blonde. Know what I mean?"

"Shitheads, shitheads."

After only a few expanding orbits from the settlement of Folsom, houses became few and far between, allowing Brad to make their circles larger and larger. Johnson Mesa loomed to the north and Capulin Mountain to the south. Glancing to the north and observing the 2,000-foot rise of Johnson Mesa, Brad spoke. "How about we go up another four thousand or so? I don't trust the currents that are likely to be coming off the mesa."

Thumbs up from Lance.

Flaps up and power applied, the craft ascended. Soon, the outside perspective looked entirely different. The table-top surface of Johnson Mesa looked eerily out of place above endless miles of volcano-pocked grassland. The mesa's sides were gouged with shadowed canyons. Basalt boulders were scattered as though flung from heaven by huge and angry hands. The 14,000-foot mountains of Colorado, some still tipped with snow, towered to the north. "Oh, my Lord, is this ever beautiful!" Brad's voice was filled with awe.

"Beautiful is an understatement, my friend. We are so damned lucky to live out here."

With their elevated perspective, Lance and Brad were able to spot specific ranch homes or buildings and fly directly to them for closer observation. One by one they eliminated the pockets of human habitation. No blue jeep and no waterfall. There were still vast amounts of territory to cover. Every instinct within Brad told him that Onias would only come here if he felt sheltered, able to hide. The land to the south and west was wide open. Buildings sat in plain view for miles. It was along the rim of Johnson Mesa, where there were chasms, gullies and brush-filled canyons, that someone wanting to disappear would be drawn. Lance and Brad kept circling, eyes straining.

Brad recalled Anna's face and again heard her voice as she told of Onias living in a barn that was part of the living quarters for a hired hand. Brad knew that what he was looking for could either be close to a large ranch headquarters or tucked away in a remote canyon. Anna had spoken of how Onias revered a nearby waterfall. He plugged that information into the mental image of the type of terrain that he was seeking. Brad's inner thoughts repeated within his mind, *Keep flying. Keep looking. There are no waterfalls out in the flats. If Onias is down there, he has to be somewhere along the rim of the mesa.*

There was no longer conversation. When one or the other would see a possibility, a simple point of a finger was all that was communicated and Brad would fly direct, circle, scrutinize with the scope, shake his head in disappointment and fly on.

Circling over the east end of the mesa, where the road descended down into the valley, Lance was the first to spot it on his side of the airplane. A dark vehicle, driving on a faint dirt trail that led from what looked to be a hayfield, into a narrow canyon. Slapping Brad's knee to get his attention, Lance practically shouted, "Three o'clock, three o'clock! Bank it hard. Bank it hard!"

Right rudder, hard, turn of the yoke, back pressure, more back pressure. The aircraft responded. Now flying with the right-wing tip practically pointed to the ground, the view outside the windscreen became wildly erratic. Within seconds, both the vehicle and the trail fell into view on Brad's side of the aircraft. But, just as Brad managed to level the aircraft, the vehicle disappeared into shadows within the small canyon. Re-establishing normal flight, Brad strained his eyes, desperate to spot the vehicle again. There was only one place the trail could go but it was invisible from his current angle. He had to circle again for proper alignment. Brad felt his heart accelerate. Something about this felt right.

Afternoon light was slanted and shadows were deepening. If Lance had not spotted the vehicle while it was moving, the flimsy excuse of a road would never have been seen. It was nothing more than ruts through tall grass. With the spotting scope to his eye, Brad brought the box canyon into his field of vision just as the vehicle came out from under a canopy of trees. No doubt, it was a dark blue jeep. Then, the remainder of the picture came into view: a small shack of a house and a dilapidated, old barn. The canyon was becoming dark and impossible to see unless observed from precisely the proper angle. Circling once again for another look, Brad saw the clincher that he had hoped to spot. A creek cascaded from the steep hillside above the barn. It was a miniature waterfall. They had found it! "Jesus H, Lance, you finally managed to do something worthwhile for a change. This is it. This is damned sure it!"

The blue jeep came to a stop and parked between the house and the barn. Afraid to blink, Brad watched as the figure of a man exited the vehicle and walked to the barn. That was it. Brad had no more angle to view the house and barn until he circled again. The next orbit revealed no additional movement about the parked vehicle or the buildings.

His heart hammering and mind racing, Brad leveled the aircraft. "Fantastic damned eyeballs, you old bastard. If you hadn't seen the jeep at the exact right moment, we would never have found the place. It's tucked up into the end of that canyon and damned near impossible to see. I'm so damned happy, I'll let you buy me a steak dinner when all this is over."

Lance laughed his relaxed laugh. "If I had a nickel for every time I've saved your bacon, I could afford to buy you a steak dinner." Lance pointed to the southwest. "Something tells me that maybe we should make our dining plans another time. I don't like the looks of those clouds over there. I'm pretty sure they're headed our way."

Brad realized that he had committed a sin that no pilot of a small aircraft should ever commit. He had taken his eye off the weather. "Good Lord, when I'm fishing, I constantly watch the sky for bad stuff. I just flat-assed became too wrapped up in this mess. I forgot to look." Brad thought for a moment. "What I need to do really quick before we head for home is get my bearings so I can find this place again on the ground. I also have to be able to give directions to the guys I'll be calling to get over here and set up a surveillance or arrest."

"Yeah, good idea cause that's gonna be a tough place to find after dark. I'm sick about it, but I have to beat the storm that's rolling in. My bird is leased for a full week beginning at dawn tomorrow morning. I just can't afford to get stuck here. Otherwise, I'd drive back out here with you tonight."

"Oh, heck, don't worry at all. I don't know what's going to happen next. I'll call the investigator in Colorado and let him call the shots. He's going to have to figure out how to round up the troops in New Mexico. They'll probably kick my old has-been ass outta here once I show them the location." Thinking for a moment, Brad turned the airplane due west before continuing. "Just a few miles this way is a church that is very easy to spot. I'm going to designate the church as the landmark for navigating on the ground. Let's start from there and take a good look at how to give directions."

"You got it. If you can fly this thing half-assed straight and level and keep us alive, I'll jot down a few notes."

"Better start jotting cause that's the church straight ahead." Brad pointed over the nose. "I'll circle over the church and follow the road back to the east. If we can calculate distances half close, I think I can talk the boys in. All the GPS nonsense in the world won't help in finding that road and house after nightfall."

"I'm with ya." Lance pulled a paper from his shirt pocket, unfolded it and gave a sarcastic look to Brad. "Just like American Express, never leave home without paper and a pen. What in the world would you do without me?"

Bringing the airplane around and over the church, Brad estimated distances as they flew. "I'm pretty sure that it's about ten miles east of the church. Paved road all the way. It's where the road twists down off the mesa that I need to see one more time before going back to the airport." They flew in silence for a few moments and Brad positioned the craft so that Lance would have the road on his side to sketch his map.

"Okay, Han Solo, gimme a little right bank if you don't mind." Brad did as instructed. Lance scribbled a few notes. He traced a dirt cutting from the pavement but seemed to terminate between two separate hay meadows. Unless one knew otherwise, it appeared that there was no passage between the hay fields. But with the advantage of having seen the blue jeep make its way across the fields and into the canyon, it was obvious that some sort of crude road did in fact exist. Straightening his back from note-taking, Lance lifted his handiwork and beaming with pride proclaimed, "Who the hell needs GPS? Ain't none of your boys going to have cell phones with coverage or enough basic intelligence to use any of that technical crap anyway."

Laughing, Brad shook his head in agreement.

"And, by the way, Brad, don't get all excited cause I called you Han Solo. I was just being nice. Back when we were on the job, the girls in the office referred to you as Chewbacca. You never knew and the guys didn't want to hurt your feelings." Lance looked straight ahead, completely serious. No hint of a smile.

Taking a last look at the terrain where Onias was hiding, Brad again turned the airplane west, heading for the airport. "One of the things I enjoy most about no longer being in the Bureau is not having to put up with people and nonsense like you every day of the week."

Lance was delighted. "Speaking of nonsense, let's see what kind of landing you can make. I tripled my life insurance before flying down here today. My wife is hoping for a real smasher. She's already found herself a shiny convertible, new golf clubs and a hot-looking golf pro to help her ease through grieving. All ten minutes of it, I imagine."

"I don't know about landing, Lance." Brad shook his head in concern. "Everything has come back fairly easy so far. Landing is a whole new deal. I don't have any ego problems. You better handle the landing. Save your insurance for another day and disappoint your wife."

"What! Are you shittin' me?" Lance began shouting. "I can't possibly land from the right seat." He was now hysterical. "Oh, my God! Why did you wait until now to tell me you're a candy ass? Darkness is almost here, we've got a storm brewing, I gotta pee like a wild man! And now you tell me you're afraid to land a little 'ole airplane." Lance crossed his arms over his chest. "Kiss my hairy ass. You better land this damned thing."

Inhaling a deep breath, trepidation mixed with wild excitement as Brad shifted in his seat and spoke into the headset. "Okay, you twenty-four karat asshole, grab the check list. Let's talk about this."

"As you say, Captain Chewbacca." Lance gave a mock salute as he beamed.

The active runway was to the southwest. In the distance, a darkening sky was beginning to appear ominous. Lighting flickered.

Sweat gathered between Brad's palms and the yoke. He was aggravated with himself that he could clearly feel his heart inside his chest. He had landed a thousand times, but at this moment, it felt like his very first. His heart pounded faster with passing seconds. Lance made the radio calls for entering crosswind and downwind. In between, he intentionally aggravated Brad by softly singing an off-key version of *When the Saints Go Marching in.*

Flaps ten degrees. Carb heat. Cowl flaps, trim.

"Turning base."

Heart thundering.

"Oh, when those saints go marching In."

Flaps, twenty degrees, descending five hundred feet per minute. Heart threatening to explode.

"On final." Lance made the radio call and then continued humming. *"Oh, when those saints go marching in."*

Full flaps, power reduced, adjust trim. Mouth filled with cotton.

Brad did not remember the runway actually rising up to meet the airplane with such alarming speed but that was sure as hell how it was looking at the moment. Over the threshold. Power off. Ease back on the yoke. Keep the nose up. Hold the nose. It was a bouncer, not a squeaker. But, by God, they were on the ground and rolling.

"You miserable son-of-a-bitch!" Brad lifted his hands from the controls. "No more. You taxi. I'm finished with this airplane. I'm sure as hell finished with you."

Lance was in his glory as he took control of the airplane. "See what I told you. Just like a bicycle. Training wheels might be a good idea. But, by golly, no matter your age and being generally fucked up, you didn't do all that bad." Lance turned in his seat to face Brad and leaned close. "Okay, you horse's ass. Next time you think about calling me before dawn, you just remember, I always get even."

Lance and Brad had flown missions together for years, but Brad had never known Lance to be so pleased with himself. He was still laughing as he shut down the engine.

EIGHTEEN

HIS HAIR DRENCHED and water trickling down through his beard, Onias lathered himself with the body wash that he had saved for so long. Finally, the time had arrived.

With vigorous use of a towel, he dried his hair and face. He chose to allow water to evaporate from the rest of his body without benefit of the towel. Onias walked between the mirrors to where he kept his scented lotions and oils. He began the treasured time of brushing his hair. Stroke after stroke, minute after minute until the last hints of shower moisture were evaporated. Onias reached for the scented oil. Once again, a special fragrance that had been saved for this night. Oiling his body and looking at her closed door, he felt himself grow hard. He craved the touch of his hand but he refrained. All ecstasy must be saved for the virgin who longingly waited for him. She was just behind the door.

Satisfied with his hair, Onias dropped his towel, leaving it crumpled upon the floor. Walking through his array of mirrors, nude and erect, he moved to the barn's opened doors. He looked to the sky's deepening grey. Lightning flashed. Anger, power and possibly destruction brewed within the clouds. Onias smiled. This was the night.

Upon closing the doors to the barn, Onias stood in darkness. Faint seams of light could be seen from where the doors met the ground, but they were quickly consumed within the blackness of the structure. From memory, he made his way through the sealed barn. Dropping to his knees, he began the process of lighting candles.

NINETEEN

LANCE BANKED his airplane for his return to Colorado. Brad watched as his friend faded into the late afternoon sky. He smelled rain. Clouds looked tumultuous. He needed to call Kurt and talk about what should be done next. As in almost all small airports, the community television remained tuned to the weather channel. Radar images of building thunderheads and the broadcaster's ominous warning of destructive weather filled the screen.

Brad felt as if he had been slapped in the face. There it was. An ordinary television broadcast explained everything. Why had this been so elusive to Brad and Kurt? The television screen spoke of rain to fall in ferocious downpours, dangerous lightning and localized wind gusts. Brad looked to the sky. "Oh, Jesus, help me!"

Thankfully, Kurt answered his phone. In a gush of words fired like an auctioneer, Brad told Kurt of what the aircraft flight had discovered. Before Kurt had an opportunity to say anything, Brad hit him with a question of which he was certain he already knew the answer. "Kurt, the abduction in Wyoming, what was the weather when it happened?" Not giving Kurt a moment to respond, Brad continued, his voice charged. "It's the weather, Kurt, it's the weather. That's the sign this goofy guy is waiting for. His signal from heaven is a big-ass storm. He grabbed Sharon Moore in a storm. Out on that ranch in New Mexico, as soon as a storm hit, he goes dancing around naked with his pecker pointing to the sky."

Kurt remained quiet.

"Folsom is famous for a terrible storm that killed a slew of people. That's why Folsom is some sort of holy place for this guy. It's gotta be. It's gotta be."

"This is wild stuff but maybe you are on to something. The guy is crazy enough to believe something like that."

Trying not to shout as he spoke, Brad took a breath. "The really bad news is that one hell of a storm is headed here tonight. It's going to hit just about the time darkness falls. This is it, Kurt. Whatever that goofball is going to do, it's gonna happen in the next couple of hours. I know it, I know it, I know it!"

"God have mercy. I ain't arguing with you. I'll call Wyoming from my car cause I'm already heading your way. I had a feeling you were going to find something. I've been on the road for a while." Kurt paused. "Son-of-a-bitch. Even with light and siren, I'm at least an hour away from you. How much time do you think we have?"

"Hard to say. I can see it brewing right out the window. I just saw a forecast on the weather channel. My guess is we have maybe an hour, hour and half at best."

"Fuck! I'm driving like a wild man. I may not beat the storm."

"Please, Kurt, get your ass down here the best way you can. I'm gonna need you no matter what happens. I'm headed back out to that barn the second we hang up. You can work a hell of a lot faster than I ever could to get help through either Colorado or New Mexico State Police. Maybe the Raton PD. Hell, I don't know. If I try it as a civilian, it will be nothing but a nightmare. Everyone will think I'm a nut case."

"I agree, there's no time to wait around. Get out there as fast as you can. Watch yourself. This guy may be goofy but he ain't gonna take kindly to an outsider interrupting whatever he has planned."

"Let me think a second here, Kurt." A pause. "I'm pretty sure I've got this straight. Folsom is in Union County. I'm here in Raton, which is Colfax County. State Police are strung out along the interstate, but God knows where they might be at the moment." Another pause. "Listen Kurt, remember that stuff I got into not all that long ago with the shithead who was trading stolen Native American stuff for sex with young girls?"

"Yep."

"Okay, that mess ended up very near Folsom. When we hang up, I'm going to text you a phone number for a police officer in Clayton, New Mexico. He's a great guy and will sure as hell remember me from that case. Robert Montoya is his name. Once you tell him what's happening, he will round up troops from county or the State Police."

"I'm on it."

Brad glanced at his watch. He was handling things that had to be handled but it was painful to sit and talk when he wanted to be moving toward Onias and Sharon Moore. A quick look outside to the sky and it was obvious to anyone that the weather was becoming more threatening by the minute. "Kurt, this guy's place is in the far end of a box canyon. It's going to be hard to find after dark. I can give you directions. Ready?"

"Go."

With easy directions to the church, Brad walked Kurt through the details of what to look for once a descent was made off the top of Johnson Mesa. "If we're lucky, I'll have cell service once I get out there and can let you know what's happening. I was in Folsom earlier today. I had strong service right in the village. This canyon is a few miles out of Folsom, so I don't know. Otherwise, just do what you can to get some people to that canyon as fast as possible."

"Absolutely. Unless I hear differently from you, whether it's me or other folks, they're gonna be coming hard." Kurt took a breath. "I see no reason for you to go sneaking around. No point in trying to be a secret squirrel at this point."

"Hell yes. I plan to go charging in like crazy. Anything to distract or frighten him at this point. If we sneak around, things are probably going to end badly for Sharon Moore. You agree?"

"Good Lord, yes, I agree. Get me that number for Montoya and I'll handle this from my car. Once I get people on the way, I'll call Wyoming just for the hell of it to check on weather conditions the night of their abduction."

"Got ya. Let's keep talking as long as we can."

"So long and be careful."

TWENTY

THE SINGLE CANDLE FLICKERED, burned almost to its holder. Sharon knew she would soon be in complete darkness. Sounds of thunder, even though distant, caused her to yearn to be outside. She wanted to feel wind and to see the sky. How long had it been since she had breathed fresh air? Thoughts of a summer storm sounded heavenly.

Contemplating whether or not it was worth the effort to rise from her cot and begin a new candle, Sharon was startled when she heard the locks of her door being opened. This was completely out of line with his usual routine. Her heart quickened.

Rising to sit on the edge of her cot, Sharon held her breath. Her instincts screamed that something bad was imminent, Sharon saw him enter. The dying candle cast just enough light that she was able to see the door swing open. She watched as he awkwardly entered her room carrying an oblong container that appeared heavy. He closed the door behind him with a kick of his foot.

Sharon sat in silence as he placed the container on her table. When he spoke, energy carried in his voice. "Good evening, my love."

Sharon remained seated on her cot. Afraid to move, she watched her captor without response and remained silent.

"Come to me. I have something special for you. A gift. You must come quickly."

The now familiar trembling came once again. With weakness in her knees and fear in her mouth, Sharon managed to stand and forced her feet to move. Each step brought his face into sharper focus as he stood over the candle. The table stood between them, her only protection. Sharon halted, waiting.

"This will not do at all." He reached for a fresh candle and ignited it from the last flickers of what had been burning. His face now clearly visible, he smiled. With a nod toward the container, he spoke. "My bride, I want you to see what I have brought you to prepare for our wedding night." He remained standing over the table, expectation on his face.

Nausea rumbling, Sharon glanced to the container on the table. Soapy bubbles floated in a container of water. Lifting her eyes, she remained silent and did not move.

"Warm, perfumed water for you, my dear." He shifted his eyes to the towel and cloth that lay untouched on her table. "Come to me. Come and stand before your husband." It was not a request. Sharon heard the threat.

Dread soured in her mouth. She moved, a single step at a time, until she stood before him, eyes on the floor.

"Look at me."

Tilting her chin, Sharon forced her eyes to look his face.

"You must be clean for our special night. This water was drawn from my Father's river. The water that falls from the mountain above where we now stand. I have warmed it for you. Its fragrance is that of lilac blossoms. I want you to bathe yourself. I will not accept you if you are not clean." He paused. "My Father will not be pleased if you are not clean." He was quiet again. "Are you listening? Do you hear the words I speak to you? Do you hear my commandment?"

A slight nod. A hard swallow.

"Give me your hands."

Sharon extended her arms, lifting them slightly.

With his hands grasping hers, she felt his incredible strength. Her hands were nothing more than sprigs of dried grass within his grip. His eyes burned into her face. "Make yourself clean for me and my Father." Pressure on her wrists tightened. "You belong to me. You are mine. Do as I command." Pressure eased. "Now, I shall leave. When I return, I want your body cleansed by the water from my Father's river." His voice became softer. "Then I will take you to the sacred waterfall. That is where you will become my wife. Beside the River of Life, that is where our life together begins." He paused and looked upward. His next words were spoken into the void of the room's ceiling. "Beside the River of Life. This is my Father's wish." He lowered his head to again look directly at Sharon.

Another nod. Another swallow. Thunder rumbled and the air vibrated. Sharon felt the strength of a gathering storm.

Releasing Sharon's hands, he reached into a pocket of his robe and retrieved a tube of lipstick. "And this also, my bride. I want your lips red. Very red." He simply looked at her, expecting a response.

A nod.

"Very well. I will leave now so that you may prepare yourself."

He walked away. Darkened corners mocked the fitful light cast by meager candle flame. The sound of securing locks on Sharon's door echoed.

TWENTY-ONE

For the second time of the day, Brad drove toward Folsom. He pushed his speed. Words from his early morning conversation with Ron Slater went through his mind again and again. Ron Slater had said Onias would need to exert control. Because of that need, he would keep his victim close by. Brad listened to Slater's voice inside his head. 'If you find the guy, you will find the girl.' It wasn't much, but it was hope. 'If you find the guy, you will find the girl.'

Brad worked his way through the climbing and winding curves to reach the crest of Johnson Mesa. Once on top, he pressed the accelerator, gaining every speck of speed that he dared. More words from Slater crept into his brain. 'As these guys progress in both fantasy and then the actual fulfillment of their fantasy, their urges grow and become more intense... If these guys go on long enough...' Gripping the wheel, Brad pressed a bit harder.

A sky of grey and black illuminated in lightning. Thunder growled, tumbling over his truck. Brad felt the presence of the passenger once again. The skeleton had returned. A cross within his fingers of chalky bone. Photos of naked women oozed from his torso. The sneering creature rode with Brad. Hallowed eyes staring straight ahead.

His truck swayed. Wind now swept over the plateau of Johnson

Mesa in ferocious gusts. Brad hung desperately to the wheel. Rain droplets sounded like pebbles striking his truck.

His phone sounded and a glance indicated a text from Kurt. Brad pulled it up.

"Montoya and State Police coming to you fast. They need one hour. I'm with you in just over an hour. Night of Wyoming abduction - storming like hell."

"Oh, Jesus, please help me." Darkness seemed to simply drop from the sky as a blanket. Johnson Mesa inhaled. Holding a deep breath in preparation for onslaught, it waited. The mesa had existed for centuries. It knew what was coming.

Directly in front of Brad's truck, lightning sizzled. Illuminated for a half second, the church appeared eerily alone, its stone walls blue grey in the ethereal flash.

The lightning flash subsided. The church disappeared as if inhaled by a single gulp of the storm. Brad sped past, the structure appearing only as a blur in his peripheral vision. "Holy Jesus!" Brad jammed his breaks. What had he seen? Throwing his truck into reverse, he careened wildly as he floored the accelerator. With erratic spins of his steering wheel, Brad brought his truck to a lurching halt in front of the church. The door was standing wide open. Brad knew it was not because of the storm. Ghostly light emanated from within the holy building. Brad felt sickness as he stepped into the church.

What had been only a glimpse as he had passed at high speed now stared at Brad with mocking defiance. A new cross had been propped against the sanctuary wall. Grotesquely out of place, Brad stared at a replica of what he had seen in the bedroom of Onias. The crude imitation stood tall, obscuring the respectful cross that had kept watch on Johnson Mesa for over a century.

Heart hammering, Brad walked the aisle until he stood directly beneath the imposter. At the base, a half circle of candles had been arranged and lit. Flickering reluctantly, the candles seemed ashamed that they were forced to illuminate such repugnance. Hanging from the cross, a nail on each side and one in the bottom, a life-sized poster towered over the church. Brad's eyes could not move, could not register. Riveted, he absorbed the photograph of a naked woman, lips painted glossy red, her tongue suggestively touching her upper lip. Seduction exuded from her eyes. Legs spread, blonde pubic hair on display for the world's gaze.

Charged by unimaginable volts of electricity, the outside sky flashed through the church windows. The strobe effect delivered a garish glow to the crucified body that smiled down from the cross.

Thunder exploded. The violated chapel shuddered. Brad stood before the display, repulsion searing his gut. A small country church, constructed by pioneer hands and hearts, now stood transformed into a cathedral of vulgarity. There was no choice. To heck with evidence and crime scene analysis. Pulling his cell phone from his pocket, Brad snapped a few quick photos before pulling the cross away from the wall and carrying it to his truck. He opened the cover over the truck's bed and managed to fit the cross diagonally on top of the camping gear that had not been touched since leaving Kurt and Sam in the mountains of Colorado. God, that seemed a lifetime ago!

Wind-driven rain now pelted with increasing frequency. Brad re-entered the church. Approaching the altar area that was now rid of obscenity, he stood beneath the dignified cross that for years had offered solace for all who came. Brad dropped to his knees, intending to extinguish the candles. Once on his knees, he couldn't move. There was no choice, he had to pray. His voice a mere whisper, the small chapel held his words before sending them on to heaven. *"God, please keep Sharon Moore safe. And please, God, give me the strength to do what I have to do."*

With short puffs of breath, the candles were doused. Brad sprinted the aisle of the darkened sanctuary, closed its door to the elements and leaped into his truck. As he cranked the engine, Brad looked to the passenger seat. He was still there, the passenger. But something was different; the skeleton held his hollowed eyes to the floor of Brad's truck. He refused to look in the direction of the church.

"You son-of-a-bitch!" Jamming his foot onto the accelerator and, in a blurred spray of rain, dust, gravel and burning rubber, Brad sped to his rendezvous with Onias Phillips.

TWENTY-TWO

In confirmation to the finality of her fate, the sound of locks being opened reverberated like a death knell to Sharon. As he entered, she heard music through the opened door. It sounded familiar but she could not place it specifically. Standing in dread beside the table, she wondered how much time would pass before she simply fainted. What would happen then?

Sharon's face and eyes startled as he came into view. Even in dim light, his hair glistened as she had never seen before. He walked regally, emphasis in each movement. She could see a shine in his eyes, a flush in his cheeks. His stride was measured in precise and perfectly timed steps. He approached Sharon as a monarch granting audience to adoring throngs.

He stood before her. Softly stroking her cheek with his fingertips, he spoke. "Hello, my bride." He scrutinized her from head to feet. Sharon's courage still holding, she held his gaze. Instead of the crude, tan-colored wrap that she had become accustomed to seeing him wear, he was now dressed in a flowing robe. Purple material, fringed in gold, glimmered with the sheen of satin. An aura of royalty exuded from the man and his garment. Sculpted pectoral muscles were visible where the cloth opened wide about his chest. A gold crucifix next to his skin shimmered in the dim light. Sharon looked at his face with fear-stricken eyes. Pleasure in his own appearance was apparent. He stood in anticipation, expecting a response from the woman before him.

What did he see in her eyes? Could he sense her fear? Feel her repugnance? Would he read her expression as adoration? Sharon fought to control the quivering in her knees. She remained silent.

"I see that you are in awe of my appearance. This is as it should be." He paused as his eyes fell to her body. "Are you clean?"

Her head scarcely moved.

Extending his arm and placing a hand between her legs, he massaged, fingers exploring. "Are you clean here?"

Sharon again moved her head.

With a slight scowl, he appraised Sharon's face. "I desire more lipstick. I want your lips to be very, very red." He lifted the tube from Sharon's table and handed it to her. "More, much more."

Praying that he would not see how her hand trembled, Sharon smeared the red gloss over her mouth. She felt she had paste on her lips. Dropping her hand from her mouth, she looked at him.

His smile. The putrid smile. "Oh, yes, that is better. So much better."

Thunder erupted with shattering violence, sounding as if it came from directly over where they stood. Sharon involuntarily felt her body jump and shock registered in her face.

He again smiled as he brushed a fingertip across her check. "Have no fear of that sound. It comes from heaven. It is nothing more than the voice of my Father. He is pleased. What you hear is His voice expressing pleasure with our marriage."

With an abrupt twist and spin of his body, he turned to face the door that had, for the first time, been left open. Thrusting his shoulders back, taking a deep breath and standing with exaggerated upright posture, he placed his hand over his chest, extending his elbow outward toward Sharon. His voice electrified, he issued a command. "Take my arm. Walk with me."

Delirious with fear, thoughts of escape flashed through Sharon's mind. They were leaving her prison home. Would she have a chance? What would happen once she was out of this horrible room? Her hand on his arm, his bulging bicep easily discernible beneath the texture of his robe, they moved together toward the door. He moved in a marching cadence. He kept time with a beat that sounded within his head.

Sharon felt herself in a fog, a surreal other-world. Step by step they walked. Leaving the room of her confinement, they moved in unison through the long hallway, a dirt floor cold to her bare feet. Music grew more distinct, she tried to place it. Finally, they moved into the cavernous void she had only been able to glimpse. Had she been right, was it a barn? What was she seeing? What was she hearing? She felt dizzy. Candles burned. Mirrors everywhere. More mirrors. Reflections, endless reflections. Thunder. The building tremored. Music sounded from the ceiling's rafters:

Shall we gather at the river
Where bright angel feet have trod

"Sit, my darling, sit." A gentle pressure on her shoulder. Sharon lowered herself as strength to stand was leaving her body.

With its crystal tide forever
Flowing by the throne of God

"I now prepare you for presentation to my Father." Feeling a damp cloth being pressed into her hand, his voice sounded as if it came from miles away. "Remove that sinful stain from your mouth. You must take away the red of temptation. Your lips are painted with lust. Remove the carnal images from your red lips before the sacrament of marriage." His voice raised. "Hear the words of the scriptures, the book of Proverbs. 'For the lips of an adulterous woman drip honey, and her speech is smoother than oil. But, in the end, she is bitter as gall, sharp as a double-edged sword.'" He glowered. "Cleanse your mouth. Now! You are about to meet my Father."

• • •

Yes, we'll gather at the river
The beautiful, the beautiful river

As though the sky had exploded, thunder roared. The barn trembled.

Her hands quaking and mind muddled in bewilderment, Sharon lifted the cloth to her mouth. She rubbed hard, having no idea what was happening but feeling relief to wipe the grotesque substance from her mouth. She scrubbed her lips with the material he had given her. After moments, she looked up for approval.

"Very good. Very good, my bride. Your lips are now acceptable."

Gather with the saints at the river
That flows by the throne of God

Wind threatened to bring the walls of the barn to the ground. Glimpses of lightning seeped through cracks of the decaying structure. Spasms of blue and green illuminated darkened corners in advance of boom after boom of thunder.

Stroking her hair, he lifted it from her shoulders and twisted it about his fingers. "Blonde hair, my darling. Do you have any idea of the lust that blonde hair brings?" Running his palm over her head, he wrapped his entire hand within her hair. "Blonde hair brings lust to the minds of men." He removed his hand. "So, my wife-to-be, your blonde hair must never again be for the eyes of any man except me." He pointed a finger at Sharon. "Like a gold ring in a pig's snout is a beautiful woman without discretion. The book of Proverbs."

A new kind of terror surged. Scissors! Sharon felt strands of her hair being lifted by the handful. A rough tug yanked her head. The sickening sound of shearing registered in her mind as strands of gold fell about her shoulders and to the floor.

Sharon's tears now erupted. streaming down her face, they dripped onto her gown. Not certain she could even speak, she forced words from her throat. "Please, I beg you, please stop. Why are you doing this to me?" In a quivering wilt, Sharon's body slumped, she could no longer hold her body erect.

Rough hands pulled at the remaining strands of her hair, forcing her to again sit straight. "Do not question my command or the wishes of my Father." Such venom was new in his voice. The scissors continued their sickening shear. In seconds, he was finished. Stepping back to admire his handiwork, her hair now in stubbled patches, he spoke with satisfaction. "Now, you shall bring pleasure to the eyes of my Father. The lascivious lust of blonde hair will now be seen only by me when I command that you open your legs to receive me." Raising his arms so that his hands were high above his shoulders, he tilted his head upward. Looking into the black void of the barn, he began a recitation, "Wives submit yourself to your own husbands as you do to the Lord. For the husband is the head of the wife as Christ is the head of the church, his body, of which he is the savior. Now as the church submits to Christ, so also wives should submit to their husbands in everything." Lowering his hands and head and, with a condescending tone, he cast a stern gaze to Sharon. "The Holy Bible, from the book of Ephesians. I urge you to remember these words."

Heart pounding within her own ears, Sharon's eyes were dazed. Countless candles burned in an endless display of mirrors. The music continued, repeating again and again.

Ere we reach the shining river
Lay we every burden down
Grace our spirits will deliver
And provide a robe and crown

"Stand, my darling." He extended a hand for assistance.

Taking his hand, Sharon's legs somehow lifted her body. She stood before him, quivering in her body, sickness in her stomach. She watched as he turned and reached for a white gown. He held it next to her body. "How beautiful my bride will be in her wedding dress." He smiled. "I will turn away from you now. I must not yet look at your nakedness. Dress yourself. Then, my love, I shall carry you to our wedding bed." He pointed over his shoulder. "Outside, beneath an angry sky, my Father shows his wrath at the sinful ways of man. While he hurls fire and fury upon the earth, so it must be that you and I shall be joined. We shall begin mankind's final hope for salvation. Our bed awaits us. We shall come together, my love. We shall come together beside the river that flows from the mountainside, The river that flows from the Throne of God. The River of Life shall be our wedding bed." He paused, smiled down at Sharon. "Ezekiel, Chapter thirty-six: I will sprinkle clear water on you, and you shall be clean from all your uncleanliness."

Her legs feeling no longer attached to her body, Sharon began to collapse. He took her arms within his hands, the power of his grip easily supporting her. He spoke softly, "The time has come. I command you to clothe yourself in this wedding gown. Do what I tell you to do while I turn away. I will not yet allow my eyes to gaze upon your naked flesh." His voice hardened. "Do you understand?"

Moving her head a fraction of an inch, Sharon became aware of the sound of rain. Torrents of water lashed. Thunder shook the earth.

"Very well. Do this quickly." He turned and walked a few steps to where he adjusted the volume of the music. Speakers mounted in every crevice of the barn now blared, overpowering even the deafening fury from outside.

He stood with his back to Sharon.

Shall we gather at the river...

TWENTY-THREE

As the road began its twisting descent from the top of Johnson Mesa, so too began ferocious rain. Sheets of water swept across the road. Maniacal forces drove wind.

Within Brad's truck, the sound was terrifying. Rain in his headlights and scorching streaks of lightning turned the road into a disorienting blur. Bursts of brilliance exposed the road in dizzying blinks before darkness swallowed everything. He was at the bottom of the mesa. Could he spot the faint road that would be to his left? Brad felt the stare. He turned to the passenger seat. The skeleton looked straight at him. Black holes for eyes, teeth white in a hideous smile. The skeleton laughed.

"Fuck you!" Brad screamed as he slammed his fist into the face of the mocking presence. Nothing but empty air.

Ahead, he saw the road that would take him between the two fields. How much mud? Could his truck make it? Four-wheel drive engaged, pressure on the gas pedal. Airborne. A violent slam into rutted tracks. Careening. Engine screaming, press the accelerator even harder. Fields turned grey in lightning, blackness again. He was still moving. Fifty yards to the road.

TWENTY-FOUR

Nodding his head in a smile of approval, he drifted his eyes over Sharon. The barn shuddered. Electricity flooded through every crack and seam. The air was charged. Candles flickered as wind found its way through walls. Aged timbers moaned, straining against all that nature hurled. Screams of a torture chamber echoed.

As if she were weightless, he lifted her into his arms. Sharon surrendered. Becoming limp, she prayed for unconsciousness. Even louder than nature's outrage, the music still throbbed.

On the margin of the river
  Washing up its silver spray
  We will talk and worship ever
  All the happy golden day

Right leg forward in extended stride, his body followed. Left leg forward, body forward. He marched. Through the mirrored maze, bride within his arms, he marched. Lifeless as a corpse, Sharon's body reflected to infinity. Candles battled the wind. March, march.

· · ·

Soon we'll reach the silver river
   Soon our pilgrimage will cease
   Soon our happy hearts will quiver
   With the melody of peace
   Yes, we'll gather at the river
   The beautiful river, the beautiful river
   Gather with the Saints at the river
   That flows by the throne of God

Wind snuffed the sputtering candle flames. As if orchestrated, the music ceased. Darkened candles spewed smoke. Absolute blackness within the fury of nature.

Reaching a small door, he held Sharon in one arm as he opened it wide. Shards of icy cold blasted into his face. Wind tore at his purple robe, the crucifix lifted from his chest as a piece of straw.

He smiled. Carrying his bride, Onias Phillips marched into the night.

TWENTY-FIVE

IN A VIOLENT LURCH, Brad's truck catapulted from the flooded hayfield onto solid road. Easing his foot from the gas pedal, he struggled to not over-steer. His truck in alignment with the road, Brad again floored the accelerator. The house and barn were just a bit further. His passenger held the cross up high. Lightning fired. The skeleton convulsed in the jolting ride.

It was upon him. The blue Jeep. Utah tags. The house, the barn. Brad killed the engine. An easy target, he doused his lights. Blackness. Shrieking wind. The barn moaned. Lightning scorched and thunder roared. What now? No time to think. Flashlight from driver's door pocket and outside into the rain. Lightning sizzled an evil hiss. For a moment, the barn stood in full light of day. Huge barn doors were sealed tight from within. Hearing his own rasping breath, Brad ran. He had to find a way inside.

Rounding the back corner, Brad saw that the barn backed up to a steep canyon wall. A door stood ajar. His flashlight seemed a mere speck in the storm. Stumbling over stones and rough ground, he sprinted to the opening. Brad was inside. Unbelievable darkness. His light terribly inadequate. What the hell? Hundreds of flashlights beamed back at him. Lights came from everywhere. If he moved, the vast assemblage of lights came right back at him, in perfect synchronization. Wheezing came from his chest. Brad remained motionless. He had to think.

Finally discerning the frame of the first mirror, everything fell into place. Understanding that he stood in a hall of mirrors, repulsive realization quickly followed. What horror had taken place within this space?

Grasping what confronted him, Brad was able to maneuver through the mirrors and their network of disorientation. His light swept over blonde hair strewn about the floor. His stomach roiled. He knew exactly what had taken place. There was a hallway, a room at the end. Sprinting again, he entered the room. Her cot, the table, a toilet and sink. Sharon had been here. Brad could feel her.

Seconds were passing. He could not make a mistake. Where to go? How to approach? Sliding a finger over the switch of his light, Brad stood in absolute darkness. He heard Anna's voice. *Onias loved the stream and how it fell, like a tiny waterfall, from higher in the canyon. He considered the stream and waterfall a sacred place. It was where he could find solitude and peace.*

Brad recalled the view he had seen from the airplane. The waterfall, a cascading stream from the canyon's rim above the barn. That is where they had to be. Whatever Onias was planning to do, that is exactly where he would do it.

His light again on, Brad dashed through the mirrors. Again exposed to the clamor of the elements, Brad took a moment to gain his bearings. There had to be a way up the hill. His beam fell upon a tiny stream. It would lead up the hill. It was too dark. There were no extra seconds. The steep and rocky trail of the cascading water was the only way to Sharon..

With no idea if his voice would carry through the din of the storm, Brad began to shout as he scrambled. "Onias, Onias, please stop. I have talked with Anna. She told me all about you. Please, stop before anyone gets hurt. Anna loves you. She wants you to go home. She will help you."

It was impossible to know if it was better to try and ascend the incline by running within the streambed itself or to get out of the water and navigate the tangled undergrowth of the stream's border. Slipping on rock and mud, Brad stumbled. He needed his flashlight. He also needed both hands to grab bushes, rocks, anything to help with balance.

Breath sounding in rattling gasps, Brad climbed, stumbled, fell, slid backwards. On all fours, he scrambled. "Onias, Onias, please listen. It's not too late. Please stop. Anna wants to talk with you."

Lightning ripped the sky as if it tore through paper. In a fraction of an incandescent second, the hillside and creek bed were illuminated in sizzling brilliance. Brad saw Onias Phillips. Poised at the crest of the incline, shoulder-length hair blowing over a spectacularly formed body, the abductor of Sharon Moore looked toward Brad. Completely nude, his penis erect, Onias stood as a statue.

Inhaling a gulp of terror, the lightning-illuminated world moved in surreal slow motion. The arms of Onias raised high into the air, a boulder within his hands. The arms came down, a deadly projectile in mid-air trajectory. Darkness again. Holding his breath in anticipation of impact, Brad felt, more than he heard, the concussion of the boulder as it smashed into the ground, inches from his body.

Terror filled his desperate gasps. Realizing it provided more target than assistance, Brad tossed the flashlight. He grabbed at anything to help pull his body up the gulch. His feet frantically clawing in mud and loose rock, Brad heard the scream. Only feet away, Onias bellowed. "How dare you violate this holy night that God has ordained!" Another boulder. Brad felt it moving air beside his head before the sickening thud as it struck the ground.

Even in the darkness, Brad could now see the naked legs of Onias. Pale flesh against black night. Clutching mud, grass, anything his fingers touched, Brad drug his body from the stream's gully onto level ground. In a spectacular crack, the night became blue. Lightning. A bed. A woman. The huge body of Onias directly over him. A boulder in his powerful grasp. Arms moving down toward Brad. Eyes instinctively closing and arms in protective cover over his head, Brad waited for the blow to strike.

It was only a sound that first registered. Like a demon from hell, enraged howls filled the air. A dog's body catapulted directly into the face of Onias. Stunned and losing balance, Onias fell to his back. Hideous screams erupted from his mouth as he struck at the dog. A vicious blow propelled the animal into darkness. Faster than Brad's mind could comprehend, the dog was back. In snarling hysteria, its teeth found traction in the face of Onias. flesh was torn from bone. Claws gouged eye sockets. Nostrils became shreds of mangled tissue. The dog disappeared.

In frantic seconds, Brad found the boulder that had been intended for his own head. Hoisting it high, he bludgeoned it into the skull of Onias. Brad collapsed over the now inert body of a naked Onias Phillips.

Sucking oxygen, realization of what had happened began to register. The nightmarish image of what he had seen in the last millisecond of lightning returned to consciousness. The bed. the woman.

Legs trembling and brain addled, Brad managed to stand. Wind, driving rain and blackness. He needed light. "Thank you, God" involuntarily fell from Brad's lips as he pulled his cell phone from the pocket of his jeans. His fingers fumbled, found the proper control and flicked on its light.

The beam, paltry in the storm, focused on Sharon Moore. Brad felt sick. Her hands and feet were tied to a bed. Tape mercilessly covered her mouth. A rain-soaked gown clung to her body. It all seemed more mirage than reality. Fear within Sharon's eyes radiated. Managing to hold his cell phone within his teeth, Brad first removed the strands of satin rope that held her hands. Returning the cell phone to his pocket, he spoke soft words of comfort.

Using the rope that had bound Sharon, Brad tied the man's wrists, bringing every ounce of strength left in his soaked and frozen body to tighten the rope. He had no idea if Onias was injured, unconscious or dead. That was something to consider at a later time.

Placing Onias's drenched and mud-splattered robe over Sharon for whatever additional protection it may offer, Brad stroked her face. His lips practically touched her skin. "It's over, Sharon. It's all over. You will be with your family before the night is over. Help is on the way. I will not leave you. I promise. Only good people are with you now." He helped her shaking hands remove the tape from her mouth before lifting her shoulders for an embrace. Holding her trembling body close, no words were spoken.

Tears finally came. Her body succumbed to sobs. There was nothing to say.

As suddenly as the storm had arrived, it abated. Torrential rain and savage winds diminished into soothing sounds of water dripping from tree branches. Tranquil stillness embraced the night. Lightning continued to flicker, fading into the horizon. Distant thunder became a peaceful lullaby. Minutes passed. Sharon simply clung to Brad.

Accepting his gentle rocking, the night transformed into calm. A star-filled heaven looked down.

Aware of movement, Brad pulled away from Sharon to look down the hill. Red lights flashed. Brad watched two police vehicles pull next to his truck. Laying Sharon back onto the bed, he stood and shouted out the name of Robert Montoya to reassure the officers of his identity. He called for blankets and help as quickly as possible. With powerful spotlights from the vehicles, a well-worn trail up the hill was quickly discovered. Voices, footsteps and powerful flashlights came toward the crest of the hill.

Again sitting beside Sharon, Brad held her hand until he saw the face of Robert Montoya break the crest of the hill. Standing to greet his friend, nothing was said as they clasped hands. Montoya swept his flashlight over the scene. Stunned silence stifled any attempt at friendly greetings from the officers. Montoya and New Mexico State Police Troopers found no words as their eyes and minds began to comprehend the scene.

Sharon Moore, her feet still tied to the bed, lay shivering. Sheared hair, soaked and matted, she appeared pathetic under the beams of light. The naked body of Onias Phillips lay within the stream of muddy water.

In the moments of silence, Brad wandered to the edge of the clearing. What happened to the dog that had saved his life? With a light borrowed from Montoya, Brad searched the darkness, straining to catch the red glint of animal eyes. Nothing. Stepping a few feet into the woods, he whistled and called out, casting his light in all directions. No response. Disappointed that he was unable to locate any sign of the dog, Brad returned to the clearing. Montoya was on his knees beside Sharon's bed. Now covered with a wool blanket, her soft voice answered questions coming from an obviously emotional Montoya. A State Police Officer squatted over Onias. The sight and sound of handcuffs replacing the rope Brad had utilized told Brad that Onias must still be alive.

Overwhelmed and feeling weak, Brad slumped his body onto a boulder and buried his face into his hands. The surreal events of the past hour seemed to congeal and press down on his body. Sounding as though the words came from another world, Brad heard the voice of a State Police Officer say that two ambulances were on the way. Pressure of a hand settled upon his shoulder. Grabbing Brad by the hand, Montoya helped Brad to stand. The two men embraced. Words were not necessary.

Having lost all sense of time, Brad became aware that Kurt and two ambulance vehicles had arrived simultaneously. While medical people and the State Police tended to Sharon, other officers took control of Onias, Brad led Kurt and Montoya into the barn. Moving through the scene of atrocity, Brad explained all that had happened. Sharon's hair upon the floor was bone-chilling. Conditions of the room where she had been imprisoned were appalling. It seemed that every corner of the barn held body oils, exercise gear, candles, mirrors, Bibles and stacks of pornography. Depravity in the extreme.

The men stood together in the haunted atmosphere of the barn. Shared repugnance and a bond of common memories offered an unspoken testament to a level of friendship few people ever realize.

While waiting for crime scene technicians to arrive, Kurt walked with Brad to his truck. It was absolutely predictable that both men looked up to the sky at the same time. Clouds had long evaporated. Frozen brilliance of millions of blue spheres, hanging in eternal suspension, looked down upon the two friends. "Jesus H., Kurt, how long has it been since we were around our campfire, looking at this very sky? That was when you first told Sam and me about this case. I can't even remember. Has it been two days, three days? Christ, maybe it's been three years. My brain is too old and rusty to keep track anymore."

"How about it was three hundred years ago? That's how it feels to me." Kurt kicked at a tire on Brad's truck. "One more time. One more time. It just keeps happening. Right now, somewhere out there," Kurt swept his arm over the horizon, "there is another Onias. Thousands of the fuckers are out there. They are out there looking for their Sharon Moore." Kurt sighed. "Let's call up those smart-ass wranglers, Bruce and Greg. I say that me, you and Sam head back up to the wilderness and live like Jeremiah Johnson. The hell with this fucked-up, totally fucked-up world."

Kurt and Brad stood quietly, both men again looking to the sky. Brad spoke. "Okay, my friend, my services aren't needed here. I'm going to make a run for Raton. How about I get us both a room? I'll shoot you a text. You finish up with the crime scene folks and come on in for some shut-eye."

Kurt nodded in the dark. "Sounds good. Coffee at nine?"

"Nine sharp. Don't be late. I don't tolerate people who are late for coffee."

Waving over his shoulder as he walked into darkness heading back to the crime scene, Kurt gave an exhausted response. "See you in a few hours."

TWENTY-SIX

Sleep had not been a companion to either Kurt or Brad. A shower, shave, dry clothing and coffee somehow managed wonders for how they felt. Kurt gave Brad a synopsis of the evening's events after they had parted company. Sharon Moore and Onias were both in the Raton hospital. Sharon's parents and fiancé had been notified and were undoubtedly with her at this moment. Kurt had talked with Sharon around midnight for a preliminary statement. A uniformed officer was posted at her room, not only for security but for the psychological comfort of Sharon and her family. Kurt planned to head for the hospital right after coffee to check on Sharon. He would square things with her statement, physicians and her family.

Kurt's voice was grave. "As terrible as her experience has been, she is a very lucky lady in some ways. She was not molested or physically abused." Kurt dropped his eyes. "But the psychological trauma she endured is a different story."

"I can't even imagine." Brad's voice was low.

"I'm with you." Kurt peered into his coffee mug. "If you had arrived ten minutes later, this would be a whole different story. There's no telling what that lunatic may have done."

"How strong is she, Kurt? Can she bounce back from this without too many scars?"

"I sure ain't no professional shrink. My experience and my gut tell me she is a very solid young woman with strong family and social support. All of that will help. She probably has a long road to walk before genuine healing happens. I'm guessing time with family and friends will be the most critical aspect for recovery. Professional counseling will no doubt figure in also."

Brad shook his head in amazement. "She's tough as nails if she gets over this experience without a bunch of help."

"Yep, I think you're right. However, you've seen it as often as anybody. The human spirit can be pretty damn resilient. That's what we have to hope for."

Shifting in his seat, Brad spoke. "We have a ton of stuff to talk about but first, tell me about Onias. I gather I didn't send him to the Promised Land since you say he's in the hospital and not the morgue. After I whacked him with that boulder, I had no idea if he would wake up pissed or wake up dead. What's his condition?"

"No, he ain't to the pearly gates yet. As of last night, the hospital was cleaning and stitching him up from where that darned dog chewed his face halfway to hell. Nothing life-threatening with that part. But with his face all chewed up, he won't be receiving any offers for modeling jobs right away. Where you hammered him with the rock is a bit more serious. He's probably gonna be okay. You knocked him goofy. He definitely has a concussion." Kurt chuckled. "Remember the old TV commercial about an Excedrin headache? I think Onias is the new poster boy for Excedrin." Both men smiled with the thought of Onias doing a television commercial.

After a swallow of coffee and a pause, Kurt continued. "The ER docs said he may have some eye damage cause that's where you nailed him, just above his left eye. But that isn't their field of expertise. They seemed to think that if law enforcement wants him moved, he can probably be transported by ambulance to a Colorado hospital in a day or two."

Brad looked surprise. "Really, that soon?"

Kurt laughed out loud. "Boy-oh-boy! Will New Mexico be glad to get rid of us. They'll have to keep a uniform posted with Onias in the hospital until he gets shipped out. Even though the goofball is hand-cuffed to the bed, that guy is strong enough to do most anything. He has to be under guard the entire time. These poor folks don't have enough manpower to handle all the trouble we dropped on them in the past few hours."

Grinning with amazement, Brad spoke. "Who in the world would ever have thought something like this would happen in a place as small and remote as Folsom, New Mexico?"

Shaking his head in wonderment, Kurt replied. "No kidding. I've been on the job since Moby Dick was a minnow. The craziness of Onias beats anything I've ever seen." Both men were silent for a few moments as they contemplated the strange twists life often takes.

"I can tell by looking at you that you have more on your mind." Kurt gave a knowing laugh. "What in the world is going through that old brain of yours now?"

Hesitation was in Brad's voice as he spoke. "You're right, Kurt, there are a couple of other things I want to run by you. Please bear with me. I have a huge favor to ask. I'm sticking my nose where it doesn't belong, but this is important to me."

"I've known you for over twenty years and shyness is not one of your virtues." Kurt rolled his eyes and chuckled. "What's on your mind?"

"Look, we talked on the phone after I left Madrid. That bedroom has to be searched and analyzed. At this point, there is no way to know if Onias has committed other similar crimes. Who knows when or where."

Kurt nodded. "Absolutely."

"I told you about the lady down in Madrid, Anna Carter. She finally told me about Onias and his attraction to Folsom."

Another nod from Kurt.

"Without her help, we would never have found Onias and his little love nest. Sharon's story would be entirely different this morning and we wouldn't even know a damned thing about it."

"I hear you and absolutely agree."

Brad absently strummed fingers over his coffee cup as he collected his thoughts. "As I've told you, Anna is an incredible lady." Brad quickly repeated to Kurt the story of Anna's life and experiences with Onias, her struggles through abuse and how she had elevated herself to become a woman of intellect and dignity.

When Brad had finished speaking, Kurt looked at Brad with a grin. A knowing tone was in his voice and a twinge of humor brightened his face. "I read you like a large-print book. We've been doing this together way too long. You want me to drive down to Madrid myself and personally oversee the search of the bedroom. That's what you're angling for. Am I right?"

Brad just smiled.

Kurt took a deep breath. "There is no doubt that the bedroom has to be searched. Someone from Colorado who is familiar with our investigation should be present during the search. New Mexico is way out of my jurisdiction. A New Mexico law enforcement officer, county, state or federal will have to help me out with this. All I can do is ask for their assistance."

"I understand. It's up to you and whoever else gets involved. It's your call whether you go for a search warrant or decide on a consent to search. I'm positive Anna Carter will give consent. That will be up to you and the legal folks." Leaning over the table, Brad's concern was apparent. "Here is all I ask. You're driving a nondescript and unmarked unit. However you decide to proceed, if you will meet your New Mexico counterpart somewhere outside of town. Go to her house in an unmarked vehicle with no patrol cars, lights or uniforms. That's what I'm asking. I'm asking that you keep everything really low key. Give a decent woman the respect she has so often been denied. She has already suffered way too much."

"She touched you, didn't she?" Kurt's eyes shot straight through Brad.

"She touched me. Yes, she did." Brad tapped his heart with his hand.

"Consider it done. I'm not sure when it will happen. It could be late tonight or sometime tomorrow. I just don't know yet."

"Thanks, Kurt. I appreciate it more than you know. I'm planning to drive to Albuquerque today by way of Madrid. I'm going to make a stop and visit with Anna. I'll tell her to expect you and tell her that you are my friend. This is going to be tough on her. She has to face this one last travesty in her life. I know you and I know your demeanor. The respect from the heart that you extend to all people is part of why I always enjoyed working with you. Having you there with Anna will help her out tremendously. It will help me out tremendously."

"Okay, it's a done deal." Kurt smiled. "What else?"

Pointing to the parking lot, Brad shook his head. "Out in my truck is a piece of really sicko evidence. You need to take custody of it and log it in to your case or give it to the New Mexico boys. Whatever you guys work out." Brad explained to Kurt about the cross he had discovered in the Johnson Mesa Church.

"No problem. I'll take it and talk things over with Montoya."

Brad shrugged his shoulders. "I'll be surprised if the New Mexico prosecutors and the folks in Colorado don't have a little shoving match over who gets first crack at this case. There's plenty of violations in both jurisdictions. How do you see it?"

"Oh, hell yes. Both states will want a piece of Onias. Who will end up going first, I have no idea. Two separate trials are on the horizon, unless he pleads guilty. I wouldn't even try to guess how that's going to work out. A New Mexico judge will be in his hospital room this morning for initial appearance. I don't know when a decision will be made about when Onias will face his music in Colorado."

Brad rubbed his brow as he contemplated the situation. "Usually in a case like this, with so much damning evidence, I would say a guilty plea would be very likely." He shook his head. "I hope I'm wrong, but I have my doubts about this one. I see a lawyer and a team of shrinks going for an insanity deal." Brad shrugged. "Who knows?"

"I'm with you. Whichever way it goes, our asses are gonna be on a witness stand somewhere." Kurt grinned across the table. "Something else is on your mind. You ain't too good at hiding your emotions. Lay it out."

Brad rolled his eyes. "First it was Elizabeth, then Juanita and now it's my old partner telling me how easy it is to read my mind."

"Come on, Brad, I can see right through you only because we've been working together for two hundred years." Kurt squinted his eyes. "Plus, your mind is pretty small and simple so there ain't a whole lot to read."

Lifting his hands in surrender, Brad shook his head as he spoke. "Okay, okay, you've got me. Here's what I want to do. I just want to stop by Sharon's room to say hello. Last night was pretty damned traumatic. I suppose some rotten defense attorney might try to make my visit an issue of witness tampering. I can live with that on the witness stand if necessary." Brad continued, a hint of self-doubt in his voice. "I'm telling you. I have to do something to begin to clear my mind of all that's happened the past few hours." Brad looked to the ceiling. "Crosses and photos of naked women. Seeing Sharon tied up in that bed in a rain-storm." Brad dropped his eyes back to Kurt's face. "The image of that naked son-of-a-bitch, holding a rock over his head, intending to smash me like a bug…" Brad shook his head and left his sentence unfinished. "These things will haunt me forever unless I can see Sharon's face in broad daylight. I want to see her so that my memory is of something other than the sight of her tied up to a bed in the black of night. Out in the elements, at the mercy of that crazy bastard." Dropping his head and his voice, Brad spoke to the table. "It's simply what I desperately need to do."

Leaning across the table, Kurt leveled his eyes at Brad. "Fuck any stinking defense attorney and the horses they ride if they want to make up a false issue about you visiting Sharon. God made chili peppers just so anyone low enough to do something like that can have toilet paper." Kurt straightened and smiled. "Strong letter to follow."

"Coffee is on me." Brad stood up, laughing. "Let's go get that cross out of my truck and head for the hospital. I need to point my truck in the direction of Madrid. I hope to make Albuquerque before Juanita tosses all my stuff out into the street."

———

A man and woman, who Brad assumed were Sharon's parents, were in her room when Kurt and Brad entered. Even though Sharon was wide awake, introductions were exchanged in soft voices. What Sharon had endured demanded a respectful tone.

A blue knit cap covered Sharon's head. In Brad's opinion, it high-lighted her brown eyes, enhanced their intensity. Sharon and Brad's hands extended simultaneously and met in mid-air. Pressure from Sharon's hand and the unspoken words that poured from her eyes were what Brad so desperately needed. They held the moment, neither speak-ing. Since both understood that an attempt at words would collapse into an emotional breakdown, Sharon and Brad allowed their silent conversa-tion to begin a healing process for both. Brad stooped, lightly kissing her cheek. With a final squeeze of her hand, he turned away.

Following words of gratitude and embraces from Sharon's tearful parents, Brad stepped from the room. Looking down the hall, he saw a man, who he felt certain was Sharon's fiancé, carrying a tray of coffees and heading toward Sharon's room. Brad didn't wait. There was nothing more to say. He walked out of the hospital.

———

The previous night's storm had cleared the air in marvelous New Mexico fashion. Morning's cool and a sky of exquisite blue felt like a balm. He breathed deep and hard. Only hours away, Juanita waited. As always, thoughts of her brought a flutter to his heart. Before Juanita, however, he knew that he had to see Anna Carter. Face-to-face. It simply had to be.

In his truck and heading for Interstate 25 that would take him south to Madrid and Albuquerque, Brad impulsively changed his mind. Making a sudden exit into the lot for the café he had visited the day before, he muttered to himself. "I'll never forgive myself if I don't do this," Brad walked into the restaurant. Minutes later, with a bag filled with bacon, egg and cheese sandwiches, Brad did not even slow as he passed the interstate ramp leading south to Albuquerque.

Brad had to make one final trip to Folsom.

TWENTY-SEVEN

DELIBERATELY AVOIDING the drive over Johnson Mesa and its church, Brad followed the highway leading toward Texas. He did not wish for any proximity to last evening's horrors. As he drove, Brad mentally calculated the distance from the Folsom Cemetery to where the dog had attack Onias. It had to be eight miles, maybe more. Intellectually, it made no sense. But, in his heart, Brad was convinced that the dog responsible for the attack on Onias was the same dog that he had seen lying on the gravestone of George McJunkin.

Thinking back on yesterday's encounter with the starving dog, Brad could not imagine the weakened creature having strength to make a journey of several miles over rough terrain. All in the midst of a ferocious storm. Those were considerations of physical stamina or logistical capabilities. Even more perplexing were the esoteric questions. Why and how could the dog have known to be at the precise location and at the exact moment necessary to prevent tragedy?

Brad approached the cemetery. Could it be possible that he would find the dog still here? Too many unanswered questions. Too many unexplained events.

Only seconds were needed for the first of Brad's questions to be answered. He exited his truck and looked in the direction of George McJunkin's grave. It was exactly the same as yesterday. The dog stood. A wary expression obvious even from a distance. But just as the day before, Brad could again see the intensity of the dog's brown eyes.

Looking more closely, Brad realized that something was dramatically different from the previous day. Squinting, he strained to see. "Holy shit!" He practically shouted the words. The dog's tail was moving. More than moving, it was wagging! In a surreal moment of exploding energy and exhilaration, the dog leapt from the gravestone. In a black blur, his body practically flew toward Brad.

In disbelief, Brad watched as the dog ran straight to him without a hint of reticence or fear. Glee emanated from his open mouth and dangling tongue. Brad dropped into a squat. The dog was in his arms, tail moving furiously. His nose explored every detail of Brad's face, an occasional lick interspersed. When Brad stood, the dog remained, sniffing at Brad's shoes and the legs of his jeans. Stunned, Brad blinked his eyes, trying to comprehend what he was seeing. It was the same dog. But what a transformation! There was absolutely no sign of starvation. The animal's ribs no longer protruded from beneath mangy skin His coat shimmered with the luster of health. The dog looked up at Brad with eyes that were bright and filled with expectation. His tail remained in perpetual motion.

Reaching into his truck, Brad extracted the bag of sandwiches. The dog stood patiently, tail moving even faster. Tearing away a bite-sized portion, Brad held the morsel between his fingers and cautiously extended his hand. With restrained manners, the dog gently took the food from Brad's hand. Chewing and swallowing, he patiently awaited the next offering. Piece by piece, Brad continued feeding until the sandwich was consumed. Stroking the black fur of the creature's ears and head, Brad spoke softly. "This is the most unbelievable thing I've ever seen. I wish you could talk to me. Tell me what's going on here." Eyes, brimming with intelligence, looked back to Brad.

Grabbing the bag of egg sandwiches, Brad began walking. "Come with me, Bud. Let's take a walk together." Heading to the cemetery's entrance, the dog happily trotted beside Brad, his nose working overtime, curious to every scent coming from the ground. Once through the gate, Brad headed straight to the gravestone of George McJunkin. The grass at the head of the marker was matted to the ground. Brad could only imagine how long the dog must have laid in vigilance over the body of this overlooked and forgotten hero.

The dog lowered to his haunches, sitting on the gravestone but never taking his eyes from Brad. Dropping to one knee, Brad spoke. "Let me tell you something, Bud. I have no flowers for your friend. I think my gift will be appreciated all the same." Brad unwrapped an egg sandwich and placed it on the gravestone of George McJunkin, directly in front of the sitting dog. Brown eyes stared at Brad, tail no longer moving. As if in respect. Brad spoke softly. "Perhaps a few birds or maybe a coyote will come along and say hello to Mr. McJunkin. I'm pretty sure they will enjoy some conversation together. What do you think?" Brown eyes blinked. A tail moved slowly. The dog looked at the sandwich. He made no attempt to disturb or eat the food that had been placed only inches from his nose.

Brad stood and looked to the dog. After seconds, Brad spoke. "I don't pretend to understand all that has happened here, my friend. But I am certain that you have been an incredible companion to Mr. McJunkin. For how long, I have no idea." The dog looked up into Brad's face, tail steadily wagging. Squatting once again to bring himself on an even plane with the dog, Brad continued in a soft voice. "I think Mr. McJunkin is saying something to both of us. He says thank you for your loyalty and friendship. It is time for you to move on. He wants you to come with me. It's time for a new life." Brad ran his hand over the dog's head.

Eyes and tail spoke their reply.

After tossing a glance to the stone that marked the grave of Sarah Rooke, Brad and the dog walked away. Side by side, they crossed the Folsom cemetery, heading to Brad's truck. So much history. So many stories.

TWENTY-EIGHT

Locusts made music of late summer. Cottonwood and elm trees patiently waited for the cool of evening to bring a whisper to their leaves. Tourists and shoppers of Madrid's main street may as well have been a thousand miles distant. Brad parked his truck in front of Anna Carter's house. The rocker sat empty on her porch. A sigh of sadness seemed to breathe from the tiny home. To Brad's ear, even the hum of locusts sounded as a requiem. Stepping from his truck, Brad waited. Her screen door creaked. She was there. Tall, proud, beautiful. The epitome of dignity. Anna's eyes found Brad's. Her questions were answered without words.

Anna stepped from her porch as Brad crossed the patches of dirt and grass that were her tiny yard. Their embrace lasted through silent seconds. When they separated, Anna looked at Brad for a moment before she found her voice. "Where is he?"

"He's in a hospital in Raton." Brad had thought for hours as he drove, rehearsing what he would say. Now that the moment had arrived, his mind became a blank. He had no idea what words to speak. "He's okay, Ms. Carter. There was a bit of a scuffle. He took a blow to his head, but I think he will be fine. I really don't know if he will remain in custody in New Mexico or if he will be transported to Colorado."

Anna studied Brad's face. "And the girl? Can you tell me about her?"

"She had a terrible experience. She was never physically harmed. Her trauma was all psychological. She is now with her family. I'm certain she will be going home today to be with loved ones." Brad paused as Anna continued to scrutinize his face. Her eyes searched for answers. "It was close, Ms. Carter, very close. A matter of minutes. Had you not told me about Folsom, a horrible tragedy would have taken place." He was quiet again. "Ms. Carter, you saved her life. Your decision, painful as it was, saved that young woman's life. I hope that knowledge will bring some level of peace to your heart."

Anna remained quiet.

Still struggling for proper words, Brad continued. "I'm not in a position to know exactly what is in store for Onias from a legal perspective. He is certainly in very serious trouble. But, thanks to your help, he was stopped before things escalated into absolute tragedy. Thank you for doing what you did. I hope you understand the good that came from your decision."

With a delicate shift of her head and a swallow of resolve, she whispered, "Thank you, Mr. Walker." Tears pooled within her blue eyes. After standing in silence for a few moments, one hand swiped at her cheeks. Anna's other hand reached for Brad. Clasping his hand, she led him toward her front door. "Please, come inside. I have something for you." Upon entering Anna's home, Brad was deluged with emotion. There was something surreal about seeing her house in the light of day. What was it? The walls of the tiny house seemed to echo the life of the woman who lived here. The pain of Anna's agonizing decision to speak the truth about Onias still lingered. Brad could feel it in the air. Their evening together seemed very long ago.

As he looked about her home, Brad felt an enhanced awareness of Anna's life. Memories of abuse, determination to lift herself above her past, her potter's wheel. Her choice to live eloquently but simply. All were the ingredients of what Brad intuitively recognized as a remarkable woman. Brad looked toward the closed door of the bedroom, the ghost of Onias lurking within the forbidden chamber. It occurred to Brad that, for months or years, Anna had lived within the shadow of his presence. With each glance to the sealed room, there had been no choice for Anna but to re-live her past and fear for the inevitable future.

Brad stood still, lost within the bafflement of his thoughts. Anna stood before him. Her voice beckoning him back into the here and now. "Mr. Walker, when you left my home after our talk, I watched you drive away. As you disappeared, I realized something. It dawned on me that our conversation had changed my life. After you left, I finally found courage to face the demon of Onias. I confronted what had haunted me for so very long. That night, after you left, I vowed that the demon that had found a home inside Onias, however tragic, would no longer control my life." Tears again trickled. "You gave me liberty, Mr. Walker. The ruins of my past will no longer determine the path of my future. I shall be grateful to you until I'm laid to rest."

In a whisper, Brad spoke as he looked at Anna. "I had no idea."

"There is something else I can tell you. After you left, I was absolutely certain that you would return. Every time I walked past my window or heard a car in the street, I have expected it to be you." Anna's eyes were mysterious deep pools as she spoke. "There was something terribly incomplete in your departure. I thank you for coming to my home once again. Thank you for returning to my life." Anna lifted her hands to Brad. "The night you left, and after my confrontation with the evil that lives within Onias, I set this aside as a gift to you. Knowing that I would see you again, I have anticipated this moment. This is what I wish to give to you. Thank you, Mr. Walker."

Brad felt a tremble as he accepted the pottery from Anna's hands. Clay given by God, shaped by human hands, the color of the very heart of Mother Earth now rested within his grasp.

Brad could not speak. Words seemed inadequate. He held the pottery. His eyes shifting from the treasure that had been placed into his hands, to Anna's eyes and back again. A smile came over Anna's face. "It's a simple vase, Mr. Walker. But vases are never simple. Vases hold things. Our ancestors created vases to hold water and food. Vases enabled them to live. Vases were made to help mankind survive. and I believe that vases hold life itself." Anna's entire face smiled. "Please think of me when you look at this vase. It holds a part of my life. I want it to hold a part of your life. You came into my house. You sat with me beside my potter's wheel. You talked with me." She paused and shook her head. "My life was changed forever that night. Together, we changed life for a young girl."

Anna was quiet for a moment. "We did more than change her life.

Because of the talk that took place in this house," she pointed, "beside that very wheel, I have no doubt that we saved her life." Another pause. "You saved my life also, Mr. Walker. I thank you. I thank you for saving my life and giving me freedom. Please, take the vase and when you look at it, remember our evening together. Remember the evening that so profoundly altered my life and the life of an innocent young woman."

Gulping, seeking a response, Brad finally forced his lips to move. "I have no words, Ms. Carter, I don't know what to say." Brad stood as if frozen. His arms remained outstretched from accepting Anna's gift. "It's magnificent."

Throwing her head back in laughter, Anna rescued Brad. "Believe me, Mr. Walker, no words are necessary. Your face, your eyes and your inability to speak are the most wonderful words of gratitude that I've ever received. Nothing more needs to be said." Anna turned and walked to her miniature kitchen. "Believe it or not, Mr. Walker, I brew coffee straight from heaven. God himself sends me his special blend of beans picked fresh daily by the angels." She laughed again. "Of course, I must trek to the coffee shop and pay an obscene amount of cash to obtain the darned things. That's the cost of divine benevolence I suppose." Anna pointed to a chair by her potter's wheel. "Take a seat while I brew heaven's nectar for us to enjoy. Then, please sit with me for a while on the porch and give me a few more details about Onias. I would appreciate knowing what I should expect in the coming days."

Watching as Anna busied herself with the process of grinding coffee beans and preparing an old-fashioned coffee percolator on her camping stove, Brad held her gift of pottery in his hands. After moments of reflection, he cocked his head to one side as he asked his question. "May we please end the nonsense of calling each other Mr. Walker and Ms. Carter? My name is Brad. That sure sounds a whole lot better to my ears than Mr. Walker."

Anna halted her coffee production efforts and turned to face Brad. With her eyes twinkling and mischief on her face, she responded. "Why, Mr. Walker, how dare you be so bold." Laughing and with her entire body more relaxed than Brad had seen since meeting her, she mockingly gave a slight bow. "Anna is my name and that sure sounds better to my ears than does Ms. Carter." Turning back to her coffee duties, she asked over her shoulder, "So, Brad, what is it that so fortuitously brought you from Colorado to New Mexico just in time to find yourself in the middle of Onias and me?"

Watching Anna work at her table, Brad explained that, as the investigation was in its beginning stages, he had been fly fishing in the mountains of Colorado with friends. "So, after we parted company in Colorado, I headed back to Albuquerque, by way of Valles Caldera, for one more day of fishing and solitude. That's when my friend, Kurt Riddle, called to ask my help with his investigation." Brad decided to wait a bit before telling her that Kurt would be making contact about a search of her home.

Coffee brewing, Anna faced Brad and crossed her arms over her chest. "And, as the saying goes, the rest is history."

With a pensive nod, Brad answered softly, "Yes, the rest is history." He was quiet for a moment. Coffee percolating made a comforting sound. With hesitation in his voice, Brad spoke again. "Anna, may I ask you something?"

Rolling her eyes in pretend exasperation, Anna replied. "My heavens, first you want to call me by my first name. Now what liberties are you after?"

Brad carefully placed Anna's gift beside her potter's wheel. He stood as he spoke. "Anna, I lost my wife some time back. We had three children together. A woman named Juanita has come into my life. Along with my children, she is the most treasured aspect of my existence. We share our lives between Colorado and Albuquerque." Brad halted, choosing his words. "I want you to meet Juanita. Maybe more importantly, I want her to meet you. Juanita has a way to see inside people. She can feel what others feel. She somehow manages to get inside people and see the world through their eyes." Brad pointed to the vase Anna had given him. "You are so right; our lives are forever within that vase. I want Juanita and you to know each other. May I bring her here? Would you please visit our home in Albuquerque?"

Coffee percolated and the clock ticked.

Brad continued. "I am very happy that events of the past days have in some way liberated you. But to be honest, you have some tough times ahead with all that Onias faces. I want to remain a part of your life. I want to help you through those days. Juanita is a lawyer. She will walk this journey with you, I promise."

"Mr. Brad Walker," Anna's entire face smiled. "Please bring Juanita here. She can teach me the law and I will make a potter of her." Anna laughed. "While we are busy together, you can mow the lawn and do house cleaning. I hope you remember. That is exactly what you proposed to do when you were here last."

"Women, women, women! You are all the same. It's a deal. When in the world do I get a cup of this coffee you've been promising. I sure ain't getting any younger just standing here listening to you concoct grand ideas for you and Juanita."

Turning to the coffee pot, Anna spoke curtly. "I refuse to offer sugar or cream. My marvelous coffee shall never be fouled by such pollutants." Handing a steaming mug to Brad and, with a wave of her hand indicating that he should follow, Anna walked to her porch. Brad collected the vase and followed.

Settled in the rockers, Anna and Brad rocked and sipped in silence. Suddenly leaning forward, Anna became focused on Brad's truck and what she saw within its half-opened windows. "What is that I see in your truck? I do believe you have a dog waiting for you. Why in heaven's name would you leave the poor creature alone in your smelly old truck? Bring that animal to me immediately. I love dogs. I want to judge for myself the quality of companionship you choose."

Placing his coffee beside the rocker, Brad stood. Not wishing to go into the details of the dog living at the Folsom cemetery and how he had attacked Onias, Brad spoke as he walked toward his truck. "I think he had been abandoned. The poor critter was all on his own near Folsom. He took a liking to me so we're going to Albuquerque together."

"Oh, I see. And what does Juanita think about this?"

Looking over his shoulder as he reached his truck, Brad grinned. "I don't suppose she thinks about it at all since she doesn't know yet. Hopefully, she will let us both inside the house. But I suppose there's a pretty good chance that I will be sleeping in the back yard while the pooch here takes over the living room." Opening the passenger door of his vehicle, the dog leapt out, nose to the ground and tail in a frenzy, he trotted toward Anna's front porch.

Smiling at the dog's happiness to be free of the truck and invited to the party, Brad was shocked when he saw his new friend suddenly freeze. His eyes laser-focused on Anna, the tail no longer moved. Brad was stunned a second time when he glanced to Anna and saw that she seemed to be having an identical reaction to the dog. She stared, an expression of astonishment on her face. The dog slowly lowered into a sitting position and did not move. Anna had ceased to rock. Animal and human, motionless as bronze statues, Anna and the dog engaged in silent, telepathic communication.

Baffled at what was playing out before him, Brad eased his way back to the porch and his rocker. Sitting quietly, he waited for Anna to speak or the dog to move. After what seemed an interminable lapse of time, Anna tore her eyes away from the dog. Looking to Brad, something between fear and disbelief shadowed her face. A quiver in her voice was undeniable as she swallowed and spoke softly. "Please, help me, Brad. Where did this dog come from?"

Keeping his voice soft to match her obviously distraught state, Brad held Anna's eyes as he replied. "Anna, I told you. He is an abandoned stray. For some reason, he had made his home in the Folsom Cemetery. I found him by happenstance and the poor creature stole my heart." Still unwilling to divulge the entire story, Brad quietly shifted his eyes between Anna and the dog.

Her hands visibly shaking, Anna covered her eyes for a moment. When she lowered them, a pleading expression was all that Brad could discern. Her voice now cracked as she spoke. "Brad, this is the very dog that Onias had as a young man. As I told you when you were here the first time, I found a dog in a shelter and thought it would be a good friend for Onias. Initially, he loved the dog dearly. But, as time went by, Onias became abusive. He starved the dog and would kick the poor thing brutally, for no reason at all. His mistreatment became intolerable. The dog grew terrified of Onias. I was the animal's only refuge. When I would return from being away for a few hours, it was apparent that Onias had done horrible things to the poor animal."

Tears again etched Anna's cheeks. "The dog would whimper into my lap and shiver violently when Onias came into his presence. One day, I took the dog outside without a leash." Anna's tears now flowed. "The animal sprinted away. The last time I saw the abused creature, he was running for his life into the streets of Albuquerque."

Anna closed her eyes, squeezed them tight.

Shocked, Brad searched for a proper response. "Anna, lots of dogs look almost identical. What you're describing happened many, many years ago. Maybe the sight of a very similar looking dog has triggered traumatic memories in your mind. This is just a stray dog that I found in Folsom. There is no way it could be the same animal."

Shaking her head, Anna's pathetic eyes were heart-wrenching. "I know you don't believe me. It is the same dog, I'm certain." Breathing deeply to gather her emotions, Anna looked to Brad with resolve. "I'll tell you what. Call him over here right now. Bring him up close." Her eyes narrowed. "On his left ear, at the very bottom, you will find that he has a circular cyst. It's not even noticeable unless his hair is pulled back to expose it." Another deep breath. "And check his tummy. Almost touching his little pecker. He has a birthmark on his skin. It's a perfectly shaped clover leaf." Anna's eyes drilled into Brad. "Go ahead, Doubting Thomas. Look for yourself. Then we can talk."

"Holy smokes, what's going on here?" Brad shifted his eyes from Anna to the dog. It was if Brad had ceased to exist. The dog's brown eyes remained fixated upon Anna. The little black creature had no awareness of anything else that surrounded him. Brad whispered to Anna, "You call him. I don't think he's going to listen to me."

Without replying, Anna leaned forward in her rocker. Softly clapping her hands in a summoning gesture, her voice carried the tone of a mother speaking to a young child. "I am so sorry for how you were treated, my dear pup. I should have taken you away from that evil boy after he first harmed you. Please, come to me. Remember how I used to hold you when you were so frightened? Let me hold you again. No one here will ever harm you. I promise." Anna clapped her hands again, softly urging the dog to forgive transgressions of the past and to trust once again.

Rising from his haunches, the dog stood, uncertainty in his eyes.

"Come, my friend, let me make up for how you have been treated."

Tail now moving with caution, the dog finally looked to Brad as if seeking permission.

Leaning forward beside Anna, Brad's eyes pled with those of the wary animal. Brad spoke. "Come on now. Remember, I'm the guy who feeds you egg sandwiches. Why don't you let this lady touch you? She is my friend. She wants to be your friend also. Come on, Bud, come on over here."

His eyes back to Anna, the dog lifted a front leg. A ginger step. Another. Nose on alert, his body stretched toward Anna's outstretched hand, absorbing her scent. The dog evaluated Anna's heart. With a quick glance to Brad and an effortless spring from his hips, the dog was in Anna's lap.

Embracing the animal in a rush of emotion, Anna openly cried but laughter mingled when a flicking pink tongue tasted her tears.

Collapsing back into the rocker, Brad shut his eyes, wanting to seal forever within his mind what he had just witnessed.

———

Two people, two rocking chairs and a contented dog passed silent minutes on Anna's porch. Locusts made music. A jetliner's contrail streaked the New Mexico sky. A magpie perched on the bed of Brad's truck. Anna's hand rested on the dog's head, gently rubbing his ears. Brad's hand rested without movement on the animal's side. Feeling the warmth and savoring the life of this mysterious animal, Anna and Brad rocked without words.

The cyst was on the dog's ear. The clover leaf was on his tummy.

———

Conversation about Kurt Riddle's upcoming visit and how he would protect Anna's privacy and dignity had been handled. Anna's vase was packed within protective folds of a blanket in the back seat of Brad's truck. The dog happily panted in the front passenger seat. Anna and Brad prepared to say farewell. "Thank you, Brad. Today is the first time that my heart has truly been at peace since the day I ran away from that rotten, bastard, son-of-a-bitch, Fundamentalist Mormon husband of mine." She smiled. "Wanna see me spit?"

After a soft laugh, Brad spoke. "I am the one to say thanks to you. How you have managed your life, in the face of so much adversity has inspired me more than you will ever know." Moving his head sadly, Brad continued. "It's happened so many times in my life and career. Tragedy so often delivers unimaginable blessing. Why does it have to be like that?"

"I do not have an answer for you. But the tragedy of Onias has given me the blessing of finally shedding my life of the past. His tragedy gave me the blessing of you," she pointed to the passenger seat, "and the blessing of my old friend coming back to me."

Anna and Brad clasped hands, holding tightly. After seconds, Anna withdrew her hands, and placing a finger over her lips, she made a motion with her hand and face for Brad to be silent and to listen. "Listen to the locust," she whispered. "It is quite rare for us to have locust. I think maybe we are too high. I'm not sure why but they are a special guest." Anna and Brad listened. With a smile, Anna spoke, "The locust sing today because it is a new beginning. They are here to help celebrate." Again, clasping hands, Anna and Brad stood together and listened, savoring the moment.

Brad entered his truck and started the engine. Jabbing his thumb toward the dog and peering over the top of his sunglasses, Brad issued his warning. "We'll be baaack! The real boss of this cattle drive, Miss Juanita, whoowee! Madrid will never be the same."

Clapping her hands in glee, Anna fired back. "You just remember to bring your lawnmower and vacuum cleaner."

TWENTY-NINE

Only an hour's drive on the Turquoise Highway and it would all be over. Juanita and home awaited. Setting the cruise control, Brad allowed his mind to wander. Juanita's copper skin, her eyes, her fragrance. His heart fluttered. The backside of the Sandia Mountains filled the western horizon, a welcome home beacon reaching a mile into the sky.

The past days were a blur. How had this all started? Was it a dream or had it really happened? Seeking mental consolation and companionship, Brad decided Willie Nelson and Dolly Parton would be perfect. Their voices blended in duet to one of his favorite songs. *Everything Is Beautiful In Its Own Way* filled the cab of his truck. A black dog, curled like a pretzel, slept beside him. Freeing his mind, Brad returned to the beginning of his unbelievable experiences with Onias Phillips and Sharon Moore. The music, a soothing balm.

When I look out over a green field of clover
 Or watch the sunset at the end of the day
 I get kind of moody when I see such beauty
 Everything is beautiful in its own way

. . .

Brad was back in the Colorado mountains, around a campfire with Sam and Kurt. He heard Kurt's voice telling of a girl named Sharon Moore being stolen away on a stormy night, heartache and anger in his words. Valles Caldera and its serenity. Centuries of Native American lives flowing within Rio San Antonio. The magnificence of wild trout and Redondo Peak became vivid in his mind.

I see a fountain flow from a mountain
  Or see April Showers bring flowers to May
  I can't help but ponder, life is such a wonder
  Everything is beautiful in its own way

Santa Fe at sunrise. The love of Margie and Jim Price. The image of Robert Oppenheimer and atomic devastation. The Moreno Valley, heavenly beauty filled with endless sorrow of the Vietnam Memorial.

Words can't describe what I feel inside
  When I see the beauty in each coming day
  What my eyes behold can't be bought or sold
  Everything is beautiful in its own way

The Turquoise Highway passed beneath Brad and his truck. His new dog slept.

When I see the clouds form a black summer windstorm
  That uproots the harvest and hurls it away
  In the midst of such anger, destruction and danger
  The storm's even beautiful in its own way

· · ·

Johnson Mesa. Devastating flood water. A telephone operator sacrificing her life for others. Prehistoric hunters, slain buffalo. A black cowboy delivering words of import and significance to a world with deaf ears.

When I see the leaves drop from off of the treetops
Or see the snow fall on a cold winter's day
My thoughts seem to wander into the blue yonder
God made all things beautiful in their own way

The ecstasy of flight, soaring above the earth. A small church standing vigil over a land vast beyond comprehension.

Words can't describe what I feel inside
When I see the beauty of each coming day
What my eyes behold can't be bought or sold
Everything is beautiful in its own way

Albuquerque appeared on the southern horizon. The dog still slept.

In its own way

Vulgarity, obscenity, fire and wind from an angry God. A naked man prepared to deliver death;.The miracle of a small dog.

Everything is beautiful in its own way.

Brad hit repeat for the song. Willie and Dolly were like old friends.
Anna Carter. So tall, so beautiful. So dignified. So heartbroken.

Anna Carter, once again smiling with new-found freedom. An eagle released from a cage.

In its own way

The Turquoise Highway blended into Interstate 40. Traffic, congestion. Empty desert on his left, afternoon light on the towering Sandia Mountains to the right. The dog now awake, sitting erect apparently fascinated by the madness of humans.

Juanita, only minutes away.

He was home. Brad killed the engine, looked to the dog and spoke. "Okay, don't blow this now. Like Momma always said, you never get a second chance for your first impression. So, don't let me down." The eyes of man and dog found each other and held. "Okay, you ready to rock and roll?"

Tail wagging, eyes bright.

Dog in his arms, Brad rang their doorbell. Juanita's footsteps, the door swung open.

Oh, my God, she is so beautiful!

Juanita's face and eyes contemplated what stood before her. Stepping aside with a motion for Brad and the unknown visitor to enter. Scooping the dog from Brad's arms, Juanita marched to their couch.

Immediately smitten, the dog returned Juanita's affection. His nose explored Juanita's face with profound curiosity. His tail a tornado of black motion.

Understanding precisely that he was being shunned for bad behavior, Brad headed to the fridge for a Moosehead. From the room where Juanita and the dog remained enthralled and completely oblivious to the existence of Brad, Juanita called out, "What's his name?"

Sauntering back to Juanita and the dog, Brad took a draw of Moosehead and shrugged. "Don't know, haven't thought of one yet."

Delivering a look that clearly indicated Juanita felt that she shared space with a moron, she summoned her mocking voice. "Well, Agent Walker, can you please tell me how you have communicated with this gorgeous creature." Casting an accusing look to Brad, Juanita continued.

"While completely ignoring the woman in your life, surely you have said something. He is obviously an improvement over most of the immature and reprehensible characters who occupy your life. I refer, of course, to fly fishers and like-minded juveniles."

Taking another pull of Moosehead, Brad was thoughtful. "I've called him Bud a few times." He shrugged. "That's all I've ever called him."

Rolling her eyes in disgust, Juanita huffed. "Bud! Did you say Bud? Bud is a name by which you refer to your camping mates as you eat sausages and expel obnoxious gasses from unwashed bodies and unshaved faces." Juanita looked at the dog with an evaluative expression. "I hereby name you Buddie." Juanita considered her pronouncement. "Perfect. I love the name and the matter is settled." Bringing her face close to the dog and looking directly into his expectant brown eyes, Juanita continued, "Welcome to your new home, Buddie. You and I shall now be in charge of all major decisions concerning this household."

Unable to conceal the mirth in her eyes, Juanita had to turn away as she concluded her rant."

Juanita and Brad broke out in laughter. Buddie wagged his tail

Placing his Moosehead on a table, Brad extended his arms. Juanita came to him. Melting into their embrace, it was all that Brad had dreamed of in the past days. Her hair, her skin, the warmth of her body. "Oh, my God, I love you." Holding her with all his strength, Brad saw in a fleeting blink all that had happened since their last embrace. "We are so lucky, Juanita. We are so lucky. I could never live without you."

Warm breath on his neck, Juanita's fragrance overwhelming his senses, Brad was vaguely aware of a tail, happily thumping on the floor.

ABOUT THE AUTHOR

Dale spent twenty-five years as an FBI agent investigating violent crimes and concluded his law enforcement career by helping establish the Federal Air Marshal Service. He then turned his energy to writing. Dale lives in Colorado where fly fishing, mountains and the grandeur of nature have been integral to him, his wife, and their three children.